I0687561

FATED MEMORIES

By

Joan Carney

FATED MEMORIES

© 2016

Joancarneyauthor.com

All Rights Reserved. This book, or any portion thereof, may not be reproduced or used in any manner whatsoever without the express written permission of the author, except for the use of brief quotations in a book review. This book is a work of fiction. While some historical events, names and locations are mentioned, other names, characters and incidents either are products of the author's imagination or are used fictitiously. Any resemblance to actual persons, living or dead, events, or locales is entirely coincident

Table of Contents

Acknowledgments

Thank you to Stacy Juba, Developmental Editor for patiently wading through my first draft and setting me on course to write a structured and read-worthy novel.

My gratitude also to all the wonderful people on Goodreads who offered invaluable comments, suggestions and encouragement to make my story come to life: in particular Deb Rhodes, Sharon Umbaugh (The Writer's Reader), and Stacy Howell.

CHAPTER 1

Kitty's hands shook and her vision blurred with tears. It didn't matter. After having read the short note three times, the words '… transfer to the second floor' had been engraved on her brain. She'd found the letter in her mail slot at the hospital where she worked, just this morning. *That's Richard's floor!* The wound from their breakup still scarred her heart. *What do I do now? Quit my job?*

The elevator doors opened and Richard Delaney stepped off surrounded by his physical therapy staff, who were tittering at one of his clever quips. Kitty wheeled around, making a beeline for the restroom. She couldn't let him or those bitchy nurses see her cry. In her haste to become invisible, she miscalculated the corner of the wall and, smacking her shoulder against it, bounced back flat on her ass. Silence washed over the unit as everyone's eyes turned to her.

Flushed with embarrassment, she scrambled to her feet, faced her audience and curtsied. "I'm here all week, folks, don't miss the show!" Then she burst through the lady's room door.

Kitty locked herself in the stall, working to salvage her dignity while dialing her cell phone for her pillar of strength; the one who always knew what to do.

"Ma?" Despite her efforts to control it, her voice still shook.

"Kitten, honey, are you crying? What's the matter, are those silly boys in school teasing you again? Should I go speak with the principal?"

"Funny, Mom, no I only need to talk to someone. Remember when I told you the hospital makes the ward clerks reapply for their jobs every few years so they can weed out the ones they no longer want? Well, it's that time again. I got my take-it-or-leave-it offer today and it says they're bumping me from the step-down unit, to the pits of the med/surg dungeon. If I don't accept it, I'll be out of a job. I don't know what to do."

Silence.

"Mom, are you still there?"

"Yes, I'm here." She blew out a long breath. "Kitty, you're a smart lady, but if you don't respect yourself enough to stand up and take charge of your life, you'll always be at the mercy of others. Remember, the choices we make follow us and decide our fate."

"I know, Mom, but…"

"The best advice I have for you, sweetheart, is to move home with us so you can go back to college and learn more marketable skills."

Kitty had battled with them before over this. In her mind, living with her parents at her age was the same as having a big red letter "L" tattooed on her forehead. "I see, okay. Um, I have to get back to work now. I'll talk to you later, Ma. Thanks for listening."

As she washed off the mascara tracks from her tears, she studied her reflection in the restroom mirror, mulling over the misery that was her life. *You're almost thirty years old, Kitty Trausch, what have you got to show for it? A man? Not since Richard dumped me last year. A career? More like a crappy job that's become unbearable.*

Kitty remembered her mom's mantra "When the world gets rough," she'd say, "remind yourself of the good things you have." She thought hard for a positive slant, but only came up with her prized closet full of shoes and salvation from her acne plague. Great, at least that and two-seventy-five will get me on the subway. Oh, and one more good thing. Rooming with Sonia allowed her to walk the short distance to the hospital and not have to ride the train from Tuckahoe to Manhattan. *Wow, I'm overwhelmed with gratitude.*

Richard had been the only highlight in her otherwise dull life. Since their breakup, the monotonous days dragged by, each a repeat of the last. She pretended it was all she wanted and feared it was all she deserved. Now even that empty, anonymous lifestyle faced extinction.

Her shoulder throbbed from hitting the wall, her head hurt from crying, and her pride was bruised from the fall. In too much pain to continue working, Kitty asked for a sick release from the unit coordinator, gathered her belongings, and headed home.

***

Most people lose their appetite when they get upset or angry. Kitty never understood that. Instead, she got hungry. And not just 'a sandwich sounds good right now' hungry. But a vicious, self-destructive, tantrum-throwing brand of hunger that could only be satisfied by the most calorie-laden, forbidden, high-fat food possible. And alcohol, lots of alcohol.

Kitty knew the hospital wanted to get rid of her. She'd rather be drawn and quartered than work on that unit.

Especially since that's where most of Richard's therapy patients were. She'd see him every day flirting with the nurses and watching them fawn all over him. Who in the world could she have pissed off enough to deserve this?

At the market, Kitty moved in a trance-like state as she laid a second bottle of *Chateau St Michelle Riesling* from the store shelf into her basket. It already contained the pepperoni pizza from Fat Charley's Italian restaurant next door, three boxes of *Mallomar* cookies, and a half gallon of double chocolate-chunk ice cream.

Even though she tried to stifle it, her mom's earlier facetious remark niggled in Kitty's brain. Bumping into the display the stock boy had just finished assembling, his cold stare ushered in the flood of hurtful memories. Jeers and digs about her five-foot-ten frame that earned her the nickname of Marmaduke rang in her ears. But the worst tormentors were the walking erections who turned her name into a disgusting, mortifying taunt. Their innuendoes landed them, bloody and bruised, in the principal's office on several occasions.

Kitty had no recollection of paying at the checkout counter until the blaring car horns and the impatient drivers' angry words jolted her back to her senses. Startled by the commotion, she realized she'd been standing still in the middle of the street. Any other day she'd have responded with a few choice expletives of her own, but even those deserted her now. Kitty shuffled the heavy grocery bags around, hurrying the last block home.

***

She reached the door to the apartment she shared with Sonia and Carlos juggling so many packages, she had to ring the bell and hope Sonia was there to open it. When she did, Kitty just stood there dripping with sweat from the muggy summer air, her arms full, and tears and snot streaming down her face. Sonia dragged her inside unburdening her and assessing her for physical damage while she used the edge of her shirt to wipe Kitty's face.

"Oh my God, Kitty, what happened? Are you hurt?"

"Did you get mugged?" Carlos demanded. "Where did it happen? Did you get a good look at him? I told you not to walk through that park!" Sonia's boyfriend since high school, Carlos, had been working for the NYPD for over ten years and made it his mission to lecture everyone on safety and security.

Kitty pulled the letter out of her pocket, handed it to Sonia, and plopped on the couch sobbing.

"Go to work, baby." She gave Carlos a gentle push towards the door. "Kitty and I need to have some girl time.

Be careful and wake me in the morning when you get home."

He gave her a serious look then kissed her goodbye. "Tell her."

"What? Tell me what?"

Sonia waved off the question as she headed to the kitchen and Kitty was too miserable to pursue it.

"So, med/surg; that's not so bad. You can handle it. You just need to stay organized. Jackie always manages to keep it under control." Sonia returned carrying two large spoons for the ice cream, a corkscrew, glasses and a handful of paper napkins.

"What do you know?" Kitty blew her nose one more time before digging in to the pizza. "You've never had to do it. You're part of the nurse's sorority who snaps their fingers at the clerk expecting her to be capable of organizing Jell-O!"

"I would never do that to you or any other clerk and you know it! If you think I have it so great why don't you go back to school and become a nurse?"

"Who me? What if I screw up the calculations on a patient's IV, or trip over my own feet with a needle in my hand and kill him? Trust me. The world is much better off keeping me in the background where I can't hurt anyone.

But I don't understand why I'm getting transferred. Sure, the nurses on my floor are stand-offish, but who cares? And the manager rarely interacts with me. What could I have done to make them want to get rid of me?"

Sonia sighed as she poured the wine. "Listen, Kitty, you know I love you, but have you considered that it might be your attitude? Ever since your break up with Richard, you've been a little… edgy. I thought those martial arts classes you're taking were supposed to re-direct your anger?"

Whenever Sonia pursed her lips and lowered her eyes Kitty knew she was hiding something. She clutched Sonia's arm, spilling a few drops of the wine. "Please Sonia, you're my best friend in the whole world, if people are talking behind my back you need to tell me. Please, that's what friends are for."

"Okay, fine. Just don't kill the messenger!"

Sonia took a long drink of her wine. "Everyone knows we're friends, okay so they don't say anything to my face, but still I hear things, you know? And from what I gather, the reason the manager avoids any contact with you and the nurses are what you call stand-offish, is because you're always so sarcastic and you have a habit of rolling your eyes and snapping at them. They think you're a bitch."

"I'M... NOT... A... BITCH!" The waterworks were starting in earnest now and the hiccupping sobs even made her put down her food. How did this happen? How did I go from a teenage wallflower too shy and insecure to talk to anyone, to an almost thirty-year-old pariah that everyone considered a bitch?

"Oh, honey, look." Sonia draped an arm around her. "I don't think you're a bitch, you're just... unhappy. You know, this thing with the hospital may be a gift. The push you need to get out of your comfort zone and on to a new direction. Maybe you should take vacation and rethink your options."

As Sonia's comforting hand moved to cover hers, Kitty noticed the ring for the first time. "Sonia! Oh my God! You're engaged! When? I mean, I always figured you and Carlos would get married someday, but I didn't know he'd proposed!"

Sonia glowed with pride. "He popped the question after dinner at Luigi's last night." She held out her hand to display the small diamond. "It was so romantic. He even got down on one knee, right there in the restaurant with everyone watching! He looked so serious I almost laughed. His promotion becomes effective with the new rotation next month, so now we can afford to buy a house, start a family." Sonia's eyes flashed guiltily and darted away.

"Oh, that's wonderful." More bewildered than happy, Kitty leaned forward reaching for her wineglass to keep Sonia from seeing the disappointment on her face. A thousand thoughts ran through her mind at once. This must be what Carlos had urged Sonia to tell her. If they were moving on with their lives, they certainly didn't need a third wheel getting in the way. They wanted her to leave. Where would she go? With her job in jeopardy she'd have to move back with her parents. *Oh, God no!* Could this day get any worse?

***

Kitty woke to the alarm clock at her usual five a.m. the next morning, emerging from her room bleary eyed, her face creased and sticky from tears. Work was out of the question today.

She stumbled out to the living room in her ratty pajamas, and her hair a solid clump of tangles. As she picked up the phone to call in sick, peeling a piece of pepperoni off the receiver, she surveyed the mess they'd made last night. Without time or talent for decorating, Sonia had filled her apartment with a profusion of odd pieces, calling it eclectic. The saggy blue sofa passed down from Kitty's parents, and the mustard-colored fake leather recliner rescued from Carlos's grandfather's house, stood between two thrift store tables topped with brown ginger jar lamps. Now the glass coffee table had melted ice cream on it, empty wine bottles littered the stained carpet, and demolished cookie boxes and used napkins lay strewn everywhere. One slice of pizza remained in the box on the couch. Kitty heard the shower running and didn't want Sonia to come out and begin her day seeing this disaster. If she had to leave, she refused to be remembered as a slob. Sick call done, Kitty nuked the leftover pizza for breakfast, got a pot of coffee going, grabbed the roll of paper towels and the trash can, and tackled the clean-up job.

Kitty had the laptop set up at the kitchen table that doubled as a desk when Sonia emerged shiny and bright-faced, looking as though she hadn't stayed up half the night letting her devastated roommate cry and whine on her shoulder. Her blue scrubs fit her trim body perfectly and her clear, light-brown complexion needed no makeup whatsoever. With her slightly frizzy hair slicked back in a ponytail, she still maintained the image of the cheerleader she had once been.

Sonia and Kitty's sister, Patty, best friends since second grade, had been the prettiest and most popular girls in school, but they'd never acted smug about it. They always encouraged Kitty to tag along to pep rallies and parties, even though she only watched the excitement from the sidelines, wishing she had the nerve to join in the fun. The two of them had even gone to nursing school together. After graduation Sonia had taken a job in the ICU at Bethlehem General where Kitty worked. Patty met Dan, the love of her life, and they'd moved upstate where she launched her career as a labor-and-delivery nurse.

Kitty counted back the years. *My God! Was that really over ten years ago? Where has the time gone?*

Sonia poured them each a cup of coffee and joined Kitty at the table with her bowl of cereal. "Not going to work today Kitty? You were pretty wound up yesterday. Did you get any sleep?"

"A couple of hours. Thanks for indulging me last night. It felt good to get that tension and anxiety out in the open. I'm more focused this morning so I think I'll check out the head-hunter job sites and see what's available."

"Mmm." She slurped her cereal. "Sometimes freeing those negative emotions is the same as lancing an inflamed abscess. You have to squeeze the ugly pus out in order for it to heal."

"Yeah, thanks for the visual."

Minutes later Sonia got up and rinsed her dishes out in the sink. "I gotta go before I'm late. Good luck head-hunting. I'll see you tonight." She kissed Kitty on the cheek, attached her ID to the lanyard around her neck, threw her humongous purse over her shoulder, and flew out the door like a tiny Puerto Rican whirlwind.

Kitty spent a few hours surfing the want ads on the net and uploaded her resume to a few agency sites. She hated to admit it, but her parents were right. No way could she support herself anywhere above the poverty line without learning more marketable skills. Her Humanities degree opened possibilities in teaching, public relations or sales, except those careers involved having people skills. Not her forte. The question still rattled in her brain, what field did she want to study? Her best subjects in school had been the science classes. Biology, earth science, chemistry, she got A's in every one of them. Games and puzzles and things that fit together were on her favorite-things-to-do list, but the problem of how they'd produce income and keep her interest for any length of time baffled her.

After a while, her surfing veered dangerously towards shopping, so she decided to check her email and then give it a rest. Maybe go to the gym where she could think while punching the body-bag. Kitty could never make her parents understand why hitting things always lightened her mood. That's when she saw the note from Maggie.

A distant cousin, Maggie McGrail had found Kitty last year while doing genealogy research on her family. While Kitty had dabbled in that, she'd never gotten too far. Eager to meet her, she'd driven to Maggie's home in Pennsylvania one weekend and they had an absolute blast. Over pizza and beer, they'd shared memories of their childhood years—good and bad—, their failed romances, and promises they'd made to themselves. Maggie's hilarious stories of goings-on at the diner where she worked had Kitty in stitches.

Although not close relatives, the cousins found similarities in their natures and circumstances with enough common ground to be at ease with each other right away. A new experience for Kitty.

Physically they weren't that much alike. For one thing, Maggie's side of the family was more generously endowed in the chest area. She had light skin, clear and smooth as porcelain, and her blue-gray eyes that she said she got from her grandma, were fringed with thick dark lashes. She had the same reddish-brown hair which she supplemented with more red highlights, making the contrast with the rest of her coloring more striking. A major blessing for Kitty, Maggie's five-foot-seven height meant she'd never be called a giant standing next to her.

Since that first visit they'd kept in contact through occasional phone calls and frequent emails. The internet made it easy to share their deepest secrets, their fears and anxieties, as well as a few laughs over everyday life. These open and frank conversations helped the cousins grow as close as sisters. Kitty became the one Maggie never had and Maggie replaced the one who'd moved away from Kitty when she got married. Maggie's only other living relative was a sweet old grandmother who had little time left to live, so it pleased Kitty to welcome her into her own little circle of family and friends.

Kitty hated dumping her problems on her, but practical Maggie always had such good advice. And, as much as she loved her mom and dad, she always felt like such a child when she ran crying to them. To make matters worse, she'd also have to listen to their sermons on how to live her life. Sonia tried, but it was Maggie who always helped her see things clearly. Her mind made up, Kitty reached for her cell.

Maggie picked up the phone on the first ring. "Hey Kitty, how's it going?"

Even with the catharsis of last night's tear fest, Kitty's voice still quivered as she spoke. "Not good."

"Why? What happened? Is everything okay?"

"My life sucks, Mags. Everyone at the hospital thinks I'm a bitch and they want to get rid of me. They gave me a take-it-or-leave-it offer for the med/surg unit where Richard works and I can't do it Maggie, I just can't. And to top it off, Sonia and Carlos got engaged and they might be moving. If I quit the hospital I'll have to go back and live with my parents. I'm such a loser."

"Never say that Kit, you are not a loser. Life is all about changes that's what makes it interesting. You've always known you were too smart for that job. This is your chance to break free, turn the negative into a positive. Spread your wings. Grow."

Kitty still wasn't convinced. "You make it sound so easy."

"No, it isn't easy, it's freakin' hard. Until they're tested, though, people don't realize their strength. I have faith in you, Kitty Trausch." Maggie's voice caught. "Speaking of strength, Grandma Margaret's is running out. She gave everyone a scare the other day when her heart stopped and they had to shock her back. Doctor Brunsting had me sign a paper saying that if it happens again they'll just let her go. She's ninety-six, Kit, and she's dying."

Kitty sat up straighter in her chair, chastising herself. *How awful of me to burden her with my whining when she had heart-wrenching problems of her own.* "Oh, I'm so sorry, Mags. Is there anything I can do to help?"

Maggie thought for a second, then her voice brightened and she talked faster. "As a matter of fact, there is. Tell those ingrates at the hospital to pound sand and come stay with me for a while. To have you here would be a Godsend for me, and then you'd have time to explore your options. It'll be good for both of us. What do you say?"

What a tempting idea. Sonia deserved her privacy, and the hospital obviously wanted her to leave, but Maggie needed her. That meant she didn't have to run back to Mom and Dad and listen to their lectures. There was no downside.

"Okay, Maggie. I'll do it. I'll put in my two weeks' notice tomorrow. Tell Grandma to hold on till I get there."

CHAPTER 2

"Maggie, would you mind switching tables with me? If I have to clean up another milkshake those brats at table four spilled again, I'm going to throttle them both." Sylvie never did have patience with kids.

"Sure, no problem. Why don't you go take your break and I'll finish up here? Then we can switch back."

"Thanks, you're a doll. I owe you one." Sylvie almost ran to the small break room behind the kitchen at Sammy's Diner.

Maggie didn't want to say anything, but Sylvie already owed her several. At least she only had one customer to be served in her section. He sat alone in the corner booth scrutinizing the menu over and over as if re-reading it might make it change.

She came to his table and gave her usual speech, "Hi, I'm Maggie. I'll be your server. What can I start you with today?"

His jaw seemed to unhinge and his eyes bulged out of his head as he tore his concentration from the menu. Not the usual response. Maggie thought it a straight-forward question, and couldn't help shifting on her feet. To make their day go by faster, she and Sylvie sometimes played a game of "Guess the Occupation." So, while he composed himself, she assessed him for what his might be. His longish-brown hair needed styling, and just a hint of a beard that hadn't fully come in yet, shadowed his face. The staring brown eyes had little flecks of green and she found his thick, dark lashes quite alluring. She noticed too that a slanting scar interrupted the hair on his left eyebrow and ran right through it. He wore nice jeans and a cotton button-up shirt, except the red plaid pattern and missing tie, ruled out an executive or an accountant. *Computer geeks get to dress casually, that might be his thing. Anyway, if he doesn't close his mouth soon I'll peg him as a doofus and move on.*

"Do you need a few more minutes to decide?"

A flicker of light went on in his head as he peered up at her. "Lucy?"

"Uh… no, Maggie." She pointed to her name badge. "There's no one here named Lucy. I'll be your waitress today. Have you decided what you want to order or should I come back in a few minutes?" He was cute, but a definite doofus.

"No, no that's okay. I'll have the French dip sandwich, fries and iced tea. Or wait, make it an Arnold Palmer. Do you know what that is? Half-lemonade and half iced tea? And please, forgive me for staring. It's just that… I think I know you."

The apology sounded genuine, and she almost felt bad for him. Not bad enough though. "Oh, I haven't heard that line before, good one. I'll be right back with your drink."

Maggie left to get the drink and saw Sylvie screwing up her face in that smirk again. "So, what's this one? From his build I'd say whatever he does involves heavy labor. Is he a garbage collector? Does he smell?"

"I don't know he's kinda dumb. He couldn't even hit on me with any creativity. It's a shame though, I think he's cute." She glanced back over to his table and found Sylvie was right. Built like a linebacker, he had wide square shoulders and arms that made the sleeves of his shirt strain as he leaned forward examining his fingernails. The view from the side showed no paunch or flab whatsoever. *I'll bet his body-fat-percentage is in the single digits*, she mused. So, if not a garbage collector, maybe he played sports? An athlete would certainly be a more interesting explanation for his physique.

When she returned with his food, he averted his eyes and fidgeted with the napkin dispenser. His obvious discomfort made her uncomfortable, so she redeemed one of Sylvie's IOU's, gave his table over to her, and retreated to the break room.

***

With only light traffic today, Maggie zoomed home from the early shift by four, leaving plenty of time to wash off the grease from the diner and grab a quick bite before her run. Keeping in shape had always been a major part of her life and, even once soccer season ended, she'd still run four to five miles a day. It gave her such an exhilarating sense of freedom and release. Maggie changed into her running gear, lacing up her hot pink Saucony's and, after a few good stretches, ran out the door and revved up her trusty CRV. At this time of day along the Susquehanna riverfront trail, the breeze made breathing the hot muggy summer air tolerable, and she loved watching the people enjoy the park. There were art shows or other festivals during the summer, but she tried not to stop and linger so she could log her miles.

Once at the park-n-ride Maggie set her fit watch for five miles and programmed the alarm to ding at the halfway point to alert her when to turn around and head back. She popped in her earbuds attached to the phone strapped to her arm and off she went.

Most times, singing along with the music in her head helped distract her from feeling fatigued or muscle sore. But today she couldn't help thinking about that guy at the diner who had called her Lucy. People say everyone has a doppelgänger, yet it made her sad to think she might resemble someone's dead wife or something. Maggie hoped that wasn't the case. Perhaps Lucy was an old friend or co-worker he liked and missed. Even though he came off as awkward and flustered, she could imagine a whole slew of circumstances that might make seeing him again interesting.

"Hey, McGrail! McGrail!"

With Rihanna in her ear and fantasies on her mind, it took a few moments for her to realize that someone had called her name.

Marshall Doyle came up fast behind her. He and his Camp Hill Rec team had beat Maggie's in the finals for the spring season championships this year. *Huh, team. The word doesn't even apply to them. They're more like a street gang with uniforms and play way too rough.* After the game, she remembered, when they went to shake hands, they taunted and jeered them to further crush their spirit.

"Go away, Doyle, I'm not in the mood to talk."

"That's okay sweet cheeks, with the view I have from here, I don't need to hear your voice."

"You're disgusting, go away." Though she tried to speed up, she was on her fifth mile and, with this heat, no longer had the kick to match his long stride. Before she knew it, he'd darted ahead and ran backwards in front of her blocking her from passing and forcing her to slow her pace.

"Come on, just because we beat your asses in the finals doesn't mean we can't be friends. Did anyone ever tell you how hot you look when you're red-faced and sweaty?" Doyle leered at her like a starving hyena eyeing his next meal. "Y'know, if you want I can give you a few pointers on how to be a better player. And how to play soccer better too!" Was that his idea of witty banter?

Maggie gave up and just stopped. She needed a drink of water anyway. Studying him while she recapped her water bottle, she saw why some women might find him attractive. Tall with a lean muscular body, Doyle's thick, dark hair, though slicked with sweat right now, looked professionally styled. His lips seemed full and soft and his shit-eating grin showed impossibly white teeth. Except he had the worst personality in the world. He reminded her of the controlling wife beaters that got arrested on TV crime shows and she wanted no part of him.

Maggie turned away while she snapped the water bottle in place on her belt. "Look, no offense Doyle, but I really do have to go. My boyfriend's waiting for me to get home so we can go to his parents' house for dinner." *Wow,* she congratulated herself. That lie came out so easily. She didn't even stumble through it! And it obviously did the trick as he shifted his feet.

Doyle squinted suspiciously at her. "Your boyfriend, huh? How come I never see you with anyone at the games? Is he not into sports or is soccer just not his game? Cause, you know, you really should be with a man who understands your interests." He had tried for an earnest expression, but it still turned her stomach.

"Oh, he understands." She knelt and pretended to retie her shoe. "He's just more the academic type. I like a man with a brain."

Maggie popped the earbud back in and stepped around him, jogging the last half mile to her car without looking back. She felt his eyes burning through her back as she left. As she reached the car, her heart pounded from the run and even more so from being creeped out by Doyle. Maggie shot a longing glance at the guy selling ice cream from a pushcart, thinking she'd love to have an Italian ice to cool down, but she didn't want to give Doyle the chance to catch her up again. Instead, she gave up on the cooling snack, jumped in the car, and drove home. She wanted to make it to the nursing home to visit Grandma Margaret this evening.

CHAPTER 3

With Mondays being the busiest days at the diner, Maggie had been run ragged. Just after the noon rush, she noticed doofus guy come in and ask to be seated in her section again. *Dumb or not, he's really hot.* She was flattered and more than a little excited that he came back and asked for her section. Though still flushed and hesitant, at least this time he made an attempt at conversation.

"Hello again." Maggie's heart pounded in her ears and she prayed he couldn't hear it. "Are you back for more of our world famous cuisine? Should I start you off with an Arnold Palmer while you decide what to order?"

"You remembered. I'm impressed. Yes, I'd like that. By the way, my name is Simon." He extended his hand and Maggie shook it, surprised by its warmth.

"Maggie McGrail. Nice to meet you. I'll get your drink while you read over the menu." The heat surged up from her feet and her hands were shaking. *What, am I fifteen again? I hope he didn't notice*!

"Ooh, look at you blushing like a school girl." Nothing gets past Sylvie. "Don't tell me you're taking a shine to the doofus garbage man."

That made Maggie's face even redder and now she had to stop and breathe for a moment before thinking of a smart-ass reply, let alone returning to the table with the drink.

"Right, because my life doesn't stink enough I need a garbage man in it. Get serious." Although that shut Sylvie up, the knowing smile stayed on her face as she watched Maggie stumble back to the table.

Simon saw she was unsteady and tried to take the drink from her hand, but it wound up spilling all over the table and his lap anyway. *How mortifying. I never spill things on customers. Who's the doofus now?!* Apologizing profusely, she grabbed a fistful of napkins and started wiping up the table, but only succeeded in pushing still more ice cubes onto his already sopping pants.

"It's okay, it's okay, really." He tried to make light of the awkward situation as he attacked his pants with the whole dispenser full of napkins, his face flushing redder. "We're having a heat wave right now so this'll cool me off."

Sylvie rushed over with more absorbent paper towels from the back and, turning aside, said under her breath, "Damn girl, ease up, will you! You're gonna scare this one away before he even gets started."

Maggie plopped into the booth across from Simon and pressed a damp towel to her own head to calm herself. If he heard what Sylvie said, she'd just claim insanity and go home. Luckily, he either didn't hear it or ignored it. Instead he led her by the hand to an adjacent dry booth and sat across from her dismissing the manager's apologetic attentions.

"Are you okay?" His warm, genuine smile put her more at ease.

"Yes, I'm so sorry. I guess I'm just a little off my game today. I'm really not this clumsy. Not ever."

"How about I let you make it up to me? I'm in town for the Gettysburg re-enactment and I have tickets to the museum artifact display for tomorrow afternoon. If you go with me I'll forget all this happened. What do you say?"

"Oh, well, I…"

Simon untucked his shirt, but it did little to cover the dark stain. "Maggie, I'm gonna be leaving here looking as if I just wet myself so I think you owe me this. Come on, it'll be fun. And I'm a real Civil War buff so I can bend your ear, I mean explain, everything on display." He reached for her hand again, peering into her eyes. "Look, I know I acted like a dork last week, but I promise you, I'm one of the good guys. Will you meet me there? Two o'clock? I promise not to spill anything on you in retaliation."

His good-natured manner settled her and she couldn't, or rather didn't want to, refute his logic. At least Maggie's past American history classes made her confident she could speak intelligently on the subject as long as she remained calm and avoided liquids. "Okay, yes, I'll be there."

Artie, the manager, returned offering him a free meal, but Simon opted for a rain check, saying he'd be back another day with drier pants. Maggie slunk lower in the booth as Artie glared at her.

Simon winked, "See you tomorrow," and left holding a towel over the front of his pants.

Maggie cornered Sylvie in the supply closet. "Sylvie, remember when you said you 'owed me one'? Well, I have a date tomorrow; at least I think it's a date. Will you cover for me?"

Sylvie continued to refill the napkin dispenser and restock the paper towels while Maggie followed her around like a cocker spaniel waiting for a treat. "You mean the guy you almost drowned asked you out?"

"Please? I'll work a shift for you another day if you want."

"That's okay." Sylvie stopped moving and gave Maggie a motherly hug. "I could use a few extra bucks. You go have fun."

***

Maggie contemplated the situation. She hadn't been on a date in months, many months, and she need time to prepare herself—physically and mentally. Did this even classify as a date? It was a museum exhibit in the middle of the afternoon, not dinner or a movie, and he'd asked her to go as payback for ruining his lunch. Maybe if she didn't think of it as a date she'd be less nervous. *Why am I nervous anyway? Good God, McGrail, you're losing it!*

Maggie came back from her morning run dripping with sweat, but invigorated and ready to face the day. After changing clothes three or four times, she chose a simple, cute, flowered sundress that flattered her figure without being too revealing and low-heeled sandals that were fashionable, but comfortable enough to walk around in for a few hours. She swept her hair up in a casual ponytail and used only a light brush of mascara to it keep it from dripping down in the heat and leaving black smudges on her face. Ready and out the door just after one p.m., she had plenty of time to find a place to park.

A whole five minutes early, she climbed the stairs to the museum and saw Simon at the entrance smiling and waving. He smoothed back his hair and Maggie realized he'd just gotten it cut and styled. Yesterday's stubble had disappeared, and the aftershave or cologne he'd used smelled like expensive leather. The light-blue shirt he wore with his khaki jeans even matched the flowers on her dress. Simon had gone out of his way to look his best today and she flattered herself that he'd done it for her benefit. Maggie let him link her hand through his arm as he ushered her inside and out of the heat.

Only a small museum, most people perused the exhibits and video presentations at the Gettysburg in a couple of hours. Simon excitedly examined each display of weapons, ammunition, uniforms and diaries. He recognized and expounded on everything with amusing enthusiasm, and Maggie countered with the tidbits she'd learned at the college. Even other patrons stopped and listened to their conversations at a few of the exhibit stations.

As they neared the exit of the museum, Maggie's stomach betrayed her with a loud rolling growl that echoed through the hall. "Oh my God, I'm so embarrassed."

"Well, I'm hungry too. I, um, passed a decent-looking restaurant not far from here; it may not be the caliber of Sammy's, but the crowd inside appeared to be enjoying their lunch. Will you join me for a bite if I promise not to bore you any more with my Civil War obsession?"

"I'd love to. And I'll try not to spill anything on you."

***

The tiny Italian restaurant had only one window in the front, but the delicious spaghetti Bolognese made up for the cramped quarters. At this time of day, the sun favored the other side of the street, leaving the restaurant candlelight-dim and cozily intimate; a perfect place for two people to get acquainted over wine and mountains of spaghetti.

"My life story is pretty mundane," Maggie said as she buttered a piece of bread. "I've lived in Harrisburg forever. I was a late-life baby. My parents thought they couldn't have children, so they were shocked when Mom became pregnant at fifty. But then they died soon after I graduated high school, within a year of each other. Mom from cancer and Dad, I think, from a broken heart."

"Wow that must've been difficult for you."

"Yeah, it sucked, but at least I had my grandma for support. I've worked at a few odd jobs here and there, got my degree in economics from Penn State then took a few classes and seminars at the local Junior College in American History. You recall my brilliant display of knowledge at the museum." Maggie rolled her eyes and smirked.

Simon cleaned a smudge off his knife before digging into the bread. "With so much education, why are you working as a waitress?"

"Well, Sammy's gives me enough to get by on, so I can spend more time at the library and on the internet following my current passion, genealogy research. Oh, and I'm a nut about fitness and nutrition. Spaghetti and wine notwithstanding."

"Huh, the family I come from is larger than most, I guess," Simon remembered. "Even so, I've always felt like an outsider, as if I didn't belong. So I can relate to anyone who's grown up as an only child."

"Why would you feel like an outsider in your own family? I always envied kids with sisters and brothers."

Simon squirmed in his chair as if all of a sudden his clothes had grown too tight. His reaction disturbed her, and she thought he sensed her unease. "I had hoped we'd get to know each other better, so you can see I'm not crazy or a weirdo, before I tell you my story. But I guess it's better to be upfront after all, because the story also involves you."

Now she was really worried. *A crazy weirdo? And it involves me?* The scary news stories that flashed through her head must have shown on her face.

"Maggie," he said, startled, "I'm sorry, I didn't mean to frighten you. Please, let me begin again. Maybe I started off wrong. Please?"

She cautiously agreed, and he began. "I was only five years old when my three older brothers and I each got these plastic toy guns from Santa. You know, or maybe you don't, but in a large family everyone has to get the same gifts so there's no jealousy or fighting." Simon put his fork down and sat up straight in his chair. "Anyway, while my brothers ran off to the backyard to play war, I stayed inside, confused. I mean, any toy from Santa is great, right? But something about it seemed wrong. As I held it, I remember getting these images in my head of a soldier going into battle with a long rifle and, somehow, I was sure that soldier was me." Simon stopped talking to sip his wine. "Of course my dad nearly fell over when I told him and, after Christmas, he took me to the library and we looked at hundreds of pictures of guns until I found the one from my vision. Turns out it was the Sharps breach loader used by Union soldiers during the American Civil War."

Maggie held her own wineglass inches from her lips. "You were only five when that happened? That would've scared the crap out of me. How did you handle that?"

"Well it was too real to me to be scared." Simon shrugged, tilting his head. "I know it sounds insane, but it's stayed with me over the years and I'm sure it was—is—a past life memory." His voice became low and husky as he leaned closer. "I can still see it so clearly. I can see the camp, my fellow soldiers, hear the deafening noise of the artillery. My leg even hurts when it rains because that's where I got shot. I can remember my battalion walking shoulder-to-shoulder towards the battle line, rifles and bayonets pointed forward with conviction in my heart and sickness in my stomach. I was there, I know it." Simon finished the wine in his glass with one gulp and signaled the waiter for more.

Maggie's hand shook, forcing her to lower her glass. "So you said this involves me, how do I figure into this?" She almost didn't want to hear the answer.

"Remember when I called you Lucy at the diner? Well, I remember being married to a woman called Lucy when I fought in the war." His head tilted with the slight, embarrassed shrug. "Your face felt... familiar."

"Hmm, interesting. So your obsession with Civil War history and the Gettysburg re-enactment stem from this... this past life memory?"

"Yes." His eyes pleaded for acceptance. "People who study these things say it's children who are most likely to have past life memories because their new life has only just begun. There've been thousands of documented cases of kids claiming to have been someone else and being confused by their new surroundings. Most times the memories fade in a few years but, for me, the memories have never faded and I've always felt as if I've been walking with one foot in each world. That's why, for the past few years, I've come here every July for the Gettysburg re-enactment. For that brief moment in time, I'm home."

Maggie sighed with relief and twirled a glob of spaghetti onto her fork. "Well that's not so bad. When you confessed to being a crazy weirdo you made me worry."

The tension in her body subsided, and she smiled again. "I've heard of this past life memory thing before and I've always been fascinated by it. It's kind of cool to meet someone who's experienced it and I see now why you're such an expert on that era. Uh, you don't physically fade in and out do you?"

"No." Simon laughed out loud. "It really is all in my head."

"Good to know. So tell me more about your family. You said you had brothers. Any sisters? What were you like as a kid?"

Simon swallowed the forkful of spaghetti he'd been chewing and leaned back in his seat, dabbing at his mouth with the napkin. "No sisters, just me and my brothers which suited my dad just fine. He owned a machine shop in Wellsboro and spent all week indoors, so when the weekends came he scooped us up and headed for the hills. Literally." Simon's whole face lit up and his eyes had a far-away look as he recalled his pleasant childhood. "We'd head for the most remote places possible, pitched our tents or sometimes just built shelters from loose branches and leaves and did a lot of hunting and fishing. Mom cooked up whatever we caught, and we'd sit around the campfire eating s'mores and singing songs. I remember it being a wonderful time. For my twelfth birthday, my dad bought me an antique Civil War musket rifle and together we researched how to use it. It didn't have the power or range of the contemporary ones my brothers had, but I got pretty good with it."

"My dad loved the outdoors in his younger days as well, but I came along so late in their lives, I missed out on all that camping and bonding stuff." A brief memory of her parents waving from the doorstep flashed before her eyes. *I still miss you Mom and Dad.* "By the time I was old enough to do those things with my parents, they were too old to enjoy it anymore, so I tagged along with my friends' families on their camping trips. It's not the same, though, as being with your own parents."

The conversation went on to lighter, more pleasant subjects as they found common interests in adventure novels and movies. Even their musical preferences ran along the same line, with "country" style being on the bottom of the list. Although their views on current events were similar, they differed on the best cut of steak to buy and how to prepare it.

Simon's warm smile and easy laugh charmed Maggie. She sensed something good starting here. But her past romantic failures cautioned her to keep her heart in check until his intentions were clear.

Three hours later they were leaving the restaurant, laughing and holding hands, tipsy from the wine, and their stomachs full to bursting. Simon walked her to the car to make sure she was okay to drive home, his lips brushed her knuckles. "I had a good time today. Thanks for listening to me prattle on so much about the Civil War and for not thinking me too weird."

"I never said I didn't think you were weird. You're just weird in a good way." He stood close, making her heart flutter away.

"Get home safe. Is it all right if I call you tomorrow?"

"Yes, of course. And thank you, I had a wonderful time today."

Later, in bed, Maggie could still hear his voice and feel the soft caress of his hands on hers. She fell asleep with the sweet memory of a perfect day and the promise of a new beginning.

CHAPTER 4

After she got off the phone with Maggie, Kitty had a new sense of purpose. It astonished her how the firm resolve to quit the hospital gave her spirit a sudden boost. With her mind freed from the heavy burden she'd been carrying, Kitty found the power to swallow her pride and ask Mom to help draft a letter of resignation that didn't sound too bitter. Just in case she wanted to use them for a reference for whatever she wound up doing. Instead of dwelling on the past, she sprang into action, making plans for her immediate future.

Close to dinner time, Kitty got off the bus on Central Avenue and found her mom waiting for her like she did when Kitty was little. A flicker of warmth washed over her when she saw her mom's face brighten.

"You're such a Mom." Kitty engulfed her in a huge hug.

"Well, it's not every day that my baby girl comes to visit and wants my help with something. Besides, it's such a beautiful day for a walk."

They strolled the three blocks to the house her parents had bought when they first got married and had lived in for over thirty years. Built in the fifties, the modest, two-story home boasted a wide front porch and a small back yard.

As they went, Mom rambled on, as usual, about her 'kids' at school. She bragged about one student in particular who had made significant strides in his studies despite the fact that he spoke little English when the term first started. Her face lit up as she talked, waving her hands around for emphasis, making Kitty envious that her mom's vocation came so clearly to her. The idea of being surrounded by a bunch of ten-year-olds all day, every day, gave Kitty the willies, but Mom thrived on it.

Kitty's long awaited decision to leave the hospital delighted her mom. And the pride of being asked to help write the letter of resignation shone on her face.

"Who else would I turn to Ma?" Subtle brown-nosing couldn't hurt, especially since she planned on asking to borrow Mom's car for the drive to Maggie's.

On the bus ride over Kitty had imagined a host of things she'd prefer the letter to say with "You can take your lousy job and cram it where the sun don't shine" on the top of the list. But, with her usual flair, Mom created a professional pack of lies that said how much Kitty had enjoyed working there over the years and how she intended to pursue other interests, blah, blah, blah. She was good and, in the end, Kitty came away with her dignity, enough leftover pot roast for another meal, and Mom's silver 2010 BMW. Mom rarely used it and kept it in the garage most of the time because of parking issues, so it still looked brand new. Kitty looked forward to driving from New York to Harrisburg in style.

Kitty broke the news of Carlos and Sonia's impending marriage which thrilled Mom. "Well it's about time. How long have those two been together? They met in high school, didn't they? At last she's getting settled. Good for her. I'm sure that will be a big relief to her parents." She gave Kitty a sideways questioning glance that clearly meant she'd love to see her own daughter get her life squared away, but Kitty ignored it.

"In any case, Ma, when I return from Maggie's I want to take you and Dad up on your offer to move back home. Only until I get another job though. Don't count on me staying here long. I just want to get out of Carlos and Sonia's way so they can make their plans without me being underfoot."

Mom's exuberant hug flustered Kitty, and she blushed with pride that she'd made her mom so happy. "Darling, this will always be your home no matter how grown up and independent you become. You can bring your things over whenever you're ready."

Ever the supportive ally, Kitty knew Sonia felt guilty for needing her to leave. To be truthful, though, the time for Kitty to move on had past long ago. She'd meant the arrangement to be a temporary reprieve while recovering from Richard's let-down, but she'd gotten comfortable and stayed way too long.

Kitty resolved to take her time loading up Mom's car while working her last two weeks at the hospital so as not to make her departure any more awkward than necessary. Her gym coach needed to be told she was leaving for a while too. Coach Robbins was the best around and, as a former Navy SEAL, he insisted on regimented discipline and refused to train anyone who didn't show up regularly. Kitty didn't want to piss him off and lose her spot in his training roster.

***

As expected, her resignation created little fanfare. "Thank you, Ms. Trausch, for your prompt response. I'll see to it that the personnel department processes this right away so you can get your final check on your last day here." Mrs. German graced her with a weak, fake smile.

"You've been here a long time dear, I'm sure you'll be missed."

And screw you too. Kitty gave her the same condescending expression back. She'd only have to spend two more weeks in this hell hole before she'd be free. *Woo hoo! Bring it on, bitches!*

***

Sonia performed a good-natured cheer routine when Kitty told her she'd decided to resign, and then distracted herself with busywork around the house while Kitty dawdled at emptying her room.

Sonia insisted on helping her pack for the trip to Maggie's and kept pulling things out of the closet and stuffing them into Kitty's suitcase.

"Don't forget to take something cute and sexy in case you ladies go out on the town one night." Her eyebrows were doing this crazy up and down dance. "Who knows, this might be where you'll meet Mr. Right!"

That brought laughter from both of them. Kitty's tinged with cynicism and Sonia's with hope. It made no sense to argue. Sonia's hand wringing and over-helpfulness just made Kitty uncomfortable so she let her put a pair of black skinny jeans and a shiny, stretchy, low-cut, black with splashes-of-green, top in the suitcase along with a torturous-looking push-up bra. Although she did make her exchange the strappy heels she wanted to lend her, for her own rhinestone studded sandals. Kitty had no intention of wearing any of that, but it made Sonia happy that she accepted them. After everything Sonia had done for her, Kitty wanted to be sure she moved out on good terms.

They hugged for the third time, then Kitty wheeled the overstuffed suitcase to the elevator and out to the car. Sonia stopped at the mailbox, giving Kitty the opportunity to get herself comfortable for the long drive.

Okay, Ma. Let's see what kind of music you have in here. Not quite three hours and close to a straight run from Tuckahoe to Harrisburg, Kitty's spirits had been soaring with anticipation for the last two weeks. Along with the classic rock stuff from her parents' time, there was also a Bluetooth device to connect to her own playlist. *Excellent.*

"Kit, honey, please promise me you'll drive carefully and be sure to call me as soon as you get there. I'll be worried sick until you do." Sonia, mail in hand, stuffed a canvas grocery bag full of snacks and drinks in through the passenger side window.

"Jeez, Sonia, I went through this with my mom and dad yesterday. I'll be fine, I promise. And I don't need all that food. It's only a three-hour trip."

"Yeah, that's what Gilligan said. Do you have enough gas?"

"I filled up yesterday." Kitty was positive her eyes had rolled so far back only the whites showed.

"How about money, do you need more cash? Is your cell phone charged in case of emergency?"

"Sonia, stop being a mother hen. My cell phone is charged and I have a car charger for backup, I have my ATM, a credit card, contingency funds, an AAA ID and a navigation app on my phone so I can't get lost. It's only a three-hour drive to Pennsylvania for Christ's sake. I'm not going cross-country. Give me props for having common sense and don't worry. I'll be fine!"

Before she could say another word, Kitty blew a kiss, waved and headed off to the highway.

***

Though she hit a minor snag in the construction zone on I-95, the decent mid-morning traffic only pushed her time-table back by half an hour as she made the connection to I-78. Kitty breezed along with Mick lamenting the wiles of those honkey-tonk women. With the windows open, her hair wild in the wind, the three hours passed before she knew it.

When she arrived, Maggie hugged her so hard it left her breathless. "Oh my God, I'm so glad you're here!" Cute and bubbly like Kitty's sister, Maggie had the strength of a body builder. "I hope you're hungry, I got fidgety waiting for you so I went ahead and made us lunch. I just need to pop the sandwiches in the toaster-oven to heat them up real quick."

"Bless you. I hoped there'd be food. I was too excited about the road trip to eat or sleep much last night, so my dinner only consisted of candy bars and soda. Now I'm famished."

'Lunch' turned out to be a feast. Stacks of roast beef with sweet green peppers, onions and melted provolone on baguettes, accompanied homemade potato salad and marinated cucumbers in sour cream. With only occasional grunts of satisfaction, they demolished the food and washed it down with lime-infused beer.

"I'm so stuffed." Kitty pushed away from the table, stifling an enormous belch. The heavy meal, on top of the long drive with minimal sleep, made her so groggy it took every ounce of strength she could muster to drag herself to the sofa.

But Maggie's energy level soared. She assured Kitty she didn't need help with the dishes as she bustled back and forth from the small dining room to the smaller kitchen.

Unlike Sonia, Maggie had a real knack for decorating. Though more of a cottage than a house, Maggie had furnished it in what might be called French-country-style or Pottery-Barn-chic. An overstuffed camelback sofa covered in cabbage rose patterned slipcovers, paired with a pale green cushy wing chair occupied most of the small living room. A few tables and an old writing desk completed the decor. She always kept a lace tablecloth on the round dining table with a vase of fresh flowers that smelled wonderful. If peace had an aroma, this would be it.

Maggie had been prattling on about something, but try as she might Kitty just couldn't keep up with her. "… confessed that he felt like such a fool for his embarrassing behavior, it took him a whole week to gather enough courage to come back and ask me out. But he knew if he didn't at least try, he'd always regret it. I'm so glad he did."

"Wait, who? I'm sorry I don't mean to be rude. It's just that my brain isn't functioning right now. I'll bet it's still processing the ton of sugar I ate last night. Did you say you have a new boyfriend?"

Maggie had a funny way of tilting her head and peering at you with open mouth and squinted eyes when she was confused, and that expression came out now. "Kit, haven't you been listening to what I've been saying?"

Luckily, the ringing cell phone gave Kitty the opportunity to close her eyes for a few minutes while Maggie talked. Two hours later she woke to Maggie calling her name.

***

"Kit. Kitty, I know you're tired, but tonight you'll regret sleeping so long. I'm going out for a run. Do you want to come with me?"

"Mmm, that's a good idea." She sat up straight on the sofa rubbing the fog out of her eyes. "I'm so sorry I fell asleep on you, Mags, just let me change real fast and we'll jump start my heart again so I can be a better guest."

Maggie drove them to her favorite running trail along the river while continuing the rundown on her new romance. Kitty couldn't help noticing that Maggie's eyes sparkled and her voice got breathless as she spoke of their first date, then their first kiss and how anxious she was to see him again. *Okay, I'm a little envious*, she admitted to herself. *First Sonia and Carlos got engaged, and now Maggie's in love. Sure, everyone's saying they'll stay close, but knowing that my friends are moving on without me, hurts. And what about me? Will I ever find the man who's right for me, or am I destined to be the same high school wallflower watching everyone else enjoy the party without being part of it?*

They started off on the trail, each listening to their own music through their earplugs, each reflecting on their own lives. Kitty knew Maggie's thoughts were turning to her new boyfriend, and she scolded herself for not being more supportive. *Oh well, I've only been here less than twenty-four hours. I still have plenty of time to atone for my jealousy.*

Two hours later they were back at Maggie's house and, soaked with sweat, Kitty headed straight for the shower. Once refreshed, she unpacked her clothes in the cozy guest room while Maggie took her turn.

Kitty chose to wear her relaxed jeans paired with a conservative white tee-shirt and her hair clipped back for the visit to Grandma. Although she preferred tapered jeans and stretchy shirts that hug the body, she didn't think it proper attire for visiting a nursing home.

Maggie did her last minute primping at the long mirror in the hall. Kitty came out of her room and the two of them laughed when they saw how alike they were dressed.

"We're two peas in a pod." Maggie gave her a quick squeeze. "I'm so glad you're here."

***

Even though it had been less than a year, Grandma Margaret struck Kitty as being much older than the last time she'd seen her. The bruise from the IV in her arm highlighted the white translucent skin and her frail frame hardly disturbed the blanket on the hospital bed. Still, she managed a warm smile welcoming her visitors into the room. "I was just thinking of you Maggie dear, and who is your lovely friend?"

"It's Kitty, Grandma, you remember her. I told you she'd be coming to visit from New York again."

"Of course, Kitty, I remember now."

On the ride over Maggie had filled Kitty in on the doctors' prognosis. It wasn't optimistic, and they wanted to lift her spirits in the time she had left. Kitty told Grandma the story of her encounter with Pete, the moron tow-truck driver who had rescued her when her old Chevy left her stranded, and the scandalous No Tell Motel she'd wound up staying in, both of which made Grandma smile with wicked delight. Unfortunately, the excitement caused the monitors to alarm, and the nurse rushed in to check on her.

The nurse took Maggie aside, reminding her of Grandma's precarious health and the need to keep her calm.

Grandma's voice sounded weak, but she insisted on speaking. "And what about those papers and things I sent you to get from the old house Maggie? Did you find them? Have you brought them with you?"

Maggie shot Kitty a guarded look and shrugged. "Uh, no Grandma not yet, I've been waiting for Kitty to arrive so she could help me."

"Oh, sure, I'll be glad to help with anything you need," Kitty said earnestly. "If you want, we can go tomorrow."

"Yeah, that sounds good." With Maggie's gaze drawn to the floor, and her hand rubbing the back of her neck, Kitty sensed she wasn't getting the whole story. Kitty knew in her heart, though, that she owed her one, maybe even two, so she'd made a firm decision to help, without argument, no matter what she needed.

CHAPTER 5

"It's what? You're not seriously telling me that the papers are in an abandoned building in a God-awful neighborhood and you want to go there at night to get them. Why can't we at least go during the day? It'll be creepy at night." Kitty had never told Maggie that she was jealous she'd found a new man, so she doesn't have a clue that she owes her. There may still be a chance of getting out of this.

They'd only been back at the house for an hour when Maggie hit her with the plan. "We have to go at night because we can't let anyone see us. When Grandma fell and broke her hip that time, I had to sell off her antiques to pay for her medical care. Then the State repossessed her house for taxes and boarded up the doors and windows." She shuffled on her feet inspecting the rug for a piece of imaginary lint. "Grandma just told me a few weeks ago about the secret room otherwise I would've gotten the stuff out years ago." Her eyes were pleading now. "I know I'm asking a lot, but it would mean so much to Grandma to have the pictures and things again. Remember how eager she sounded when she asked for them?"

Christ, she was like a wounded puppy, and she'd played the Grandma card, damn it, how could Kitty get out of this now? "Okay," Kitty sighed. "If you promise me we won't die there, I'll go."

Maggie hugged her all excited and bubbly again. "Oh, thank you, it'll be such a great adventure!" Kitty wondered just how far eyes can be rolled back before they come around the other way. They were planning on trespassing? Burglarizing? Grandma Margaret's old house tonight, so they scarfed down an early dinner of simple pasta and left the dishes for later. Kitty still got the willies just rehashing the plan in her mind.

After three wardrobe changes, the ladies were ready for their little crime spree. They had decided upon black yoga pants for freedom of movement, black long sleeve tee shirts and black knit hats. Kitty had to borrow the pants from Maggie so they didn't reach her ankles.

"We're dressed like two spies or cat burglars," Kitty judged as they checked themselves out in the long mirror by the door.

"Well, if the name fits…"

"Oh huh, I get it; cat, you're funny. I'm almost laughing."

Maggie scrunched up her shoulders for a tee-hee giggle, but stopped when she noticed Kitty's shoes. The only running shoes she'd brought were neon orange. It had to be those or her rhinestone sandals.

"You can't wear those; your feet will glow in the dark. I think I have another pair of black ones you can borrow."

Kitty reminded Maggie of her big clodhopper feet. "Are they a size ten?"

"Hmm no, we'll just have to stop and buy you a new pair."

"But you said no one would be around to see us. What difference does it make what color my shoes are?"

Maggie wasn't happy with it, but she resigned herself to the situation. Kitty was right, and she should be happy enough Kitty even agreed to go with her.

"So, how did you come up with this plan anyway? Did you get it from an old I Love Lucy rerun?"

"No silly, of course not."

"Then why do I feel like I'm Ethel Mertz and you're Lucy in this scenario?"

"Lucy! That's what Simon called me that first day at the diner." With a sly smile, Maggie checked out her back view again. "Hmm, maybe he hit on something."

"Yeah, he hit on you! Let's get out of here before I rethink this and change my mind."

***

At twilight they entered the target neighborhood. The neglected environment spread like a virus to surround the simple row houses and highlight the obvious decline of the community. Overgrown yards, downed fences, trash in the streets; all stood in sharp contrast to Maggie's neat little section. They parked the car on an empty street and Maggie pointed out the house.

"There, not the brick house on the corner, but the white wood frame next to it. That used to be Grandma Margaret's house. It was somewhat run-down before, but since it's been vacant for so long, it's really gone to pot."

White was being generous. It might have been white at one time, but not now. The boarded up front windows and door, and the broken or missing upstairs windows, convinced Kitty it was vacant though. Two large trees along the narrow sidewalk obscured the front of the houses so no one should be able to watch their amateur raid. *God, I can't believe I'm doing this.* At first Kitty thought the two houses were attached until Maggie pointed out a gate leading to a pathway between them. Still the houses were so close the residents could've spit at each other from their windows.

"I scoped out the place last week and that path leads around back where there's another door covered with loose boards. We should be able to get them off without a problem and enter that way. It seems Grandpa Joe built a secret room upstairs for the things dearest to them when the neighborhood began to change. The things Grandma's been asking for should be in there."

Kitty had to admit it. Although scared stiff, her whole body tingled with excitement about doing something so contrary to her boring everyday life. *This is freakin' illegal, and my dad will be so pissed if I get arrested. Well, Sonia told me to bust out of my comfort zone, and this is as far out as it gets.*

Still sitting in the car, they waited and watched until they were satisfied no one else was in the area. "Okay, it's dark enough," Maggie announced. "Let's go."

She led Kitty along the narrow path and around the back of the house while the theme from Mission Impossible played in her head. The boards on the back door were half off and easy to remove just as Maggie said. Had someone else broken in here lately? They each put on the black neoprene gloves they'd bought at the sporting goods store last night and the dust masks that Maggie was smart enough to remember. "The place has been vacant a long time and God knows what kinds of creepy stuff is growing in there."

Inside, their little Maglites shone on a small old-fashioned kitchen strewn with empty fast-food containers and bags. The sudden influx of light made a thousand cockroaches scramble back into the dark recesses of the filthy room, sending shudders of disgust up their spines. The masks helped with the dust particles, but the smell of wood rot, mildew and old food still viciously attacked their nostrils.

"I guess we're not the only ones who've trespassed here." Even Maggie shivered at this sight.

"I don't hear anything," Kitty whispered. "Do you think anyone is still here?"

"No, I think we're okay."

In the next room, they found an old, dirty mattress on the floor littered with more fast food bags.

"Whoever's been camping here is a hungry little bugger," Maggie chuckled.

"Let's just get what we came here for and get out. I'm getting the creeps." Kitty's skin itched as if cockroaches were crawling all over her and her nerves were making her as giggly as Maggie.

The staircase to the second floor was just to the left, and the trespassers started up with caution. So much for being quiet. The dry, old, wood stairs made loud creaking noises they were sure could be heard on the next block. They held their breath, cringing with each step.

They opened each door on the second floor and found what were once bedrooms, but were now only furnished with leaves and debris let in from the broken windows.

"Grandma said we could access the room from this hall." Maggie jiggled the wall sconces trying to activate a door.

As they scanned the walls, their Maglites showed nothing but cobwebs and dust. A huge spider web that spanned the width of the hall reflected in Kitty's light with the biggest spider she'd ever seen scurrying across it. Her over-developed imagination warned her of a mutant spider attack, and she freaked. In her anxiety to escape, she tripped over her own foot and crashed into Maggie sending them both flying up against the wall. Heaven knows what happened on their way down, but, as they hit the floor, a door slid open and they fell headlong into the room.

A quick scan with their lights showed them in more of a big closet than a room. Stuffed inside they found a rack of vintage clothes, shelves of gorgeous antique clocks and figurines, piles of old boxes and books, several lamps, and two ancient steamer trunks. A tarp, crusted with dust, hung halfway off an ornate mirror.

So much stuff crowded the tiny space that, as Kitty bumped into a hat tree, she knocked it over and spooked a nest of rats. The rats went scurrying across the floor, making her wobble on her feet again, and her Maglite fly out of her hand. Kitty screamed, Maggie screamed, they even heard the rats scream. Kitty's eyes bulged wide, and she breathed so hard the cup of her dust mask got sucked up against her lips.

"Shit, shit, shit, shit, shit!" Kitty could only repeat that one word as she scrambled to find what she now considered her most vital possession. For her, the only thing worse than seeing the rats, was not being able to see them. Grateful for the gloves, her hand found the little flashlight under the dress rack and her breathing slowed to a near-normal rate.

Maggie set her hands on her hips and shook her head. "If you think you can stay on your feet for a few minutes, I need you to open that trunk and check what's in it. I'll tackle the one over here."

Maggie picked beautiful, handcrafted linens and embroidered towels out of the trunk she had opened. "Oh my God, Kit, come here, look at these things, they're gorgeous."

"No Mags, you come here, I found what we're looking for." Inside her trunk, Kitty found several old framed photographs and loosely bound scrapbooks.

Maggie danced over, doing a Stevie Nicks twirl with the lacy scarf rescued from the trunk she had scoured. She stopped mid-step and knelt again to inspect Kitty's discovery. The gilded frame held the image of a woman wearing a long, dark-colored satiny dress with a sweetheart neckline and off-the-shoulder short sleeves. She held a small bouquet in front of her. Kitty couldn't decide if the splotches on the old, faded photo were part of the dress, or a discoloration in the paper. The woman wore her brown hair pinned up high with dangling curls and, at her throat, hung a delicate locket with roses in the center. Even in black and white, the photo was stunning. The name engraved at the bottom said Margaret McGrail.

Kitty stared at Maggie in astonishment. "It's you."

Maggie touched the photo with reverence. "No, silly, it's Grandma Margaret. I always thought we kind of resembled each other."

"Kind of? Y' think?" Kitty's head jerked up and her ears twitched like a dog on alert. "Maggie, listen, I hear people talking."

"The living room must be right underneath us. Let's get this stuff together and get out of here." Maggie loaded armfuls of linens into the trunk with the pictures.

"Won't they see us?" Panic crept into Kitty's voice again.

"Not if we're super quiet. Grab the handle on the other end and help me get this down the stairs."

As they stepped out of the room the door slid closed again and vanished.

"Huh, it must be pressure activated," Maggie decided. "You must have to step on the right spot to open it."

The overstuffed trunk made their descent somewhat awkward, but they made it to the first floor without incident. Loud voices echoing through the empty house from two men in the living room masked the stairs' creaking boards.

"I guess we found the campers," Maggie whispered as they made it to the back door. "There's still enough distance between us and them so if we run out now I bet we can make it to the car before they can stop us."

Kitty doubted that, but she feared if they waited and the poachers found them inside, they'd never be seen or heard from again. Damn, this was even worse than getting arrested!

They each gripped a handle of the trunk and bolted out the door, surprising two more men who were less than three yards away.

"Hey! Who're you? What're you doing here?" The men hurried forward.

Now it was Kitty's turn to even the odds. She turned to Maggie with a stern voice, "Take the trunk; go. I've got this."

Maggie hesitated for a second, then made up her mind and hurried off, dragging the trunk by one handle along the path towards the car.

Kitty turned and faced the men who were now almost in front of her. One of them reached for something behind his back. If he had a weapon, she'd have to act fast. Her neon-orange running shoes flashed in the air as she landed a succession of good roundhouse kicks, surprising the hell out of both of them. Not wanting to wait around for a rematch, or their reinforcements from the living room,

Kitty made a mad dash to the street while they were still out of action. She found Maggie struggling to lug the heavy trunk into the back of her CRV.

"Hurry, they're right behind me," she called out as she raced toward her.

"Help me, this thing weighs a ton!"

Together they got it secured and were screeching away from the curb as their attackers made it to the middle of the street.

They drove for several blocks, checking the mirrors and peering behind them to be sure they hadn't been followed. Kitty's heart raced from her brush with the squatters, and her breath came in ragged gasps.

When they were a mile away from the house, they stopped at a traffic light and Maggie glanced over at Kitty. "Are you okay there, Ethel?"

She thought for a moment then nodded. "Yeah, I'm good, Lucy, you?"

Their smiles turned to giggles that progressed to full-blown belly laughs, clearing the tension in the air. They laughed so hard and so long, they missed the green light and had to sit through another red one. After catching their breath, they drove the rest of the way home, still reliving their narrow escape from the old house.

"Thank God you handled that, Kit. When I saw them coming so close I thought we were finished. And I'll never forget that expression on your face when you said 'I've got this'." She mockingly deepened her voice, making it sound like The Terminator. "You were such a different person, so in control and focused. I knew you'd get us out of there alive! You have no idea how amazing you are." Maggie reached over with her free hand and gave her shoulder a quick squeeze.

***

They carried the trunk into Maggie's house and dropped it in front of the sofa where they both collapsed. "Wait a minute." Maggie jumped up and ran into the kitchen singing to herself and returned with two glasses and a bottle of cheap champagne. "I bought this for us to celebrate." She popped the cork with flair and poured them each a good size glass.

Maggie raised her glass, "To a job well done." They clinked glasses and took long draughts of the cold bubbly liquid.

Kitty countered with, "To not getting killed or arrested."

"I'll drink to that."

There were several more toasts that got sillier each time and the champagne disappeared quickly.

"Let's check out our booty and see what we've got." Maggie unlatched the trunk and rifled through it. "These old linens are amazing. Check out the intricate embroidery, it must've taken months to finish these things."

Though not Kitty's style, she tried to sound impressed for Maggie's sake. "Well, I guess there wasn't much to do for entertainment in those days, though I can't imagine how hard it must've been to do that close work by candlelight."

Kitty waded through the old pictures again. The one of Grandma Margaret intrigued her. It was amazing how much she resembled Maggie. There were also a bunch more of people she didn't recognize. Still, seeing the faces matching up with the names inscribed below, made them come alive.

"Are any of these photos of the ancestors we have in common?" It occurred to her that the possibility existed.

"I don't know. I'll have to recheck my research and see where they connect."

As Kitty dug deeper into the chest, examining each photo and spreading them out on the floor, a small ornate jewelry box caught her eye. Filled with lovely antique pieces, each one had to be worth a fortune. Among the items, attached to a thin gold chain hung an antique oval shaped locket that showed two roses, one pink and one red, on a cream-colored background encased in ornate gold. The roses appeared to be made from a thousand tiny chips of colored stone and Kitty marveled at the craftsmanship needed to have created the image. She inspected the photo of Grandma Margaret again, comparing it to what she held in her hand.

"Maggie look, here's the locket your grandmother wore in this picture. It's even more gorgeous now that you can see the colors."

Maggie stopped examining the linens and removed both things from Kitty's hand. "Oh wow, you're right, it is." She released the catch, revealing a miniature of both her grandmother and her grandfather on each side. Tears formed in her eyes and Kitty plucked a tissue from the dispenser on the side table for her.

"Help me put it on, I want to wear it."

Kitty knelt behind her on the floor and connected the ancient catch. It hung at her throat just as it did on her grandmother in the photograph.

"I'll bet it's been many years since Grandma's seen this. She'll be so happy that we found it. Let's gather up as many of the documents and binders as we can and we'll bring them to Grandma tomorrow when I come home from work. I'm not sure what she was looking for, but it must be among these things."

Maggie's next day at work flew by as she relived the escapade over in her mind. Grandma had been rambling about getting something from an old trunk for weeks and, after scoping out the house, Maggie realized she needed help to retrieve it. The original plan was to recruit Sylvie, but Kitty's misfortune at the hospital turned out to be a blessing, turning a potential disaster into a successful mission.

What a shame her grandma hadn't been lucid enough to mention that room when the bills poured in from her surgery. Those gorgeous antique clocks would've gone a long way to help pay for the hospital and aftercare. *Hmm...* With the experience they now had under their belts, Maggie wondered what it might take to cajole Kitty into going back for another crack at them. It made no sense leaving those poachers sitting on that gold mine.

***

When they arrived at the nursing home that evening, the clerk at the nurse's station told them the doctor was with Grandma Margaret right now and they should stay in the waiting room. She gave assurances he'd speak with them before he left.

Doctor Brunsting turned out to be a rather large, heavyset man in his sixties, with gray hair and a warm voice. He came into the waiting room wearing a grim expression.

"Maggie, I'm so glad you're here."

After Maggie introduced Kitty, Doctor Brunsting settled in the chair facing them. "I've just been examining your grandmother, Maggie, and I'm afraid the update I have on her condition isn't very promising. Since that last heart attack, her condition has taken a sharp turn for the worse. Your grandma is an extraordinary woman, but, as you know, age catches up to all of us and it appears her time is short." Doctor Brunsting closed the chart on his lap. "Right now, she's still awake and I'm sure she'll be glad to see you."

"Thank you Doctor Brunsting. You've been so kind to my grandma and me. I appreciate everything you've done."

He patted her hand and gave them both an apologetic smile then left to complete his rounds.

Kitty let Maggie cry on her shoulder for a few minutes.

"I don't want to waste too much time out here." Maggie blew her nose and calmed her breathing. "I'll never forgive myself if she passes away while I'm sitting out here blubbering. Let's hurry up and get to her room."

They carried the old trunk down the hall between them, the excitement of showing the contents to Grandma Margaret dissipating with the doctor's words.

In the room they found Grandma half sitting up, her face pale and worn, the nasal prongs for oxygen in her nose and an IV running in her arm. The dimness of the room echoed their sorrow and heightened the foreboding atmosphere. Even so, Grandma gave them a warm, welcoming smile and tried to act as if nothing was wrong.

"Maggie, Kitty, so nice of both you to visit." Her labored breath made her voice weak. "What's that you have there?"

They were both so glad to hear her speak they almost forgot about the heavy trunk they'd been carrying.

"Grandma." Maggie started sniffling again and ran over to hug her.

"Oh dear, you've been talking to that silly doctor haven't you." She patted Maggie's back like a baby. "Don't worry baby, everything will be fine. Your Grandpa Joe's been waiting a long time for me and you have your own life to live without hanging around an old lady."

Kitty fished the old photograph of Grandma Margaret out of the trunk and carried it over to her bedside. "Grandma, we have a surprise for you. We went to the old house as you asked and we found this picture with your name engraved on the bottom in the trunk with the papers and other photos. You looked so beautiful. Do you remember taking it?"

"Get my glasses from the table and let me see." Kitty helped set them right on her face and placed the photo in her shaking hands. "Oh my, yes, look at me. I was quite a looker in my day you know." She puzzled over the old photograph for a few minutes. "But no, I don't remember posing for this. I'm just not sure. There are so many things I don't remember anymore." A note of regret and frustration tinged her voice. "Getting old is such a bugger!"

Maggie and Kitty couldn't help smiling at her brashness.

Grandma studied both of them as she weakly shook her finger. "Remember to take every opportunity that comes your way because it might not come again. Now I'm not saying to be reckless of course, but if you stay on the safe road all your lives you'll never have any fun. And what good is getting old if you don't have any fun to remember?" A devilish smile flitted across her pale lips as she gazed at Kitty and then over at Maggie. The moment disappeared, though, as an expression of alarm froze on her face.

Grandma's hand lifted, and she brushed the locket around Maggie's neck with her fingertips. "The locket, you found it." she whispered. The lines on the monitor spiked higher as she spoke. Her voice regained a little strength, and her eyes filled with wonder at the sight. "I bought this in Philadelphia at an antique shop on Broad Street on my sixteenth birthday. I do remember that. You know how I love to shop for antiques. Ah, I was so young then, so adventurous, just as I hope you ladies are." Grandma's wistful smile was contagious. "Those lovely roses with the pearl white background drew such envy from the ladies in Paris when I wore it."

Maggie's brow creased. "Paris? I had no idea you'd visited Paris, Grandma."

"I went back to find earrings to match," Grandma continued without acknowledging Maggie's question. "But I couldn't find the store again. I searched up and down the street where the shop had been, even stopping at other shops to inquire, but that little antique store had just vanished into thin air. It was so disappointing."

"Anyone can understand why the other ladies would be so jealous, Grandma, the piece is stunning. And I love that you put pictures inside of you and Grandpa Joe. I'll treasure it always."

"Yes, and remember to hold on to it very tightly dear, very tightly." Grandma sunk back into the bed fatigued from the effort of speaking. "It's such a wondrous thing. It took me anywhere my heart desired."

As they talked, Kitty dug out other photographs and assembled the important papers for Grandma's attention. By the looks of things, time was running short.

"Maybe we should let you rest Grandma, you're looking exhausted."

"Tired, yes, I'm very tired."

Maggie didn't leave her grandma's side, but sat there with her cheek resting on her grandma's frail hand.

Minutes later the slow beeping became a steady tone and nurses swarmed into the room. As Maggie wept, Kitty saw her grandma had passed. What do you say to someone who's just lost the one person who's been their lifeline for the last several years? Even as old and frail as she was, just knowing there was someone nearby who knew you intimately, who could understand and comfort you, be your crutch and confidante when you were at your lowest, meant all the difference in the world to Maggie after her parents died. The two women had become so close over the last year, more like sisters than cousins, and the painful scene before her made Kitty's own problems seem insignificant. There were just no words to comfort that emptiness, so enfolding Maggie in her arms, she rocked and cried with her.

"Thank you Kit, for being here with me, I can't imagine how I'd have handled this by myself." Maggie struggled to hold her emotions in check.

"Seriously, Mags, if I wasn't already here you know I'd have dropped everything and flown here in an instant. I'd never leave you to face this alone, best buds forever, right?" Maggie rewarded her paltry effort at humor with a weak but grateful smile.

The nurses were kind enough to let them stay in the room as long as they needed. A couple hours later, the paperwork signed, and the mortuary notified, Maggie and Kitty made their way back to the house, drained of emotion.

***

The next few days went by in a blur. Kitty had only planned to stay in Harrisburg for two or three weeks, but she couldn't walk out on Maggie now. She called her parents to tell them what had happened and that she'd be staying as long as Maggie needed her and not to worry. They sent their condolences with a huge basket of flowers. In fact, Maggie's house resembled a florist shop from so many well-wishers.

There were no other family members, but Maggie's many friends from the diner and the rec center attended the small memorial service she held at her house, bringing gifts of food and bouquets of flowers. Kitty assumed the role of hostess, welcomed the well-wishers, and accepted the thoughtful gifts on her behalf so Maggie could relax as much as possible with her friends. And at long last Kitty got to meet Simon. He'd been keeping his distance because Maggie had told him she'd be busy visiting with her cousin, but there was no way he'd miss such an important event. Maggie clung to him for support and introduced him to her friends.

He definitely looked hotter than she described and Kitty hoped that sometime she'd get the chance to discuss the past life memories Maggie had mentioned. Not tonight though, Mags really needed his attention and Kitty didn't want to distract him.

The guests didn't stay too long so by nine o'clock the leftover food had been put away. Kitty had just finished up the last of the dishes when Simon came into the kitchen.

"Kitty." Simon put his arm around her shoulder and led her back out to the living room. "You've been such a great help to Maggie tonight, but now I want you to get off your feet and come have a drink with us. We need to toast her grandma's exit from this world as she begins her journey to heaven."

"I'm not a religious person, so the whole journey to heaven bit is lost on me but, I have to admit, the drink sure sounds good."

Simon poured from the bottle of wine he had stashed away from the other guests and the three of them touched glasses. "To Grandma," Maggie said with a noticeable catch in her voice. "Thank you for all you've done for me over the years, and may you find the peace you so deserve."

"To Grandma," Simon and Kitty repeated.

Against Kitty's arguments otherwise, Maggie insisted on going back to work the day after the memorial. "The sooner I get back to my normal routine the sooner I'll feel better. Besides, the diner is such a busy place I won't have time to focus on anything else.

Her protests wore Kitty down and, she agreed to spend the day cataloging the documents in the trunk.

"I can't look at those things just yet, Kit, but if you could go through them and make a list of what's in there, it would be so helpful."

"Okay, fine, I can do that. We can go for a run afterwards too."

***

Kitty's mom had called to check in and they'd talked for hours. She'd filled her in on what had happened and Mom had news of her own.

Sonia and Carlos had set their wedding date seven months from now, in January. Although they planned a small event, Kitty and her mom both knew that Sonia's huge family would never stand for it. Kitty shared the details of Grandma Margaret's demise and glossed over the vacant house caper to keep her from worrying too much and launch into one of her unbearable lectures. At one point Kitty tuned her out, her mind wandering to the contents of the open trunk while her mom babbled on about Kitty having a new man in her life. She'd never had much luck with men to begin with and, after her crushing defeat with Richard, she thought she never would. She wished her mom wouldn't keep bugging her about it.

Kitty was still knee-deep in paperwork when Maggie came home in high spirits. She couldn't believe it was five o'clock already.

"Simon came by the diner today and invited both of us to go to this dance club he found that features a karaoke contest every Saturday night," Maggie said. "Remember when we did that at Christmas? We had so much fun."

"First, let me say I'm glad you're feeling well enough to consider going out to have fun. That being said, there is no way in hell I'm going with you. For one thing, I'm not going to be a third wheel on anyone's date and secondly, I'm not getting up to sing karaoke in a bar. In front of family for fun is one thing, but I refuse to be jeered at by a bunch of drunken strangers." Kitty poured the last beer from the refrigerator into two glasses for them to share.

"Oh, Kit, come on, it's not a date. It's only three friends getting together for a drink." Maggie talked faster as she followed Kitty back from the kitchen, sounding like a kid trying to get her mom to let her use the car. "Besides, I don't know where this thing with Simon is going yet. I mean, I'm attracted to him, very much so actually, but he doesn't even live here. He said he's only in town for the Gettysburg re-enactment and we haven't discussed it, but I guess he'll go back to his business and his life up in Wellsboro, when that's finished."

Kitty resettled herself on the living room floor to continue digging through the paperwork she'd been organizing. She had no intention of giving in no matter how much Maggie nagged.

"And I can't leave Harrisburg, not yet anyway," Maggie continued. "This may be just a casual fling on his part so I'm afraid to get too close. I need you to be there as a buffer to help me keep this on a casual level until I figure out if something is happening between us or not."

Kitty understood her reluctance to get herself into a situation where she might get hurt. They'd both had their hearts incinerated before and were now quite cautious. Still, claiming to have lived before is pretty spooky. She hoped this guy didn't have any other deep dark secrets.

CHAPTER 6

Having the backbone of a wet noodle, Kitty caved in with just a few more feeble arguments. She'd been so busy helping Maggie, and running errands, that music and a few drinks sounded like a good idea. The distraction would be a welcome stress reliever for both of them and she'd been washing and wearing the same clothes over and over again for so long, it would be refreshing to get dressed up for a change.

Maggie whistled when Kitty emerged from her bedroom. "Woo hoo, look at you, hot mama! And that eye shadow highlights the green in your eyes so well. You're so beautiful."

"Oh yeah, Angelina Jolie watch out, Ethel Mertz is on the prowl."

She wore the black skinny jeans and black-and-green stretchy tee-shirt with the push-up bra that Sonia had insisted she bring and had used Maggie's curling brush to fluff up her hair. She even applied a dab of mascara along with the green eyeshadow she'd found at the drug store. Pleased at Maggie's positive reaction, she twirled to give her the full-effect and nearly fell off her low-heeled sandals.

"Careful with those twirls there Ethel, Ricky's waiting for us at the club and I don't want to have any 'splaining to do."

Maggie's skinny jeans were similar, but hers reached her ankles like they were supposed to, and her white, silky knit top with keyhole cut-outs at the shoulder clung to her curves just enough to emphasize Mother Nature's generosity. She hadn't taken the locket off since she'd found it and it now hung at her throat skimming the neckline of the top, the gold-encased roses standing in stark relief against all that white. Another drugstore find was the shiny, red, ceramic rose earring studs she wore to match the locket.

Maggie handed Kitty the teardrop jade earrings she'd admired from grandma's jewelry box. "Here these are for you. I'm sure Grandma would've wanted you to have them and they'll match your outfit."

Tears started in her eyes and she willed them away to prevent mascara from running down her face. Kitty fastened on the earrings and fluffed her hair back to admire them. "What do you think? Do they look as pretty as I feel?"

"They, and you, look wonderful. Now let's get out of here before I get emotional."

Kitty fastened the strap tighter on her sandals to keep them secured better. If she was unsteady sober, she could just imagine how she'd be after a few drinks. They decided to take her mom's BMW to eliminate the temptation to overindulge, knowing she'd have to drive home. Kitty's other reason she kept to herself. She thought that if Maggie and Simon stepped up their relationship tonight, she'd at least have a familiar car to drive home. Not that she thought Maggie would ever leave her stranded; she only wanted to give her the freedom to follow her heart.

The roadside club was just off the highway and Kitty paid special attention to memorize the route in case she wound up driving home either alone or with a passed out companion. Loud music and laughter resounded all the way to the outer edge of the gravel parking lot, where they found an open spot, and emerged from the car amped up and ready for a good time.

From the outside the club looked tiny, but once inside the door, the room opened to a huge cavern packed to capacity. A strong smell of alcohol with a mixture of colognes permeated the air. The DJ played eighties rock with a heart-thumping bass, and so many people packed the small dance floor they seemed to blend into one gyrating person. Off to one side, three bartenders worked hard to keep up with the orders. Somehow, Maggie spotted Simon waving to them from a bar-height table he'd commandeered at the edge of the dance floor. They made their way over to him, squeezing through the crowd. Kitty was pretty sure she'd gotten felt up at least three times on the way, but in this crowd, who could say for sure whether it was intentional or not? Besides, with so much padding in the push-up bra, she couldn't feel much in that vicinity anyway.

Once they reached their seats, a waitress appeared to take their drink orders. Maggie gave Kitty the fish eye when she ordered a vodka and cranberry juice.

"I thought you weren't going to drink tonight, *remember*?"

"Trust me, I haven't forgotten. I'm going to have this one drink to loosen up and that's it. I promise not to embarrass you. Or Simon." She flashed a smile Simon's way.

"Don't worry, ladies, there are so many people in here no one will notice anything you do, unless you fall flat on your face on the dance floor."

Maggie lifted her eyebrows at her as a reminder to be cautious. Regardless of her clumsiness, Kitty came here to have fun, so she stood her ground on the drink. After a long sigh Maggie gave in and ordered her own. "Scotch rocks for me please." Orders taken, the waitress somehow teleported herself back through the crowd.

After getting used to the noise and finding the right speaking level, Kitty cornered Simon. "So, Maggie told me you've had past life memories that took you back to Civil War times. That sounds incredible. Can you tell me about it?"

Simon's mouth opened then closed as he fixed Maggie with a sideways stare. "Well, a toy gun I got for Christmas one year triggered the memory. I was just a kid and didn't know I'd said anything unusual until I saw the dumbfounded look on my father's face."

Kitty couldn't help smirking. "I'll bet. That's a hell of a thing to hear your kid say. What about the kids at school? Did they tease you because of it?"

He glanced at Maggie then lowered his head. "No, it wasn't something I went around telling just anybody."

Simon's discomfort got a momentary reprieve as the waitress reappeared at their table without spilling a drop of their drinks on the tray she carried. She rolled her eyes as they argued over who got the bill for this round, and since Simon won the argument, she disappeared again with his credit card.

The bartender had gone heavy on the cranberry juice and the first sip made her pucker. Kitty stirred the ice cubes to dilute the tartness while she continued to interview Simon. On the surface he seemed okay, and Maggie was obviously smitten, but she was too important to let her get mixed up with a nut.

"So, tell me more, what was your name? Do you remember it being different? Were you someone famous like a general or something?"

"No, no, nothing of that sort. You know many people claim to remember past lives, but I've always been skeptical of those who claim they were Cleopatra or Attila the Hun or some king. In reality there've been a helluva lot more of us common folk than otherwise so, seriously, what are the odds of remembering to have been a famous historical figure?" Simon had a head start on the ladies and downing this second drink eased his discomfort on the subject. "My memory puts me as a rifleman-sharpshooter assigned to the infantry. I guess in today's military terms they'd be called Special Forces. I'm sure that's why the toy gun initiated the memory. As far as a name, though, I have no idea. I can't remember knowing it or having anyone call me by it."

So not General Grant riding in on his gallant steed to save the day; at least that lent credibility to his madness. Kitty still didn't buy his story though. There's been so much in the news lately celebrating the heroics of the Special Forces, he may have gotten it from there. "Maggie probably hasn't told you much about me, but I'm a sci-fi nut and odd things like this arouse my interest. I've also read there are ancient Eastern Indian religions who believe we're doomed to be reincarnated over and over again until we either learn all the lessons living can teach us, or until we apologize for whatever heinous misdeed one of our ancestors committed that passed the bad karma down through the generations. I'm going with the lessons learned part, since I'm clueless as to why I'd need to apologize." She slurped the rest of her drink through the straw.

"I thought I remember you saying you weren't a religious person." Kitty caught the air of challenge in his voice. *Okay, I probably deserve it from the way I've been pressing him.*

"I'm not. Not in the familiar sense of the word anyway. Don't get me wrong, I'd never judge anyone else for their personal beliefs, it's just that science and cosmology are more credible to me." She leaned forward so he could hear her better over the increasing level of the music. "Have you ever read any of Carl Sagan's books? He says we're all made of stardust from comets carrying organic DNA that crashed into the earth millions of years ago and spread their seed so to speak. To me, that supports the idea of a cosmic universal relationship that lives in and among all of us; as though we're spiritually connected somehow. My brain can't digest the concept of an omnipotent supreme being overseeing our lives, nor do I feel it necessary to perform the rituals or attend the services of organized religion. So no, rather than religious I guess I'd call myself spiritual." She rested back in her seat again giving him time to digest what she'd said. Challenge met.

Maggie had slipped away to the restroom for a minute, but now she was back and pleased to see Kitty and Simon in deep conversation and getting along so well.

"Okay, I'm back, you can stop talking about me now, did I miss anything important?"

"Kitty was explaining the universe to me."

"Oh, well I'm glad you've been brought up to speed on that important issue. I'm ready for another drink, how 'bout you guys?"

Through all the noise in the club, Maggie's words 'another drink' carried to the waitress's ears, and she magically reappeared.

"Another round for everyone?"

"Make mine a virgin vodka and cranberry," Kitty said.

"That's just cranberry juice you know."

"Oh, huh, so it is. That's okay, I'm driving."

With the DJ taking a break, the MC for the night introduced the karaoke contest with an open invitation to take part.

Amid the cheers and whistles several people hurried forward to put their names on the list. Without the music, the decibel level decreased to a near normal level and only the talking and laughing of people having a good time lingered. Maggie and Simon had their heads together in a private moment. Not wanting to interrupt, Kitty excused herself to the ladies' room.

"Hurry back, Kit, don't be too long."

"Okay, don't get excited, I'm only going to the ladies' room."

"Yeah, but hurry back." Maggie's eyes were wide and pleading as she jiggled in her seat.

Jeez, is she that afraid of being alone with him? He'd impressed Kitty as weird, but not dangerous. She had planned to give them some private time, but she'd come back sooner if she could get through this damn crowd.

As Kitty made her way back she noticed Maggie craning her neck watching for her. Something made her very nervous. Kitty wished Simon would take a break so she could get Maggie alone and find out what the hell it was.

The decibel level had dropped now except for a few laughs and cheers as this poor half-drunk guy onstage sang this comedic version of The Black Eyed Peas' "My Humps". Kitty admired his nerve and self-confidence to even get onstage, drunk or not. She clapped and cheered the same as everyone else when he finished. But she was floored when the MC called out, "Okay, thanks Alan, next up we have Maggie and Kitty singing "Wannabe." Let's give a big O'Malley's cheer for Maggie and Kitty!" The room erupted with shouts and chants of "Magg-ie, Kitt-y, Magg-ie, Kitt-y." Kitty broke out in a sweat as the walls began to close in on her.

"Lucy!" She accused her, "You're freakin' kidding me! Tell me you didn't do this."

"Lucy?" Simon did a double take when he heard Kitty call her that, but Maggie impatiently waved him away.

"I knew that if I'd asked you first, you would've said no, and then you'd have missed out on all the fun." Kitty couldn't tell if Maggie's face had turned red or if she was just seeing red.

Simon waved his arms pointing to them and shouted, "Here they are, over here."

The crowd practically carried them up to the stage. "Listen, you can kill me when we get home," Maggie murmured. "Right now everyone's expecting us to sing, so let's just go with it."

Kitty's anger now turned to fear. "Maggie, you know when I'm nervous I have a tendency to lose my balance. What if I fall on my face on stage? I'll be mortified."

"Oh honey, don't worry. It's just for fun. Look around, everyone's so drunk they couldn't care less how we sound, and I specially chose "Wannabe" because we did it at Christmas and I knew you were comfortable with it. Remember how you fought with those men at the old house? What did you do to gather your courage then?"

Kitty considered that for a second and, as the music started, she squared herself up as though getting ready for a fight. Which, in a sense she was; only the fight was with her own fears. A few seconds into the song she understood Maggie's point. No one was listening at all because they sucked and still the crowd yelled and cheered them on like rock stars. Her heart thumped in time to the music, her arms waved with abandon, and she smiled so wide it hurt. But she didn't care. They strutted back and forth across the stage as if they had rehearsed and performed the song a dozen times. The most remarkable thing to Kitty was that she stayed on her feet the whole time!

No drug in the world could have duplicated the high she experienced as she left that stage. She could've conquered this world and the next single-handed, outrun a speeding bullet, leapt tall buildings in a single bound. Superman had nothing on her.

"Did you see that? Did you see us?" Maggie hugged Simon so hard Kitty thought she'd break his ribs.

"Of course I saw it. You girls were awesome."

Kitty started to raise her hand for the waitress, but she was already there. This woman was spooky.

"Another virgin vodka and cranberry for me please. And it's my turn to buy this round so don't you dare take a dime from either of those two." She handed over her credit card, and the waitress melted back into the crowd.

Kitty felt a hand on the back of her chair and turned, thinking this couldn't be the waitress coming back so soon. Nobody could be that fast.

"Heeyy, McGrail, you never told me you were a Spice Girl, and who's this lovely lady with you?"

Okay, he had her complete attention. Right height, athletic body, stylish, gorgeous eyes, and he'd called her lovely. All the perfect components. Except that drawn out 'hey' blew right into her face boosting her blood alcohol level a couple of points. This guy was seriously lit.

"This is my cousin Kitty. Kitty, Marshall Doyle." The bland expression on Maggie's face didn't match her congenial voice and Kitty wondered if these two had a history. She shook his offered hand anyway, and he took that as an invitation to join them, slithering right into the vacant chair beside her.

"And this must be the brainiac boyfriend, huh?" Doyle extended his hand to Simon who took it without enthusiasm.

"The name's Simon. And I'm not sure you'd call me a brainiac..."

Maggie linked her arm through Simon's and leaned her head on his shoulder. "Oh, honey, what Doyle means is that I told him you were more the academic type." She stroked his muscular arm. "While you're obviously fit, you're not so much into sports as I am, that's all."

Simon caught on and played along. "Oh, yeah, right." He patted her hand. "Maggie outshines me in sports, but we have other things in common. Don't we, sweetheart?" He kissed her chastely on the lips.

This overacted performance turned Kitty's stomach and Doyle didn't seem too happy at that kiss. She tried to divert his attention, pointing to the stage and moving her finger right in front of his eyes so he'd have to follow it. "Oh my, check out that guy on stage. He's so into that song isn't he? Do you know who he is?"

"Yeah, that's one of my buddies, he's okay." He stayed hyper-focused on Maggie, who clung to Simon's arm and avoided Doyle's gaze as much as possible. Since that little distraction hadn't worked, Kitty would have to try another tack.

"So, Doyle is it?" She rested her hand on his arm and squeezed it to get his attention. "What do you do for a living, Doyle?" Before he could answer, the magical drink fairy came back to their table.

Once she'd served everyone, Simon took up the question with Doyle. "You were going to tell us what you do for a living, Doyle."

"Oh, yeah, well I'm a project engineer with Rawlings, one of the local companies here. I do feasibility studies and job cost analyses, that sort of thing," Doyle explained in a self-important and condescending voice, slurring a little. "And what about you, Professor, what do you do?" He glared at Simon with eyebrows raised as if challenging him to come up with something better.

What an asshole. Now Kitty understood why Maggie didn't like him. The polite banter was a sham to keep the atmosphere pleasant around Simon, but she must be itching like crazy to tell this guy to bug off for good.

Familiar with the game being played, the muscles in Simon's jaw set tight, and his eyes bore into Doyle's. He answered in a casual tone as if it wasn't impressive at all. "My brothers and I own a thriving sheet-metal fabrication plant up in Wellsboro. It pulls in just under a couple mil a year."

Doyle had no reply, his eyes narrowing as he nodded in return. She didn't know Simon well enough to say he was telling the truth, but shutting Doyle down like that was awesome. *You go, Simon!* Kitty sent him telepathic cheers while Maggie gazed up at him doe-eyed.

Doyle's buddy had finished his song, and the MC announced the next contestant. "Next up is Simon. Simon, where are you? Come on up here my man."

"Is that you?" Maggie asked, startled.

"Yep, that's me."

Maggie and Kitty stared at each other, reading each other's mind, the dread clear in their faces. If Simon went up on stage he'd be leaving them here alone with creepy Doyle!

Doyle's arrogant smile returned, and he clapped Simon on the back as he rose. "Go ahead, man, do your thing, I'll keep these lovely ladies company while you're gone."

Simon hesitated a moment, giving Doyle a dark, menacing scowl before making his way over to the MC.

For a moment, Kitty thought there'd be a fight which, in this crowded room, would be disastrous. She didn't know if Doyle was an angry drunk or not, and didn't care to find out, so she thought it best to wait a few minutes, to not make it obvious, then ask Maggie to come with her to the ladies' room. They'd make a graceful exit and decide what to do when they got there.

Simon appeared to be negotiating with the MC as he thumbed through the music listing.

"There's been a slight change in the program here, people. Instead of "Changes", Simon's going to wow us with "Love Shack". It's a duet y'know, buddy. Do you have a partner or do you need a volunteer?"

Several women waved their arms in the air, offering their services. "No, no thanks," Simon said with a self-satisfied grin. "I brought my own back-up singers. Maggie, Kitty, come on, let's show them how it's done."

Simon, you are a brainiac. He had rescued them from drunken asshole hell. The ladies gave each other the same knowing smile and this time Kitty was excited to get up onstage. The euphoria from their last performance coupled with the prospect of an easy escape, had them running with their arms in the air and wings on their feet to join Simon onstage. Neither of the girls knew the song, so they read the words from the screen, faking it as best they could. They kept smiling, sashaying around, and making a show of it like last time. Not that anyone in the club cared. Maggie was right, it didn't matter how they sounded, everyone just wanted to see a show and have fun and they did their best to oblige.

The song ended with a shout of 'Love Shack' which they did in unison with their arms raised. Simon grasped them each by the hand and, after stepping off the stage, led them towards the exit as fast as possible. The threesome laughed so hard, they crashed into a couple standing by the door and almost fell.

Out in the parking lot they headed straight for Kitty's mom's car, laughing and reveling in amazement at their performance and the audacity of their little deceptive end run.

"Hey, McGrail, hold up. Where're you guys going?" Damn, if it wasn't Doyle again. He left the three guys he'd been talking to and stumbled over towards them. *For crying out loud, can't this guy take a hint?*

Still in the grip of the rush, Maggie had a hard time being serious. "Oh sorry, Doyle," she said still laughing. "We're outta here. See y'around, bye."

As Maggie stepped away again, Doyle seized her by the shoulder, spinning her around to face him. As he did so his finger caught the chain she wore, breaking it and sending the locket flying to the ground. "You're not going anywhere."

Maggie dove to retrieve her precious heirloom and rose, clutching it in her hand, her eyes wide in shock and anger. Kitty stood riveted to the ground, unsure whether to start a parking lot brawl or to sweep Maggie away and run.

Simon responded with a crunching blow that sent Doyle reeling to the ground, blood spurting from his nose. Doyle's companions saw the confrontation and headed towards them. Outnumbered now, they wheeled around and Simon jerked each of them by the arm.

"Let's get the hell out of here… fast."

They raced off, Simon still holding onto each of them. The sensation of falling, as if off a steep cliff, hit them in slow motion. The music from the club had disappeared, and the world had gone dark.

CHAPTER 7

"Kitty, wake up. Kitty, come on, wake up. Are you okay?"

A man's voice came to her from a distance and she felt someone shaking her shoulder. For a disoriented minute, she imagined herself back in her room with her dad getting her up for school. But it wasn't Dad's voice. It was Simon's. "What? What is it? Why are you here waking me up?"

Through bleary eyes Kitty saw they sat on the ground with a heavy mist around them. *What the hell?* She remembered being in the parking lot of the club en route to her mom's car, then nothing but a blur of Doyle stopping them. "Where are we? Are we still at the club? Where's my mom's car? And what is that smell?"

"That smell is you… and us." Maggie stood and brushed off her clothes. "It seems all three of us threw up and, good God, look at you, you're covered in it. What did you do, fall into it?"

A quick assessment showed vomit plastering down her hair on the left side, and more dried on the same side of her shirt. "But I only had one drink. I never throw up after only one drink."

"That's the least of our worries." Simon helped her to her feet while he scanned their surroundings. "It's obvious this isn't the parking lot, and I can't even see the club from here. I'm sure we weren't that far from the door. We'd only just left."

Kitty had become lucid enough to focus on what Simon described and realized that, instead of the gravel parking lot, they stood in an open grassy field with the heavy mist of dawn around them. A solo, wide, old oak tree broke the flat landscape. Underneath lay enough acorns scattered on the ground to keep a family of squirrels fat and happy for several winters. "What the hell? That can't be the sunrise. It couldn't have been much past midnight when we left the club."

"We must've passed out." Maggie surveyed the landscape, just as confused as the others. "It's cold. Let's find the road and get out of here. Which way should we go?"

"One way's as good as another I suppose," Simon said. "I don't know, should we split up, you think? Not too far, I mean, maybe for a hundred yards or so to see what's around? We might have a better chance of finding it that way."

"No!" Maggie and Kitty were emphatic about staying together and their simultaneous response made that clear.

"Okay, well then it's lady's choice, I'll follow your lead."

Maggie and Kitty glanced at each other and shrugged. "This is your city," Kitty said, "you decide."

After a moment's consideration, Maggie closed her eyes and turned in slow circles with her arm pointed out until she got dizzy. "That way." From where the sun was rising it appeared she pointed due west.

Simon placed his hands on his hips and shook his head. "Very scientific. Okay, let's go."

After a few feet Maggie yanked off her shoes because her spiky heels kept sinking into the loose, grassy soil, and Simon snatched them from her hand. "Wait, I have an idea. If you're not going to wear them, let's hang these shoes on a branch of that tree so we'll know if we come back to it again we've been walking in circles."

"Ooh, Doyle was right, you are a brainiac." She reached up and gave him a quick kiss, eliciting a proud smile while Kitty's eyes disappeared in her head. Two low branches made the climb easier, and he chose a sturdy one for crawling out to the edge. They each stepped back a few paces to check his handiwork.

"Huh." Maggie crossed her arms and her head tilted to the side as though examining a museum piece. "The shoes are a little hard to see. They blend in with the tree." Her gaze shifted to Kitty's feet and then to her face.

"You want my shoes?"

"Maggie's right. The rhinestones on yours will catch the sun and we'll be able to see them from farther away. If it makes you more comfortable, I'll leave mine here too and we'll all go barefoot."

A long sigh accompanied her eye roll. "Fine, whatever. Anything to get us home and into the shower faster."

By the time they'd left the tree, it had three pairs of shoes tied onto it. Simon hung one of Kitty's on the east side and one on the west so they'd catch the sun coming and going for the best visibility, his on the north side and Maggie's on the south.

"Okay, no matter which direction we're coming from we'll be able to see the shoes and recognize the tree." With his head held high, Simon crossed his arms over his puffed up chest.

Maggie caressed his arm and brushed the debris from his hair. They linked arms again and started off in the direction they had decided upon earlier. "Now let's go find that highway and get the flock outta here!"

Kitty still couldn't figure out how they'd lost the freakin' road in the first place. "Wait, aren't you guys even a little curious about how we got here? We're in the middle of nowhere, for Christ's sake."

"Of course," Simon answered. "We're as bewildered as you are, but standing around worrying won't get us any closer to an answer. We have to find a road or a landmark. Something that will give us a fix on our location so we can get out of here. We need to keep moving."

They continued along at a steady pace, Maggie and Simon led the way and paid little attention to her comments. Simon put his arm around Maggie's shoulders and pecked her on the cheek in reassurance.

"Look, Kit, a house!" Maggie's excited grin lit up her face. A house was better than a road. None of them were getting any cell service, but there must be a phone inside to call a cab for a ride home. They'd only been walking for about a half hour, so this wasn't such a huge ordeal after all. Relieved at the sight, they picked up their pace, practically skipping the rest of the way.

As they got closer they saw that the house was a simple white wood frame with a covered porch, outside shutters adorning the windows, and a smaller utility building off to the side that might have been a garage or a small barn. Chickens clucked from somewhere nearby and the red flowers edging the porch made for a sweet serene setting. Hulking at the door stood a man close to Maggie's height, wearing what once might have been a white shirt that had yellowed, with sleeves bagged to the cuffs and buttoned up tight to the neck, and loose fitting brown pants with suspenders. A moustache and long beard obscured half his face, but Kitty guessed his age at around forty. Simon slowed their pace, nodding to the long rifle the man had alongside him.

Kitty tugged on Maggie's arm and lowered her voice. "I thought the Amish were non-violent."

"Good morning, sir." Simon stepped forward while they kept a safe distance. "I'm sorry to disturb you, but the ladies and I have gotten lost. May we use your phone to call a cab to take us home?"

The man at the door didn't respond. His suspicious eyes raked Simon up and down before fixing Kitty and Maggie with a scandalized and disgusted scowl. Their appearance had to be dreadful as they both stood there damp and shivering, and Kitty had vomit on her. At this point Kitty didn't care though, and she moved forward to plead her case.

"Don't." Maggie grasped her arm. "Let Simon handle this. I get the impression this guy isn't so happy to see us."

"Are you here for the enlistment?" He tore his eyes from Maggie's shirt that clung to her chest from the dampness and addressed Simon again.

"Uh, yeah, the enlistment." Simon nodded and looked back at his companions with raised eyebrows.

"Oh, that's it," Maggie whispered. "He's with the Civil War re-enactors and they must be getting ready for a rehearsal or something. That explains the rifle and how he's dressed."

"Oh, okay, I get it. So is he going to let us use the phone or not? I can't stand the smell of myself anymore."

"Well, I'll be on my way to the camp presently with supplies for the soldiers. I'll be glad to give you a ride up there if you don't mind waiting till after I've had my breakfast, but the whores will have to go back to whatever brothel they came from. Whores are not welcome in the camp or in my house."

"Excuse me?" Maggie's voice exploded with indignation at this comment.

"Who the hell do you think you're calling a whore?" Kitty shouted. "You've got some damn nerve!"

Simon had to block the women from marching up onto the porch and getting into the asshole's face. "Calm down, calm down, I'm sure it's only a misunderstanding." He lowered his voice to a whisper, "That's a real gun he has there, so let's not provoke him, okay? Let me handle this and go along with whatever I say. Please?" He searched their faces for acceptance and got eye rolls and nods from both of them.

Turning back to the porch, he began again. "Sir, again I apologize for the early hour. I'd be most grateful to take you up on your offer of a ride, but I'm afraid you're mistaken, the ladies are not whores." Simon studied their disheveled appearance, racking his brain for a plausible excuse for it. First he pointed to Kitty. "This lady is my, um… sister, Kitty, and this lady." He came closer to Maggie and whispered something even Kitty couldn't hear. "This lady is my beautiful wife, Maggie. The three of us were attacked and robbed yesterday evening and spent the night out in the field. As you can see, we're still wet and dirty from it." He gave Mr. Porch Guardian his most imploring expression of honesty, hoping he'd pleaded a good enough case.

A woman they assumed to be the man's wife, came up behind him and they whispered back and forth for a moment. Freckles covered the woman's plain facial features, and she had on the period costume worn by most women in the mid-nineteenth century. The ankle length calico dress with the little round collar fastened below her chin with a narrow ribbon bow, and her drab brown hair peeked out from under her lace cap. Together they could have posed for a Norman Rockwell painting.

"Set upon and robbed, you say? You and your... kin." He pointed to Maggie and Kitty with a hint of skepticism in his voice. After a moment's hesitation he said, "Well, come along then, my wife, Mrs. Blandford, will help you get cleaned up and fed breakfast before we start out for the camp."

The prospect of being fed eclipsed all insults and the three of them scurried behind Mr. Blandford into the house. Neither of them cared what made him believe Simon's story, they were too relieved at being allowed inside to get dry and clean. Not to mention the prospect of replenishing their empty stomachs with food.

The inside reminded Kitty of Maggie's place with the same style of antique tables and handmade accessories. Maggie's face glowed with excitement from the sight.

Once in the kitchen, a delighted squeal escaped her when she saw the huge cast iron stove set into the far wall.

"Oh, Mrs. Blandford, your house is amazing. Where did you ever find that stove? It must've cost a fortune! And these cast iron pots and things, I can't believe my eyes." Pots and bowls hung from a rack over the stove and more cluttered the wooden counters and table. Maggie marveled at and brushed her hands over everything in sight.

To Kitty it looked like a museum. She couldn't imagine why anyone wanted to live this way, even for a short time. These re-enactors were world class role players.

Mrs. Blandford blushed at Maggie's fussing, and after ushering them into a small mud room off the kitchen, she poured water from a large pitcher into a basin. A few towels and a bar of soap were laid out for them as well. She frowned and tsked at Kitty, then set out an extra basin with another pitcher alongside it for her to wash her hair. The ladies guessed they were too stinky and dirty to use the bathroom. This would have to do until they got home and into a long hot shower.

"You poor dears, did those hooligans steal your clothes as well? It's becoming so dangerous around here these days with all the strangers come into town. My daughter left a few things here when she went to Washington a few weeks ago. She's a nurse you know, doing her patriotic duty. We're very proud of her." She peered up at Kitty from her diminutive height, curious at the difference. "I'll see if I can't alter one her dresses to fit you ladies. No sense you going around wearing that." She gestured at their clothes, wrinkling her nose with disgust.

"Oh, you don't need to go to any trouble," Maggie said. "We'll be…"

"Nonsense." Mrs. Blandford cut Maggie off in mid-sentence with a wave of her hand and left them to get cleaned up while she finished preparing breakfast.

"Okay," Maggie finished.

Kitty sighed and shook her head. "Aren't they carrying this charade too far? I mean, role playing is one thing, but you've got to break character sometime."

"You're right, I know. Let's just play along for now. We'll be out of here soon."

They washed up as best they could with the basins and towels Mrs. Blandford had provided. It wasn't easy using bar soap instead of shampoo, so Maggie helped Kitty with her hair.

As they cleaned off their clothes, Kitty noticed that Maggie no longer wore the rose locket. Since her grandma's passing Maggie had become so attached to it, Kitty knew she'd be devastated at losing it.

"Maggie, the locket, it's gone. It's not on your neck anymore, do you have it?"

"It's in my pocket. When I woke up I had it clutched so tight in my hand it left an imprint." She examined her palm to see if the imprint was still visible. "The chain was missing, so I put it there for safekeeping until I get a new one."

"That's a relief. Listen, I don't mean to sound like a broken record, but do you have any idea what happened last night? The only thing I remember is a scuffle in the parking lot with that drunk, and then I woke up covered in vomit. When did we leave the parking lot? Did I black out or what?"

"I wondered about that myself. I have a hunch we all blacked out because neither Simon nor I remember anything after that tousle in the parking lot either." Maggie paused, mulling over the possibilities. "Y'know, I wouldn't put it past Doyle to bribe the waitress into drugging us, then after staging that fight, he and his friends carrying us off and dumping us in the middle of nowhere. That might explain why we threw up, too."

"Oh my God, you're right. Why was he out there anyway? We'd left him at the table."

"Exactly. You know, he's been chasing me for months and I've been ignoring him. I'll bet he got jealous seeing me with Simon and pulled this dirty trick for spite." Maggie slammed her hand on the counter. "Wait till I get my hands on him, I'm gonna wring his conniving little neck."

"Okay Lucy, you take his neck, I'll aim a little lower." Despite their jest, something still nagged at the back of Maggie's mind that she couldn't pinpoint. Something didn't smell right, and it wasn't their vomit. The last thing she needed, though, was for Kitty to go into one of her frenzied meltdowns and get them shot. She'd best stay positive and not let on that she had misgivings.

Back in the kitchen, they found Simon sitting at the table, his face pale and worried. He'd spent the last several minutes defending their virtue. Mr. Blandford had put the rifle away and now drummed his fingers, signaling for everyone to be seated so he could dive into his breakfast. Pewter platters of fried eggs with thick slices of bacon, fresh made biscuits, a steaming bowl of baked beans and a pot of hot coffee waited on the table to be devoured. They tried to be polite and take small portions, but it tasted so good, their hunger got the best of them. They drank the coffee black in their little tin cups and gorged themselves on the butter and honey, slathering it over the biscuits. While everyone else ate, Mrs. Blandford sat off in the corner absorbed in the task of sewing extra lengths of fabric onto her daughter's old dresses.

Aside from the sound of their munching and the occasional compliments to the chef, the table remained quiet. Kitty broke the silence. "So Mr. Blandford, your wife tells us your daughter is a military nurse. My older sister is a nurse and I've been working in a hospital for the last several years myself. It seems we have a lot in common."

Still scowling, Blandford considered Kitty's statement with his fork suspended in mid- air. "I doubt that, but it's good to know. They'll need you up there."

Up there? Up where? What the hell did he mean by that? Simon's eyes stayed glued to his plate and Maggie shook her head at Kitty's skyrocketing eyebrows. This guy would never win any personality contests, but at least he wasn't calling them whores anymore.

After breakfast Mrs. Blandford led them to a tiny bedroom to try on the dresses and the undergarments she'd laid out.

"This is my daughter's room." Mrs. Blandford's wistful fingers stroked the end rail of the old and chipped white iron bed. At first Kitty felt sorry for her and then for her own mother who'd also had trouble adjusting to an empty nest. That is until she remembered the role-playing gimmick.

"What's your daughter's name, Mrs. Blandford?"

"Aurora. That means sunrise you know."

"How beautiful, is she your only child?" *Oops, I guess I hit a nerve.*

Mrs. Blandford's face dropped by a mile. "We lost our son early this month in Virginia. He's buried up there on the hill behind us. We're told he was a brave soldier, but that's little consolation for his loss. His death made Aurora offer her services to the army, to honor his memory and support his comrades. I only hope we won't be burying her alongside her brother." She retrieved a wrinkled and balled up handkerchief from her pocket, dabbed her watery eyes, and sucked in a deep breath, re-gathering her dignity. "I'll just give you ladies some privacy so you can change. Unless you need help?"

"No, no, that's quite all right," Maggie assured her. "We've been dressing ourselves for a long time now. I'm sure you have things to do."

As Mrs. Blandford closed the door behind her Maggie and Kitty marveled at the melodramatic performance they'd watched. "Oh, my heavens, look at the clothes she left us, they're period costumes the same as hers, and so authentic." Maggie got that Lucy look on her face and Kitty knew she was getting ready to launch a scheme. "So Ethel, what do you say? Want to be part of the re-enactment?" She flaunted one of the dresses in front of her. "It's what Simon came to Harrisburg for in the first place and now we can join in as well. I've never done it before, but I've seen hundreds of people coming to join in year after year, so it must be fun or else why would they keep on doing it?"

"Your Lucy logic scares the hell out of me, but okay. I guess I'm learning to trust you on the 'fun' part."

Kitty let Maggie think she talked her into this though, in reality, adrenaline rushed through her veins at the thought. They'd be like kids again playing dress up and prancing around pretending to be their great-great grandparents. At least it wasn't something that would get them arrested or killed doing like Lucy's—uh, Maggie's— other schemes.

It was such a relief to peel off the grungy clothes. The push-up bra Kitty wore had wires poking into her ribs that drove her crazy. They put on the costumes in the order they found them, starting with the craziest underpants the girls had ever seen. The legs reached their shins and the waistband tied with a drawstring, but the back was slit open without a middle part. No crotch, just legs and a waistband. They nearly burst from trying to keep their laughter from being heard in the next room. Over that went a full-length, loose cotton slip with short sleeves, topped by a front laced corset with shoulder straps. The corset was made of sturdier cotton than the slip and inset top to bottom with corded stays.

"Great, I get to trade the pushup bra's underwire for stays that go all the way to my hips." Once she got it on though, it wasn't that bad. "The support actually feels good as long as I don't breathe too hard. I wonder if this corset is the nineteenth-century version of Spanx."

Maggie admired herself in the mirror stand from every angle. "I hope Simon gets to see me in this before we go home. I think it's sexy. Maybe I'll send away for one of those fancy ones I've seen in catalogues for those 'special' moments. After all, he did call me his wife."

Kitty started to ask what Simon had whispered to her when Mrs. Blandford knocked at the door. "Are you ladies ready? Mr. Blandford wants to be leaving in a few minutes so if you don't hurry you might miss your ride."

"Oh, yes, okay, we're almost ready. Quick, Kitty, put on the petticoats and the dress. We can pin up our hair in the car."

They hurried to button, lace and squeeze themselves into their costumes, and stashed their dirty clothes into the linen sack Mrs. Blandford had supplied. Their dresses came with a large pocket sewn on the inside, reachable through a slit in the skirt, and that's where Maggie hid her locket for safekeeping. Kitty copied her good sense, depositing the jade earrings in her own pocket.

Costumed and ready, they arrived outside in time to see Mr. Blandford hitching two horses up to an open wooden wagon with a high bench for the driver while Simon waited on the porch. "Really, no car?" Kitty asked. "Okay, let's hear it for authenticity." Simon still wore his now scuffed and stained khaki Dockers and blue shirt, but his face paled with worry.

His obvious discomfort concerned Maggie. "Simon, are you okay? Are you sick? I can ask Mrs. Blandford if she can get you something if you want."

"No Mags, don't. I'm not sick. At least I don't think so. Something is wrong though and we need to talk, in private, as soon as possible. It's nothing dangerous. Only strange. When the three of us are alone we can discuss it. Just keep going with the flow for now."

Simon helped the women up into the bed of the wagon where they sat on top a pile of quilts surrounded by baskets of fruits and vegetables, then climbed into his place on the bench. Mr. Blandford met Simon's attempt at conversation with occasional one-word responses. After several minutes of that, Simon gave up and leaned back.

The sun had risen higher in the sky now with only a few clouds to block its welcomed warmth. Kitty lay back and relaxed. If this was Doyle's doing as Maggie said, then his little scheme backfired because they were making the most of this adventure. Still, she wondered what had Simon so upset, and why he wanted to talk to them in private.

CHAPTER 8

After a brief, bumpy ride, Mr. Blandford maneuvered the wagon up to the guard post at the tall wooden fence. He advised the sentry on duty that he carried supplies and enlistees for the camp and was waved inside the gate.

"I wonder where we are." Maggie scanned the sea of canvas and smoking campfires for a sign or familiar landmark. "I've never seen this place before. I had no idea the people who ran this gig were so organized. Look at all these tents, there's got to be over a thousand people here. It's going to be so exciting to be a part of this." With a delighted giggle, she squished Kitty's shoulders in a tight hug.

The three of them dismounted from the wagon into a slushy muck that oozed through their bare toes, making them wince with disgust. It seemed setting the camp somewhere that had paved roads wasn't realistic enough for these actors. They found themselves in front of a large teepee shaped tent that opened wide in the front. The sparse office furnishings included a wooden desk, a side table, a bookshelf, two chairs and a wood stove in the middle. Two soldiers in full Union regalia maintained their posts as an officer rose to greet their driver.

"Mr. Blandford, it's good to see you again sir. And you've brought more desperately needed donations for our men. That's wonderful, our sincerest thanks to you and your wife for your continued generosity and support. We're forever in your debt, sir."

The three passengers tried to thank Mr. Blandford for his help as well, but he ignored them, speaking straight to the officer instead. "Got another enlistee for you here, too, and these whores say they're nurses."

Blood burned in Kitty's ears as she whirled to face her accuser. "Why you mother-fu..." Simon's hand came out of nowhere leaving her sprawled on the ground in shock. Simon bent to help her up and whispered through gritted teeth. "You can't use that language here, you're gonna get us all in trouble. Just be quiet for Christ's sake and let me do the talking." Blandford smiled for the first time, displaying a mouthful of yellow teeth as he drove the horses to the supply tent.

The officer stood by with his mouth hanging open and eyes bulging, watching the kerfuffle. "Please sir, you'll have to forgive my sister. She suffers from an unusual affliction that makes her lose control and blurt out the most outrageous obscenities to the embarrassment of our whole family. The doctors call it Tourette's syndrome and we've learned that the only way to stop the flow of filth is a sharp blow to the mouth shocking her back to her senses." He sent her a withering look, daring her to say anything.

The officer bought Simon's explanation, but issued an ominous warning that would have a lasting effect on them. "There's an insane asylum on the east side of the camp where she might get help, but, if your sister's to stay in this camp, she must behave herself. Commander Biddle doesn't approve of the men using foul language, and he certainly won't put up with it from the women."

An insane asylum? That got Kitty's attention. *Tourette's or not, I'm not the one who's insane here.*

"Biddle? Did you say Commander Biddle?" Maggie's head wheeled around, her eyes flashing from one side of the camp to the other and then back at Simon in disbelief.

Simon seemed to read her mind. "I don't know. We'll need to discuss it later."

Meanwhile, the officer went back to his desk and asked their names to record in his log. Back on her feet, Kitty noticed that he was a short man, as the two other soldiers in the tent towered over him. Unkempt long, dark hair floated around his head in disarray, and a full beard and moustache covered most of his face like Mr. Blandford.

"My name is Simon Reiger, sir, and the ladies are my sister Kitty and my wife Maggie."

Kitty thought the officer might fall over backwards as he looked up at her. "Yes," he drawled studying her up and down, "I can see the resemblance. I guess size runs in your family." The officer drew himself back to the matter at hand. "Well, Mr. Reiger, ladies, welcome to Camp Curtin. Where are you from?"

"Wellsboro, sir, Tioga County."

"A northerner, splendid. We have a regiment of soldiers from the northern counties who call themselves the Bucktails. Sharpshooters, every one of them. Are you good with a rifle, Mr. Reiger?"

Simon swallowed hard as his pallor faded once again. "Y'yes sir". Simon must be impressed by this man, Kitty guessed, to be so shaken.

"Well, sir, the Union thanks you for your support and desire to preserve our great nation. Corporal Barnes, find Mr. Reiger and his family suitable quarters while they await induction. And see that the quartermaster issues them shoes, I won't have any volunteers walking around the camp barefoot."

"Yes, sir, Colonel Kane."

"Colonel Kane?" Simon cleared the high-pitched squeak from his voice.

"Yes, Mr. Reiger?"

"N… nothing, I…, thank you sir."

***

With the first order of business being shoes, Corporal Barnes led them back around towards the front gate to the Quartermaster's office. Simon and the corporal walked a few feet ahead of the women in deep conversation. Although the corporal did most of the talking and Simon just nodded. Barnes stood over six feet tall, and Kitty guessed his age to be sixteen or seventeen. Pale blond hair stuck out from under his hat and his light eyelashes were almost invisible. At least he didn't have as much facial hair as the other men in the camp. It amazed Kitty that any of them could even eat around all that hair. If Barnes had grown a beard though, it might have gone a long way to cover the pock marks on his face that Kitty assumed were remnants of a raging case of acne. *Poor guy, I can sympathize.* The most distinguishing feature, though, the one that caught Kitty's attention the most, was the enormous Adam's apple that kept bobbing up and down in his neck as he spoke. She found it very distracting and kept wanting to reach out and grab it to make it stop.

Once inside the wood shack that served as the supply office, Corporal Barnes relayed the colonel's orders to the desk clerk. "Will you women be working in the hospital or the laundry?" the clerk wanted to know.

The laundry was out. As far as they'd gone to keep this authentic, it was a sure bet there were no washing machines or dryers here and Kitty had no intention of hand washing anyone's dirty drawers. She could do first aid for a few days though. How hard could that be? Maggie and Kitty nodded to each other in agreement. Hospital.

"Well then Aunty Jackson will supply you with what you need there. I'll just get you the basic camp supplies."

"And shoes, don't forget the shoes," Kitty called after the clerk. "Anything you have in a ladies' size ten, preferably something without too high a heel." The clerk ignored her and continued towards the back room. The others gaped at her in stunned silence.

"What, I've got big feet okay? I want to make sure I get the right size."

Moments later the clerk returned with a pile of stuff for each of them. They each got the same exact pair of plain brown leather ankle boots that laced up, two pairs of brown woolen socks and a messenger bag he called a haversack containing a frying pan, a canteen, a tin plate, cup and utensils. A blanket was folded on top of each pile.

Kitty's cold, wet feet were crusted with mud from walking through the camp. "I'm not putting these on without washing my feet first Corporal, where are the showers?"

Mystified, Barnes gazed up to the sky.

Her patience waning, Maggie snapped at Barnes that she'd meant the bathing area where they could wash. Barnes hesitated, disturbed at her attitude. He pointed over to the western edge of the camp, asking them to wait while he checked to see if the designated bathing area was available. It would be scandalous, he explained, to subject the ladies to the sight of naked men in the midst of their own ministrations.

Satisfied with his inspection, Barnes motioned them over to the shoreline where they made their way past several tents as large as the colonel's office. Many of the tents had graffiti all over them with banners and signs indicating the soldiers' assigned units. A few men, dressed in casual pants and shirtsleeves, milled around campfires in front of the tents and gawked at them as they passed.

***

Fidgety and shuffling on his feet, Simon dismissed Barnes and ushered the ladies over to sit on the rocks near the riverbank. "Thank you, Corporal, we can take it from here." He and Maggie hadn't had any privacy since arriving at the Blandford house and now, at last, they could talk. Kitty lifted her voluminous skirts to her knees, dangling her feet in the cool, refreshing water of the river.

"Simon, what the hell is going on?" Maggie demanded. "The historical names, the primitive camp, Blandford and that horse and wagon, everything is so realistic. It's scary. Are these re-enactors really that good? I thought it would be fun for me and Kitty to play a part in it, but now they're just making me nervous and you look like you've been walking on hot coals. Would you stop hopping around and sit down with us, please? You're making it worse."

Simon slumped onto a rock, his anguished head in his hands. "I don't know," he groaned. "This has never happened before. My memories have always been flashes, lasting no longer than a few minutes, just enough time for me to experience a particular incident or a moment in time. Never for this long. And people I know in the present have never been in the memories because I didn't know them then. But you're both here and that Corporal Barnes

Simon's yammering got on Kitty's nerves. *What the hell? Am I losing my mind or is he? What did his so-called memories have to do with any of this?* "Am I missing something here? I don't know what the hell you two are talking about, but you're scaring the daylights out of me. Anyone want to explain?"

"Kitty's right, honey, you looked as if you'd eaten something bad earlier, but since you and Barnes talked on the way to get our shoes, you've been a nervous wreck. What in the world did he say to you?"

Simon took a deep breath, hesitated, and then stared them both in the eye. "I thought something was weird when I talked to Blandford and now Barnes has confirmed it. Barnes has never heard of the battle at Gettysburg. He's a farm boy from Dauphin County with a third grade education. These people are not re-enactors at all and the date today is June 28th, 1861. Gettysburg hasn't even happened yet. We are here, physically, somehow, in what is the past for us and the present for everyone else around us."

***

Corporal Barnes came back to escort them to their quarters before they could continue their bewildering discussion. Kitty wasn't sure if she and Maggie were on the same wavelength, but Simon appeared to be having some kind of breakdown. He couldn't seriously believe they'd travelled back in time. Science fiction may have been her favorite genre, but she could still tell the difference between fantasy and reality.

Their luxury accommodations turned out to be one of the big teepees they'd passed on the way to the river. The furnishings included a wood stove, like the one in the colonel's office, and six rope-laced cots with only a quilt on each for a mattress. It smelled as if a hundred men who had done hard labor in the sun without bathing slept in here for a week straight. At least it had a wood foundation under the canvas floor to keep out the ground moisture and mud.

"You're lucky I found this for you," Barnes admonished Kitty when he saw her pinched expression. "One of the regiments shipped out the other day and no one from the smaller tents in back has claimed it yet."

"Do you have a separate privy or latrine for women here?" The last time Maggie and Kitty had relieved themselves was in the small outhouse at the Blandford house and, after being in the river, they both needed to go.

"Oh, no ma'am, there ain't but a few women here so we all use the same facilities. It'd be best if you have your man here be look out for your, um, privacy. If you know what I mean. Oh, and you'll find the chamber pots under the beds."

"Speaking of privacy, there are six cots in here, Barnes," Simon interjected, "I hope you're not setting me and the women up with other soldiers."

"Oh, no sir, that wouldn't do at all. This'll be just for you and your kin. Mind, it's only temporary now. There'll be some shuffling done when the regiment comes back."

"What regiment is that?" Simon asked.

"Colonel Biddle's, sir. He took his Bucktails and a regiment of infantry and artillery units down to Cumberland. They're sure to see action there." Barnes graced them with a huge yellow smile, showing a missing front tooth.

"Thank you, Corporal Barnes. If you'd please excuse us now, the ladies are tired."

"Sure thing, I'll come back after a while and take you ladies to meet Aunty Jackson. She'll show you around the hospital and explain what your duties will be." His voice lowered to a confidential tone. "Oh, and those blankets you got from the quartermaster. The men haven't been using those 'cause they're infested with lice." Barnes tipped his hat at them and left.

"So where's Cumberland?" Kitty asked, waiting to be sure Barnes was out of earshot so she wouldn't sound ignorant again. Holding it gingerly with two fingers, she tossed the already inhabited blanket off into the corner of the tent. "Is that where they stage the fighting scenarios? Do they call it scenarios or something else?"

Maggie studied Simon for a moment and then perched on the edge of a cot. "Kitty, I don't know how to break this to you, but Simon is right. Cumberland, Maryland was the site of one of the early battles of the Civil War. I remember reading a brief entry about it in one of my American History textbooks. Nothing major happens there, so no one ever re-enacts it. I think this is for real, I think we are in 1861. Don't ask me how or why, I don't know and I'm sure Simon doesn't." She threw a questioning glance at Simon who shook his head. "We need to try to figure it out."

Kitty eased herself onto the edge of another cot and narrowed her eyes at Maggie. "Are you serious, or is this another Lucy scheme? Because if it's a scheme to get me hyped up for the activities or whatever, you can save your breath, I'm already there."

A moment of uneasy silence filled the room before Maggie spoke again. "Okay, let's look at this logically for a moment. What's the last thing we all remember that makes sense?"

"That's easy," Kitty answered. "That dimwit drunk, Doyle, tried to attack you in the club's parking lot and Simon punched him. I remember thinking we needed to get the hell out of there, and then I woke up covered in vomit."

"Mmm hmm, me too. I panicked when Grandma's locket fell off. I thought if it got lost or broken, I'd lose that part of her forever. When Simon yanked our arms to run away, I was holding it in a death grip. Then I had this weird sensation of falling, like in a slow motion dream. What about you, Simon?"

Simon had gotten up to pace as Maggie recalled her viewpoint and didn't answer right away. His face had paled again, and he looked as though he might puke.

"Simon?" she prodded.

"Well it was just one of those random thoughts, you know, like everyone has now and then." His hands waved around for emphasis as his pacing became faster. "Nothing ever comes from those thoughts. How could it? How could I know this was the one and only time it would happen?"

"Simon." Maggie used that same voice all mothers do when they want you to confess that you're the one who knocked the lamp over and broke it and your sister had nothing to do with it, because she'd been upstairs in her room the whole time.

He exhaled a long sigh. "Okay, as I said, it hit me out of the blue and it was something to the effect of 'If I was in 1861 right now, none of this would be happening.' There, that's it. So now you can say it. All this is my fault."

This is absurd. Kitty's laughter broke the uncomfortable silence. "Okay come on, guys, you got me. You can drop the charade now that's enough."

Simon sat beside Maggie, drawing her close as she sobbed into her hands. Neither of them spoke. Simon handed Maggie his handkerchief to blow her nose, and it dawned on Kitty that her tears were genuine. She wasn't faking, this was really happening.

"What, you're serious?" Kitty's mind raced with confusion. Images of her mom posting their pictures on telephone poles and milk cartons swirled through her head.

Kitty sprang to her feet, her muscles tense and mouth dry. She couldn't decide whether to cry or scream. "You did this? You wished us here? Who does that kind of thing? What, are you some kind of alien or something? You take it back. You wish us back right now. I want to go home."

Simon wavered on his feet, responding in a thick, husky voice. "I told you, I have no idea how this happened, and I'm just as freaked out about it as you. Don't you think that if I knew how to get us back home I would already have done it? My memories..."

"Your memories! I'm sick of hearing about your asinine memories. You're a freak! A freak who hit me! You're still due some payback for that, you know."

Maggie intervened to keep the tension from escalating further. "Stop it, you two. Fighting isn't going to help. Simon, I'll give you the benefit of the doubt that you were trying to prevent her from swearing in front of the officer, but if you think you can raise a hand to either of us in anger, we're going to have a problem."

"I didn't mean to hit her I just wanted to make her mouth stop moving. I am not that guy. I would never..."

Kitty didn't give him a chance to finish. "Bullshit. I was on the receiving end of that smack, and it felt perfectly real to me."

Frustrated, Simon placed his hands on his hips and stuck out his jaw. "Fine. If it's revenge you want, go ahead. Hit me."

Maggie stepped to wedge between them, but she was too late. Kitty's fist landed square on his jaw, sending him staggering back a few steps.

The result disappointed her. Rather than the satisfaction she'd anticipated, her heart instead filled with despair and defeat. Maggie was right. This time, fighting didn't help.

As Kitty turned towards the tent opening, Maggie caught her arm. Her voice came out in a hoarse whisper. "You can't leave, Kitty, there's no place to go."

Kitty's lips trembled and tears streamed down her face with the reality of her words. "I just need some space, Mags. Please, just let me sit outside alone for a few minutes. I promise not to go anywhere."

***

Kitty's tears flowed in silence as she sat in the small patch of damp grass near the tent. She thought her life sucked before, it never occurred to her that it could get worse. If only she could wake herself up from this nightmare.

A sudden gust of wind brought a rank whiff of sewage to her nose. Her attention drawn to her surroundings now, she noticed a lot of uniformed men passing amongst the tents. Their curious stares made her uncomfortable, but not enough to go back in the tent. In addition to the muddy paths and the stink, the condition of the grounds resembled a refugee camp rather than a military compound with haphazard laundry lines and trash strewn around it. Not far away, a man stood urinating onto the muddy path near his tent. *Nice. Thank God they gave us shoes.*

Knees drawn up, Kitty rested her head on her folded arms. She had nearly dozed off when a loud clap of thunder sent a deluge of rain pouring down on her. Still she sat there, too numb to move. The loud downpour did get Maggie and Simon's attention, though, and they rushed out to drag her back into the tent.

Maggie scolded and fussed over her, but her voice seemed so far away. "Christ, Kitty, I know you're upset, but you could at least get out of the rain."

It had come down so fast and so hard, her saturated dress dripped rivulets onto the floor and her hair lay plastered to her head.

Was it the sudden chill? The rain? Her nerves? Kitty broke out in a violent shiver.

"Simon, hurry. Can you get a fire going in the wood stove? I think Kitty's going into shock and we need to get her dry and warm right away. Come here, honey, let me help you with your clothes. Kitty, look at me, are you okay? Kitty?"

***

Everything after that was a blur. She awoke the next morning mummy-wrapped in a quilt, with Maggie hovering over her smoothing her hair. A bugler's reveille sounded in the distance. Maggie's eyes shone with tears, but a smile curled her lips.

"Are you okay there, Ethel?"

"No. We're still here."

A tear spilled down her cheek. "Yes. Simon and I talked for hours last night, but we couldn't come up with a rational explanation."

Simon. Just the mention of his name made Kitty's jaw tighten.

"He went out to scrounge up food and coffee for us," Maggie continued. "Your clothes were sopping wet, but I managed to dry a few things. It would be a good idea to sit up and put something on before he gets back."

The chemise and the dress were wearable, but the other things were still too damp. Kitty had just finished finger combing her hair and tying it up with a strip of fabric torn from the bottom of a petticoat when Simon returned.

While at the commissary, he'd met a company of men whose three-month militia commitment had ended and would be mustering out soon. They'd bequeathed him their field supplies, a table and three chairs. Among the items were raw coffee beans, instructions on how to roast them, and a battered pot to brew them. Still more listless than helpful, Kitty remained inside the tent while Simon built the campfire and he and Maggie prepared the raw rations that had been distributed. Once the coffee started brewing, though, the aroma brought her out to join them.

The empty chair was next to Simon and, as she sat, he covered her hand with his and leaned closer. "I know this is hard, Kitty, and you have every right to be angry with me. But believe me, I never meant any of this to happen. I can promise you, though, that I'll do everything in my power to keep you and Maggie safe until we figure a way to get out of here."

Kitty searched his face for reassurance. The creased brow, the sad, yet hopeful, eyes shadowed with dark circles, and his slumped shoulders said he meant every word. She didn't have to be happy about it, but continuing to punish him wouldn't do any good either. He was obviously just as worried and confused as everyone else. She squeezed his hand in return and nodded.

As they picked at their food, Simon filled Kitty and Maggie in on what he'd learned from the few people he'd talked to in camp. "That insane asylum Colonel Kane mentioned yesterday is real. I saw it. It's a big house just across the tracks from the eastern side of the camp. If we're not careful about fitting in, and not letting anyone know our true circumstances, we may wind up there."

Maggie inspected the hard square biscuit that came with the meal and pushed it aside. "Yesterday Kitty and I agreed to work in the hospital. I guess we can check that out and see if there's anything we can do. Are you still okay with that, Kitty?"

"Sure," she said with a rueful smirk. "I fall a hundred and fifty years into the past, and I'm back working at a hospital. If that isn't karma I don't know what is."

Simon leaned closer to her and lowered his voice. "And Kitty, I don't mean to single you out, but you need to think before you speak. Ladies don't use that kind of language in this time. If they brand you a whore, we might all get thrown out of the compound, and then we won't even have the food and shelter it provides. Okay?"

She nodded in agreement. As irritated as she was with him, at least his knowledge of the era would help them survive.

With the threat of the insane asylum looming over their heads, Maggie and Kitty decided to go ahead with their original plan of volunteering at the hospital. A job helped them blend in and gave them credible respectability. Since

Colonel Kane had indicated that Simon could wait for the Bucktails unit to return before being formally inducted, he'd be available to coordinate the logistics of their survival. Though not a religious person, Kitty still thought it wouldn't hurt to pray for help to find a way home. Just in case.

CHAPTER 9

Corporal Barnes never did come by to show them to the hospital, so Maggie and Kitty found it themselves. Since the camp had only a few wooden structures, it was easy to narrow down their choices. Inside they found a large open floor space that had been divided into two rooms, one for the injured and one for the sick, as well as several prep stations and desks. It made them sad to see so many young boys, many of them teenagers who should still be in high school, lying sick and injured in the beds. The sick far outnumbered the injured, with complaints ranging from simple fevers and diarrhea to typhus, measles and pneumonia. Camp Curtin also kept a separate hospital for the smallpox victims on the opposite side of the grounds.

The staff called the matron in charge "Aunty" Jackson. Kitty and Maggie pictured a short, fat, woman with gray hair drawn in an austere bun from her plain face, wearing a long, black dress and bustling around the hospital shouting orders. Instead, they met a pleasant, middle-aged woman with dark hair, tucked under her lace cap, showing only a few streaks of gray. A white pinafore apron covered her plain white cotton dress. She matched Maggie in height, had a slender build, pleasant features and a soft voice. Mrs. Jackson received their offer to volunteer with sincere appreciation and didn't mind in the least that they had no previous medical training.

"All you need dears is a warm smile, a gentle touch and a willingness to do what's necessary," she explained. "These boys, most of them, are away from their homes and families for the first time in their lives. They're sick, they're injured and in desperate need of whatever comfort we can give them. If you have it in your hearts to do that much, then we can easily train you to do the rest."

An instant kinship to these patients settled in Kitty's heart. With her family so far away, she could use a little comforting herself. The vision of the soldier urinating into the pathway flashed in her head. The challenge would be to stay healthy long enough to make it back to them.

Mrs. Jackson retrieved two white uniforms from the linen closet. "I prefer my nurses to dress alike in these plain dresses so the men are not distracted by the fact that we're women. You understand. But, I don't think I have one long enough for you, Miss Kitty. You are rather tall for a woman."

Kitty cringed and steeled herself for a repeat of the taunting she'd received in school about her height, but Mrs. Jackson continued in her warm, genuine way.

"Perhaps you ladies could go into town on a few errands for me today. While you're there, you can take the dress to my seamstress who can lengthen it for you. And yours as well Miss Maggie."

Kitty's ears perked up with that. *What? Would we mind getting out of this sewer they call a military base for a little while?* "Why sure, Aunty Jackson, we'd be glad to go."

***

Simon wouldn't hear of them going off into town alone, it was too dangerous. To be honest, Kitty thought he was just as curious to see how the town looked in this time as she and Maggie were. Since he hadn't been formally inducted into a regiment yet, he was issued a pass to be off base for the day. Aunty Jackson gave them a list of places to visit and sent the three of them off on the one-mile-walk to the city of Harrisburg.

Redbud and cherry trees, still blossoming due to a late winter storm, lined the mild downhill grade of Ridge Road. Their bounty of magenta, pink and white petals like painted fingernails against the blue of the sky and green of the fields. Once outside the influence of Camp Curtin, they could take a deep breath without assaulting their senses. For the first time, they noticed how fresh and sweet the air smelled without the pall of smog and exhaust so prevalent in their own time.

They chose to visit the seamstress first, so she'd have time to work on their dresses while they made the rest of their stops. Maggie recognized the house on Front Street right away as a historical landmark.

"This is the Brunswick house. I've passed it a million times, though I don't remember it ever looking this good. Local history was never a favorite pastime of mine, so I never paid much attention to it. I only remember something about old Brunswick being this railroad tycoon and an abolitionist, but I can't tell you if they designated it as an historical site because of his notoriety or because the house was so old."

Intrigued, Simon said, "Historical site, huh? Maybe I can get a tour while you ladies get fitted for your nursing uniforms."

The view from the outside showed three stories with four dormer windows protruding from the sloped roof, along with several chimneys. Set back from the road, a low stone fence enclosed a beautiful and fragrant rose garden.

Without a doubt, whoever lived here didn't depend on the income from altering dresses for a living. Kitty imagined herself sitting on the wide front porch in the evenings with a glass of red wine, enjoying the view of the Susquehanna while fireflies danced over the rose garden.

An ebony-skinned maid answered their knock at the door and allowed them in when they said Aunty Jackson had sent them. Their eyes popped when she showed them into the huge parlor. Ornate molding rimmed the high ceiling, and over a grand piano hung a gold chandelier decorated with little cherubs and long leaves. In one corner they discovered a small alcove with floor to ceiling windows, just big enough for the table and two chairs that occupied the space. Huge mirrors and paintings graced the walls, and an oriental rug decorated the parquet wood floor. It was so stunning they hesitated to sit on the little settee the maid gestured them towards that they might get camp dirt on it from their clothes. Instead, they walked around the room gawking at everything as if in a museum.

After a few minutes, the maid came back with a tray of tea and cookies, followed by the lady of the house. Mrs. Carole Rose Brunswick, not quite five feet tall and slender, had honey blonde hair that hung in curls around her face. The dress she wore resembled the ones Kitty had seen in the history books. Made of brocade satin, it laid flat in the front, wide at the hips, and pouffed out in the back with a bustle. Wide sleeves began just below the shoulder under a narrow ruffle.

She waved away their protests to sitting on the settee with their dusty clothes where they exchanged pleasantries over the tea and cookies. Mrs. Brunswick gushed with delight at their intention to volunteer at the camp hospital.

"My, such dedication, I just don't have the constitution myself to attend to those poor sick boys, but I help in any other way I can. I've been active in organizing the Volunteer Relief Fund and our family collects and donates food and blankets from the good people of Harrisburg. Now did you say Mrs. Jackson sent you with dresses to be altered? You ladies come with me and I'll show you the brand new machine for sewing Mr. Brunswick bought for me." After arranging for Simon to be shown the rest of the house by one of the staff, she whisked the ladies off to her sewing room to display her new toy.

"I do a lot of sewing and this wonderful invention just makes it so much easier and faster. Jerome, Mr. Brunswick, bought it for me because he says I have a real knack for designing dresses and he loves to see me in the ones I create." She adjusted a few pins on the half-finished dress on the dummy form. "I'm going to wear this one to a dinner party we're hosting next month when the governor comes to visit."

Changing into their uniforms, the dresses, or rather the skirts and blouses that Aunty Jackson had provided, hung in loose folds. If Mrs. Jackson had been aiming for the androgynous look, she'd achieved it for sure.

"I wonder when they invented scrubs." Maggie's eyes flew open as she spun her head around with a cautionary gasp. *Oops, I guess I said that out loud.* Good thing Mrs. Brunswick wasn't paying attention.

With Mrs. Blandford's dresses back on, Maggie and Kitty met up with Simon in the parlor. Mrs. Brunswick said she'd start on the alterations right away and they promised to return in the afternoon to retrieve them.

***

With only three other short stops to make, they wandered around the Capitol grounds and side streets where Maggie pointed out the few things she recognized.

"About a hundred and fifty years from now, the building on that corner will house my favorite Italian bakery. They make the best cannoli in the world," she sighed.

Simon let out a deep moan. "Did you have to mention food?"

Maggie reached into the rucksack they'd been given to complete their errands and produced a couple hunks of bread and three apples she had "requisitioned" from the commissary before they left. "It's not cannoli, but it will keep us from falling over until we get back to the camp for supper."

They sat on the steps of the Capitol building in the warm sunshine, devouring their small lunch as they watched people pass. Many young recruits loitered on the steps as well while they sought induction into the army. The shabby clothes that hung on their thin bodies gave Kitty the impression that joining the army would be an improvement in their lives.

Simon licked his lips. "I could really go for a cold beer right now. It's such a weird feeling to be broke. I've never been without cash in my pocket before."

"Well, I for one, am going to bring food to every homeless person I see when we get back," Maggie brushed the crumbs from her dress. They took stock of the sad state the people around them were in and nodded in agreement. As Simon had warned them earlier, as long as they kept a low profile, they'd at least be assured of food and shelter.

They dropped the letters off at the post office and then stopped at the apothecary shop for the lint dressing squares, bandages, and salves, Aunty Jackson had on her list. Their final stop was at an address on Market Street that turned out to be a saloon. Simon cautioned Maggie and Kitty to wait outside while he fetched whatever they were supposed to get. Mrs. Jackson had only said to mention her name there, and they'd be given a package to bring back to her. After what seemed a long time, they heard banging noises and men shouting coming from inside the saloon.

Maggie wrung her hands nervously. "Should we go in? What if there's a fight inside and we get in the way?"

"What if there's a fight inside and we can help?" Kitty countered.

They cast aside their fears, making a mad dash into the saloon intent on rescuing Simon from whatever he'd gotten into. She may still be resentful that he pulled them down this rabbit hole, Kitty reasoned, but what if he was the only one who could get them out? They elbowed and pushed their way through the circle of men who were shouting and stomping their feet, both of them afraid of what they'd find.

As they made it to the inside of the circle, they found Simon arm wrestling with a long-bearded brute at one of the tables. At least, from what they could see, the men looked evenly matched. Both of them showed muscles bulging in their arms, their grimaced faces red from the effort of the contest. The advantage wavered from one to the other, delighting the audience who exchanged bets on the outcome while shouting encouragement to their chosen champion. Sweat stood out on Simon's brow, the strain and determination clear on his face. One more dip towards the brute's side and then a startling grunting shout from Simon as he pounded his opponent's hand down to the table. A sudden chorus of cheers filled the saloon with a round of backslapping and congratulating as money exchanged hands to pay off the bets.

Simon noticed Maggie on the sidelines and, encircling her waist, he planted a solid kiss on her lips, eliciting more cheers and backslapping from the crowd. Clearly, the heat of the moment had him pumped. Maggie came away breathless and red-faced.

In the press of the crowd, a groping hand traveled down Kitty's back, and hot, fetid breath tickled her ear. Her new drunk friend struggled to stay upright. Kitty faced him, gave him a sugary smile, then grabbed his testicles, twisted and pulled. His mouth dropped open, exhaling more of the foulness of his mouth into her face. At first his eyes shot wide open then they rolled up into his head as his whole body did a little jiggly dance. As he stiffened with pain, the beer mug fell from his hand and he passed out. Drunk and distracted by Simon's floor show, no one in the saloon noticed their little encounter. More than likely they assumed the drink caused his indisposition which, given the circumstances, was not too far a stretch. They shoved him out of the way and continued their business.

Simon circled with his unused arm raised like a victorious gladiator who'd just slaughtered the lion. "Barkeep, my family and I are thirsty, bring us our drinks." Simon led them to sit as the server brought three large glasses of the local brew to their table.

Maggie reclaimed her senses after that passionate kiss. "Are you out of your mind? What in the world possessed you to arm wrestle that guy? He could've broken your arm."

Simon shrugged. "I was thirsty."

***

By late afternoon, their errands accomplished, and Simon's pocket jingling with his hard earned coins, they arrived back at the Brunswick house. This time the maid had cold meat sandwiches, a pitcher of lemonade for the ladies and a glass of beer for Simon waiting for them. They devoured the small feast like cavemen, showering her and the cook with praise.

When Mrs. Brunswick swept down the stairs she not only carried the white uniforms they'd asked her to alter, but also another outfit for each of them. "You ladies are sacrificing so much for the cause I wanted to do something special for you. I found these in my stash half-finished and, since I already knew your measurements, I adjusted them to fit. One can never have too many dresses, you know."

Their hands shook with gratitude as they accepted both calico cotton dresses. The one Mrs. Brunswick handed Kitty had blue and green motifs, and Maggie's had lavender and pink ones. After all the recent stress, her unsolicited act of kindness made their eyes mist with tears.

Now that evening approached, Mrs. Brunswick directed the butler, Joseph, to drive them back to Camp Curtin in the carriage so they wouldn't have to face the dangers of the road in the dark. When they arrived at the gate, Joseph handed Simon a wrapped parcel, per Mrs. Brunswick's instructions, and bid farewell.

Maggie tore open the package as soon as they settled into their tent then rested back, solemn and quiet. In addition to the loaf of sweet bread and jar of cherry preserves, their benefactor had packed toothbrushes and toothpaste, a hair brush, a jar of hand lotion and a bar of lavender soap. Though certainly meant as a helpful gesture, and aside from the embarrassment of noticeably needing them, the supply of personal hygiene items lent an air of permanence to their position that gripped their hearts and reaffirmed their plight.

A palpable silence hung in the air as irrational thoughts whizzed through Kitty's brain. What did this mean? Were they being maneuvered as pawns in some sick cosmic game? Reincarnation, she thought, meant an old soul becoming a new person. If it was true that they were here because of Simon's past life memories, how did a new person become the soul he used to be? Would they ever be able to find a way out of this mess?

CHAPTER 10

After breakfast the next morning, Simon suggested he head back to the tree where they'd landed, hoping to find a clue to their mysterious dilemma. "We didn't search that field before we left it. There might be a portal access we missed. It's worth a shot."

"Yes it is," Maggie agreed. "Kitty and I will keep up appearances here and report to the hospital as planned. And if you run into Doyle out there, beat the crap out of him for me, okay?"

Aunty Jackson thanked them for the package they'd brought back from town for her and introduced them to Miss Luisa. She would acquaint them with the procedures and issue their assignments for the day.

"Oh, please. Call me Lulu." She hastened a few steps ahead, leading them out of the office and onto the ward.

"Oh good, and you can drop the 'Miss' with us as well. Just Maggie and Kitty will do."

Lulu had a cute, bubbly smile, and dark eyes that danced when she spoke. Her slim, girlish figure and thick dark hair, barely contained under her white cap, gave the impression of a girl just out of her teens.

First she brought them to the preparation nook where they stored and dispensed the medications, bandages, and other supplies. "Put these aprons on over your dresses to keep them clean. Things sometimes get messy around here and you'll appreciate it come laundry day."

The aprons tied around their waists in the back and she gave them a few straight pins to hold the top up over their bodices. "Pin-afore." Kitty couldn't help chuckling at the revelation. "Huh, I never knew where that word came from before."

A hundred or more patients were divided into wards of about twenty-five each, with two to three nurses or orderlies attending them. Corporal Barnes' duties must've also extended to the hospital as Kitty recognized him helping a male attendant bandage a soldier's leg wound.

Maggie studied the treatment room worriedly. "A lot of these men have communicable diseases, Kitty, are you going to be okay with that? Why don't we ask to only work with the injured men? The last thing we need is to get sick."

"Well, unless you have a hazmat suit hiding in your pocket, I don't think it'll make a lick of difference. This whole compound is so unsanitary, even the injured men are likely to have cooties. Wherever you're assigned, just make sure you wash your hands a lot. I mean it, *a lot*."

Their duties were light compared to the responsibilities of the nurses Kitty had worked with at Beth Gen. There were no IV's with complicated calculations to check or shots to give, no mountains of paperwork to keep updated, and thank heavens, no trachs to suction. Although they still had the unpleasant chores of bedpans and dressing changes to deal with, and they assisted in bathing and feeding the men. But sitting at a soldier's bedside, listening to him describe the family he missed, was Kitty's favorite hour of the day. She helped the ones who couldn't manage it write letters home and read the ones that came back to them. There were also newspapers and books donated by the Women's League to distribute and read. Most often, the soldiers were grateful just to have somebody nearby, and she realized that, by comforting them she also comforted herself.

During the second week of working at the hospital, Kitty attended the first of many dying patients. Chaplain Lawrence, Lulu's husband, sat with her at the bedside of Private Dern during his final moments. A devastating bout of dysentery had left him dehydrated and barely conscious. The chaplain prayed softly while Kitty, not a believer, silently cursed the circumstances that brought this poor boy here.

He'd answered the call to duty, as the rest of the men here did, been subjected to filth and bacteria, given meager rations, and housed in close, primitive quarters. Antibiotics didn't exist yet and, without an understanding of germs and viruses, antiseptic practices lagged. It made her heartsick to see the bodies of once healthy men, ravaged by disease due to ignorance and sheer negligence. From the beginning she had tried to start a campaign of basic hygiene by installing hand-washing stations in the prep areas. For the most part, though, her advice went unheeded.

***

Since Simon's warning about getting thrown out of the compound, Kitty had kept her swearing habit in check. Only one time in those first few weeks someone heard her slip. She had gone to the preparation counter to put together a dressing for a soldier who had scratched a rash that became infected. Corporal Barnes, and his teenage buddies, stood socializing a few feet behind her as she dug through the drawers and cabinets looking for supplies.

Tired from a poor night's sleep, and frustrated at not being able to find what she wanted, a mild expletive escaped her mouth. "Damn it, why the hell can't I find the freakin' lint?"

As soon as it fell out of her mouth she remembered the group behind her who were now silent. She twisted her head to see the three boys gaping at her bug-eyed. Right away it struck her that Corporal Barnes had been in the colonel's tent that first day, when Simon bestowed the diagnosis of Tourette's on her, and showed how he managed it. Barnes' jaw set, and, instinctively she sensed, rather than saw, his hand rise up to hit her in the mouth. She blocked his hand with her left, shot the heel of her right hand to his chin and Barnes went down like a felled tree.

Furious, she stood over him with the heel of her boot in his crotch, and glared into his face. "If you ever try to raise a hand to me again boy, I will snap you like a twig. And don't think for a moment I can't do it. Is that clear?"

No answer. She dug her boot deeper into his crotch. "I said, is that clear?" He nodded his head almost in tears. "And that goes for the rest of you too."

"Yes ma'am," they mumbled, still shocked at the scene they'd just witnessed.

Kitty grabbed the supplies she'd found, then stormed off swearing under her breath.

***

Regardless of their predicament, Simon and Maggie's love blossomed into a more intimate relationship. Sometimes you meet two people and know right away they were meant for each other. That unmistakable aura surrounded these two. Even if you never noticed the shine in their eyes when they looked at each other, or saw their tender touches, you'd know their hearts were synced to beat as one.

Maggie deserved the security and happiness Simon offered but, even though they tried to be considerate of Kitty's necessary presence, the rustling and soft murmurs coming from their side of the room at night only magnified her loneliness. Adept at being a third wheel again, and for her own well-being, Kitty tried to give them more private time by staying later each evening on the wards, though she always returned before nightfall. It was dangerous for a woman to be out alone that late.

***

It had been busier than usual on the ward that day, and darkness approached as she carried the last of the chamber pots to be emptied to the latrine. Though her shoes made sucking noises as she walked through the mud from the constant drizzle, she sensed someone behind her. Kitty spun around and found Barnes lurking a few feet away, a glint of steel in his hand.

His neck disappeared into his shoulders, and lips thinned to a straight line, as his voice grated. "A woman needs to be respectful of a man. You need to be taught a lesson."

Leery of the knife, she threw the chamber pot. He ducked, and it missed his head by inches. She whirled around to run, but the mud felt like quicksand tugging at her feet allowing his long legs to reach her in seconds. Kitty used the moves she'd learned in martial arts class, managing to deflect his attempts to stab her and landed a couple of good rib shots. As they wrestled, mired in the sludge, neither of them could get a good foothold and they kept sliding and hanging onto each other. A sharp blow to her face sent her reeling onto her back. When he dove forward to pin her under him, she rolled then elbowed back as hard as she could, jarring his head and knocking him unconscious.

She'd never been this late before and Simon had been getting ready to search for her when Kitty limped into the tent. She stood swaying on her feet, covered in mud, her filthy wet uniform torn and dripping, her face throbbing where she'd been hit.

Maggie's hand flew to her mouth. "Oh my God, Kit, what happened to you?"

It was her own fault. She knew it. A torrent of sheepish tears flowed from her eyes as she explained the earlier confrontation with Barnes and then his retaliation near the latrine.

Maggie dabbed her face with a wet cloth and made shushing noises at her, but Simon's eyes glared with anger, his fists balled at his sides as she told the story and confessed her involvement. When she'd finished, he silently shoved his way through the door of the tent and into the night.

"Simon?" Maggie watched him leave. With a heavy sigh, she turned her attention back to Kitty and her wretched condition.

Not more than an hour had passed when Simon returned, his demeanor brisk and business-like. After leaving his muddy shoes at the door, he went straight for the wash basin to scrub his hands and face, then led Maggie to the cot where Kitty sat, waiting for her lecture.

Wedged in the middle, his arm drew each of them towards him. "Don't worry. He won't bother either of you again."

Kitty didn't find out that night what Simon said or did to Barnes to keep him away, but he was right. They never saw him again.

CHAPTER 11

While the women worked at the hospital, Simon offered his services as a weapons instructor for the new recruits using the experience he'd gained from hunting and shooting with his father. The boys he'd been working with had never used rifle muskets before, but, through Simon's patient coaching, they developed enough skill to be effective in battle.

Kitty questioned Simon as to the wisdom of this early one morning over coffee while Maggie slept. "What if a student of yours kills a person who might have lived had you not intervened? What if that person, or one of his descendants, would have made some great contribution to the world?"

Simon put his cup on the table and leaned closer, lowering his voice. "And what if one the patients you care for at the hospital lives because of your efforts, and changes history? The possibilities are endless, you're right. Have you ever heard of the 'butterfly effect'?"

"You know I'm a science fiction nut. I loved that movie. It's based on a Ray Bradbury story isn't it?"

"Well, yeah, he used it in a different way, but the premise is the same. Basically, it suggests that even one small change could have a drastic influence on future events. The classic example is of a butterfly flapping its wings and causing or altering a tornado at a later date. Our being here will make an impact somewhere, somehow, but there's nothing we can do about it." Simon paused for a moment studying the sediment in his cup. "At some point we may have to face the fact that we're stuck here and do the best we can to go on living."

His tone was gentle, but the words still stung. "You and Maggie are strong enough to do that, but I'm not. Life in our own time was hard enough for me. I'll never be able to survive here."

Simon's lips curled with amusement. "Kitty, we're not any stronger than you. Everyone has doubts and fears and insecurities. The trick is to not let them fool you into thinking you're incapable of overcoming them."

"Not true," she groused. The echo of her dad's words made her uncomfortable, and she leaned back hugging her arms. "The two of you always know what to do. Maggie dreams up her spur of the moment Lucy schemes and dives in, regardless of the consequences. The only thing even close to a rash decision I've ever made was to quit my job and visit Maggie. And look where that got me." Simon lowered his head and rubbed the back of his neck.

God, there I go again, being a bitch. I knew his guilt ate at him, and still I twisted the knife. Now I feel guilty.

"You're wrong, Kit." Maggie stood at the entrance to the tent. Kitty wasn't aware that she'd even come out or how long she'd been there. "Remember at Grandma's old house when you saved us from those squatters? I thought I'd crap my pants, but you took charge and got us out in one piece. And what about when we heard all that commotion at the saloon in town? I hesitated, but you insisted we had to save Simon." Simon's head perked up at that and Kitty briefly met his eyes.

Maggie moved to the table and sat with them, making Kitty unfold her arms so she could hold her hand. "Look, Kitty, it's time you got over feeling sorry for yourself for that crap you took as a kid, and realize that they did you a favor."

She pulled her hand away and refolded her arms. "Yeah, right, they did me a great favor. Now I'm lucky enough to lose my balance whenever I get nervous."

"Maggie's right," Simon interjected. "Adversity builds strength. You just need to trust yourself enough to use it."

"Is this an intervention, or what?" The direction of the conversation was getting uncomfortable. She needed to change the subject. "I'm starving, I'm sure there's a line at the commissary by now and they'll be waiting for us at the hospital. Let's get this day started. See? There, I made a decision."

***

Their jobs kept their hands busy, and their minds distracted, but life still went on around them. Colonel Biddle and his regiment, along with the Bucktails, returned from their campaign in Cumberland with a few sick men, but no casualties. Colonel Kane had expected Simon to join this unit and mustered him in as soon as they returned.

Maggie and Kitty stood through the ceremony fidgeting and chewing their lips as Simon swore his oath. "He's really going through with this, Mags? Isn't there any way he can get out of it? If he joins the army, he'll have to fight."

"Yeah, we discussed that. He understands the implications, and yes, he's nervous. But I think he's also excited to live out his memories."

"His memories? You're freakin' kidding me, right? What about you? What about both of us? What if something happens to him? Where does that leave us?"

Maggie's replied without emotion. "It leaves us here. In the same place we are now, trying to figure out how to survive."

"How about that tree, why not try checking that out again? Maybe the twentieth time is the charm."

"He did the best he could with that, Kitty. It was a dead end. No portal, no magic mirror, no clue. Only our weather beaten shoes marking our arrival."

Because of his advanced education and the service he'd rendered as a weapons instructor while waiting, Colonel Biddle commissioned Simon the rank of Sergeant Major, and moved them to a large tent closer to his new unit. Though arranged in the same layout, their new digs now contained a desk and writing materials for Simon to do his reports.

A fun-loving group, the Bucktails regaled anyone who'd listen with exaggerated yarns of their last battle. Stories of their lives before the war revealed a few had worked in the logging camps in Tioga County. With those camps being so close to Simon's home town of Wellsboro, he had to be cautious of any reference points that may not have existed in this time. Evenings spent around the campfire, the ladies maintained their backstory of wife and sister. They asked questions and listened rather than contribute to any conversations related to pre-war activities.

As messmates, their new Bucktails friends joined them for meals, sharing the meager rations of hard tack, cakes of desiccated vegetables, and either salt pork or pieces of tough beef. Forage from the surrounding fields, midnight raids on local farms for chickens and eggs, and donations of sweet breads and jams from the good people of Harrisburg rounded out the menu.

Aside from the family of three, their table seated five others. Cal Jackson, a gray-eyed, black-haired raftsman from Warren county, was older than most of the others. At age thirty-seven, he'd been married twice, had six kids, and joked that he joined the army to get some peace. Short and wiry Ezra Carlyle, a shoemaker by trade, a cunning hunter by choice, with a keen eye and a quiet demeanor, seemed out of place among these rowdy men. John Gruber and David Isaacs, cousins from Tioga County, grew up together and worked as lumberjacks since their teens. Now in their late twenties, they each had the solid muscular bodies gained from years of swinging an ax and the ruddy complexion of men who had spent most of their time outdoors. Gregarious and witty, Gruber was a dangerous temptation for Kitty and she avoided him as much as possible. With his dark, flashing eyes and exotically fluid body movements, he could entice her into things his wife would not appreciate and she'd regret forever. A Bucktails corporal, Stanislaus Maxwell, or 'just Max' as he preferred, formed an instant connection with Simon and became a favorite visitor to their campfire in the evenings. At six foot three, he was barrel-chested, kept his long dark hair plaited, and was the most animated story teller. "My wife, Hilda," he'd boast scratching his thick, full beard, "is the finest cook in the whole county. And my three sons are so smart; they'll be running this country soon." An avid pipe smoker, Max carried two hand-made corn cob pipes on him at all times, just in case one should get lost, along with a pouch of fragrant tobacco. How he kept from setting fire to that overgrown bush on his face mystified Kitty.

***

For the most part, these men treated the women with respect, but one soldier from a nearby tent gave Kitty the willies. She'd always find John Leahy, with his long, stringy hair and stooped shoulders, popping up without warning or watching her from a distance. When he did speak, he'd stand too close, forcing her to step back.

As she hung the laundry on a miraculously dry morning, Kitty jumped when his voice whispered behind her ear. "Miss Kitty, beautiful day for once, isn't it?"

She stepped away, extending her hand to keep him at bay. "John, you have to stop sneaking up on me. I don't like it."

Instead of stopping, he grasped her hand and moved forward, the reek of stale alcohol strong on his breath. Kitty squirmed away from his other arm that reached around her. "John, stop this, right now. You're drunk and I don't want to hurt you."

Leahy laughed at her weak threat, twisting her arm up behind her and using it to pull her closer. She turned her face from his heavy disgusting breath, eluding his determined attempts at a kiss and writhed away from his insistent body. Her knee jerked up hard to his groin causing him to release his iron grip.

"If you ever try that again, John, you'll be peeing sitting down for a long time." She ran off before he could recover enough to test her.

She told Maggie about the confrontation as a warning to stay clear of John Leahy, but they agreed to keep it from Simon. It had been weeks since Barnes disappeared, and Simon still hadn't said a word.

***

Suppertime meant a community stew that included contributions from everyone. As days wore on, what started out as tasteless sustenance became even less appetizing, but the choices were limited. At least by combining their meager rations with whatever could be foraged or stolen from the surrounding farms, they could stretch them to fill everyone's stomachs. While gathering for supper late one afternoon, Jackson, Max and Carlyle discussed the meat wagon waiting on the train tracks for clearance to continue.

"Didja see the cattle car on the track with all the hogs on it today? There must've been a hundred-head easy of big fat sows. And here we are getting the same old salt pork and beef bits for our supper."

"Someone oughta lighten the load on that train, if you get my drift," Jackson answered in an off-the-cuff way. He never imagined anyone might act on his idea.

But soon a round of "I'm ins" filled the air and Maggie's eyes started doing their Lucy dance again. This time they'd get no argument from Kitty. A meal of fresh pork chops or ham sounded too enticing to refuse. No way was she missing out on that. In fact, she pictured herself floating on the scent of roasting meat like a cartoon character. The drool hit her chin as she imagined the juicy meat and crisp skin after roasting it on a spit. *God, I'm hungry*. Even Simon needed little encouragement and, before they knew it, they'd hatched a workable plan to rescue one of the hogs to satisfy their desperate appetites.

Under cover of dark, they made their way to the edge of the camp where the train tracks were. The pickets had been double-posted on that side to guard against enemy soldiers sneaking up on the tracks, so they had to be careful, and take slow, quiet steps. Locating the right car was a snap. They just followed the stink and the snorts.

Maggie and Kitty took positions as look-outs while the men selected and butchered a nice fat specimen. They loaded it onto their makeshift litter and covered it with a sheet Maggie had appropriated from the hospital. Now the trick was to retrace their steps to the campfire with their prize.

With visions of pork chops dancing in their heads, they made a lot more noise on the way back. Enough so, that they spooked a sentry who demanded they halt and identify themselves.

An expert at thinking on his feet, Simon spoke up first. "We have a severely injured railroad man on this litter who will die if we don't get him to the hospital by the shortest route. We didn't want to risk taking the time to go around to the front gate for fear he might not survive long enough to be treated."

"That's right," Maggie added. "I'm Lucy and this is Ethel, we're the nurses sent to tend him while he's on his way." She yanked Kitty closer so the guard, straining to see in the dim moonlight anyway, might be more inclined to fall for this sham.

The picket guard hesitated for just a moment before he waved them through, not wanting his indecision to cause a man's death and plague his conscience.

"Oh my God, I can't believe he bought that," Maggie whispered.

That near miss made them more diligent about being quiet as they stole from the railroad tracks towards the camp proper. Who knew if the guards still ahead of them were as dumb as the last guy? They took their time pushing forward, measuring their steps as best they could so as not to arouse anyone's attention. The heavy litter bore a couple hundred pounds of prime pork, so the six men in their little raiding party took turns carrying it. No one wanted to lose an ounce by tipping it over or dropping it.

At the rear of the caravan, Kitty noticed Max kept falling further behind. Every few minutes he'd stop to catch his breath, and it now came in ragged wheezes. She asked

Carlyle to pass the word up to Simon that she needed his help and made Max sit next to a tree.

"You sound like you're having trouble breathing, Max, are you sick? Does your chest hurt? What can I do to help you?" She undid the top buttons of his shirt.

"Asthma," he wheezed. "My pipe."

She patted the pocket of his vest where she knew he kept it. "It's still there. Don't worry about that now. We need to get your breathing under control first." Kitty tried to sound calm and reassuring, but her heart raced with panic. She only had a vague idea of what to do. "Concentrate on my voice, Max, and try to take slow, deep breaths."

Thankfully, Simon responded right away and knelt beside her to see what his friend needed. Max reached out, squeezing Simon's arm, his voice a ragged whisper. "My pipe… Hilda's… medicine… helps."

Simon removed the pipe with the little pouch of tobacco from Max's vest and held it up to him. "Is this it?"

Max nodded. "Please… light it… for me."

"No!" Kitty gripped Simon's arm to stop him. "He told me he has asthma. You hear how he's breathing, if he fills up his lungs with smoke, it'll just make it worse. He could die."

Watching his friend's pleading gestures, Simon's hesitation lasted only a moment. His eyes riveted her as he held her shoulders, whispering. "Remember the conversation we had about interfering? If this is his usual way of managing his asthma, we have to let him do it. I understand your reasoning, it makes sense, but people treated all kinds of diseases before… us." He shot a glance at Max. "I'm going to light the pipe, and you need to let him smoke it."

Simon filled the bowl and used the matchsticks he found in the pouch to light it. Simon puffed hard to get it going, and choked on the unfamiliar, pungent taste of the tobacco herbs. "I've seen him smoke this stuff many times. It hasn't killed him yet, so maybe it does help."

He passed the pipe to Max and faced Kitty again. "I have to help the others get that pig to camp, but I'll come back for you as soon as I can."

"What? You're leaving me here?" The panic rose in her throat again.

"Just for a little while. I'll come right back, I promise. Max needs someone to stay with him, but I need to help the men to carry that litter. You're better at things like this than Maggie. Can you do this, Kit? Can you be brave and stay here in case he needs help?"

Kitty looked over at Max, the smoke from the pipe now encircling his head. "Yes, I can be brave," she lied. "Just don't forget about me."

Simon drew her close and laid a reassuring kiss on the side of her head as she'd often seen him do with Maggie. "You're my sister, how can I forget you?"

Though she tried not to let her quivering insides show, Max still sensed her nervousness as she sat back beside him. "Thank you, Miss Kitty," he wheezed.

"Shh, don't speak. Everything will be okay, Max." She didn't know who needed convincing more, her or him.

To Kitty's surprise, it didn't take long for the herbal mixture in that pipe to do its job and Max insisted on talking. Between puffs he told her that his wife, being half Shawnee, had been taught the traditional Indian healing methods by her mother. In their hometown, people sought her out for all sorts of remedies.

Now that Max's breathing had returned to a near normal rhythm, only the fear of being left alone in the dark lingered.

After a while Max dozed off and Kitty waited, on high alert for any sign of danger. It seemed an eternity had passed before she heard footsteps through the brush. She recognized Maggie's voice and called out, directing them to her location. Simon had brought John Gruber along, in case he needed help to get Max to his tent. Now they bolstered him between themselves and, regardless of his protests, helped him along the narrow trail.

Maggie's hug was tight, but comforting. "I'm proud of you, Kit. It was so brave of you to stay here. I'm sure I would've been a basket case sitting in the woods alone watching someone who couldn't breathe. I don't know how you did it."

Neither did she.

The dizzying aroma from the pilfered pork, roasting on the spit when they returned, made Kitty's mouth water. Even men from the surrounding tents floated over, eyes bulging and tongues hanging out, begging for a share. Isaacs took charge of the picnic doling out large portions to be cooked at the other campfires. He also set aside several good sized hams to trade in town for other supplies.

His breath restored, Max told the awestruck soldiers how Maggie and Kitty had come up with the idea to steal the pig in the first place, and then concoct the story to get them past the guards. The poor undernourished men gazed at the women with such admiration and gratitude they couldn't deny the tall tale. Listening to this fictionalized account confirmed Kitty's suspicion that the battle stories they'd been told had also been blown out of proportion.

By the time they'd finished cooking the meat and filling their stomachs, and the story of their adventure twisted and told a thousand different ways, only a few hours remained for a nap before reveille. The little gang of thieves settled for coffee in the morning and, feigning illness, passed their breakfast rations to the grateful soldiers who hadn't taken part in last night's feast.

CHAPTER 12

It was early September, and Kitty couldn't wait for this miserable Indian summer to end. The foul odor of garbage filled the hot, sticky days, and the only life in the muggy night air came from the abundance of biting insects that drove everyone mad. Not mad enough to give up their evening entertainment though. The group used branches to wave the smoke from the campfire and deter the bugs, and still met to relax, laugh and discuss the topics of the day.

Simon had been brimming with excitement all evening, but refused to give up his news until the rest of their friends had gathered.

The last to arrive, Isaacs became the object of the group's amusement.

"Where've you been Isaacs, for Christ's sake?" Max jeered at him. "Didja get your ass stuck in the latrine again?" That had actually happened to him once, and no one had let him forget it. The comment started snickers and sneers from everyone.

While they all settled in, Simon poured himself a fresh cup of the local moonshine being passed around. "Okay, come on guys, enough. I want to share the important information I heard today." All eyes focused on him as he continued. "It looks like we're being assigned to General McCall's division and moving from Camp Curtin to the Washington area. The brass thinks we'll see plenty of action there."

Cheers, handshakes, and testosterone-loaded shouts of bravado gushed around the campfire from everyone except Kitty and Maggie. They'd been dreading this inevitable event, but now there were serious considerations to be addressed.

Maggie put her cup down and laid her hand on Simon's arm to get his attention. "What about me and Kitty? Should we stay here by ourselves, or can we go with you? What are we supposed to do?"

"No, of course you'll come with us, both of you." He reached to reassure Kitty as well. "The regiment always travels with a medical attachment and you two can come along as field nurses." Maggie had her doubts it would happen so easily, but at least Simon's earnest insistence sounded encouraging. "I'll see to it, I promise. You're my family, I'm not going anywhere without you."

Maggie's suspicions proved valid. Simon had made it sound way too easy. Permissions to get re-assigned as field nurses had to be secured from everyone up the chain of command to the Sanitary Commission in D.C. Paperwork needed to be filed, tests taken, and interviews passed.

Coming down to the wire, they didn't receive their approved applications until the day before the company's scheduled departure. Carole Brunswick promised to send them frequent care packages as they said goodbye to their few dear friends in and out of camp. Then, right before dawn on a cool early September morning, the regiment set off on foot for their new home in Tenallytown, just outside Washington DC.

***

A brigade strong, the Pennsylvania Reserves Division, the artillery, cavalry and sharpshooting Bucktails made an awesome sight as they started off, drums beating a marching cadence, on their one-hundred-mile trek from Harrisburg to Tenallytown, DC. Maggie and Kitty had hoped to walk alongside Simon, but Colonel Kane forbade it, saying they'd be a liability in case of attack. So they walked next to the medical wagon being driven by Lulu and her husband the Chaplain, wearing the comfortable trousers and shirts they'd asked Carole Brunswick to sew for them, the worry of what lay ahead still heavy on their minds.

As usual, reveille sounded just before dawn. After a meager breakfast of hard tack, coffee and salt pork, which did little to ease their grumbling stomachs, they started on the road at sun up each morning. The cool early morning air, though, soon turned into thick muggy heat, replaced by steamy showers in the afternoon.

The march left everyone hot, tired, and crabby by evening, with still plenty of work ahead of them. Maggie and Kitty were pressed into service right away as the medical wagons gathered for an impromptu clinic. For the most part, only minor ailments that had come up during the day like blisters, bug bites and sunburn were treated. They did have one casualty though. A poor soldier with an unknown allergy to bee stings went into anaphylactic shock. With epi pens or other life-saving treatments unheard of in this time, Kitty could only watch him swell up, suffocate, and die. She swallowed the angry tirade that welled up inside her, stomping off to where she thought no one could hear her, to jump up and down and scream in frustration. Since they hadn't gone more than twenty miles yet, an ambulance wagon shipped his body back to Camp Curtin. It would rejoin the group later for the casualties of the battles yet to come.

***

Three days later their regiment trudged into Darnestown, Maryland, wet, bedraggled and hungry. Kitty's nose dripped constantly, her muscles throbbed, and her back ached from sleeping on the hard ground with just a tarp around her for shelter. In no mood to listen to anyone else's complaints, she convinced Maggie to help with the evening clinic without her.

"You look miserable, are you sure there's nothing I can do for you? I am a nurse you know," she said playfully.

Kitty sat huddled in the lean-to they'd made with the tarp, hot and shivering at the same time. "Yes, make the rain stop. I keep soaking it up through my feet and blowing it out of my nose. I think when we get home I'm moving to Southern California where it never rains. At least that's what the song says."

"Well, I can't do that, but I can bring you back something to eat and maybe something warm to drink. Here, put this shawl around you, it'll help with the chills. I won't stay too long tonight."

Max had been seen at the clinic for the blisters on his feet and, when Maggie told him Kitty had fallen ill, he came by to check on her. He brought her a cup of the hot herbal tea his wife made for him whenever he had the sniffles. "I'm not sure what the little leaves are, but my

Hilda's famous for making teas for all sorts of ailments. She stocked me up good when I left for the war."

Kitty welcomed the kindness, remembering how Hilda's botanical mix had helped Max's asthma. With her nose stuffed up and runny at the same time she couldn't smell or taste it, but the soothing warmth, and the comfort of having someone tend to her for a change, felt good. Max's thoughtful ways more than made up for his lack of physical beauty. *You're a lucky woman, Hilda.*

After she finished the tea Max refilled her cup with whiskey from his flask and got his pipe loaded and lit. "I brought my dominoes too. Are you well enough to pass the time?"

Kitty remembered playing dominoes as a kid with her sister, Patty. *She could never beat me and always swore that I cheated. I probably did.* Such a simple memory, but, perhaps heightened by the dreariness of the incessant rain, or the misery of her head cold, it made her heart ache for home. She'd given up bitching at Simon about it. It didn't do any good. Their being stuck here meant they had to get along and rely on each other for support. But it didn't mean she had to like it.

Max had the pouch of tiles out, but before he could spread them on the ground she stopped him. "Not tonight, Max. I'm just not up to it. I'm sorry."

"Do I want to know why you're apologizing?"

"Oh Simon stop, leave her alone. Can't you see she's not feeling well? Here honey, I brought you willow bark tea for your fever, drink it while it's warm." Maggie handed her another cup of tasteless liquid along with a tin plate of rice and beans mixed with smoked ham. Kitty was sure all the fluid going into her would make her pee like a racehorse tonight.

As Simon and Maggie sat under the tarp with her, Max rose to go. "I guess I'll leave you then to your supper and get in the mess line for my own. Good night to you Miss Kitty, I hope you'll be better soon."

"Thanks again for the tea Max."

Rather than eat, Kitty only wanted to stretch out and sleep. She crawled to a spot where she could stretch her legs, wrapping the shawl around her shoulders. She lay back, closed her eyes and let sleep overtake her. Between the fever, the whiskey, and all the tea, she was out cold and didn't wake again until Maggie shook her at reveille the next morning. The sound sleep must have done the trick because, even though her nose still felt stuffy, the fever and body aches were gone, leaving her better able to face the coming day.

***

A stone's throw from their destination of Tenallytown, the brigade received orders to stay at Darnestown another few days while some organization took place. They appreciated the rest. Although housed in more primitive quarters, at least they no longer had to suffer the stench of garbage, stagnant water and overfull latrines that permeated Camp Curtin.

Colonel Kane kept the soldiers busy during the day with drills and rifle practice. He wanted them on their toes and ready for whatever action might present itself. The nurses reported for duty at the field hospital.

Near suppertime, Maggie and Kitty cleaned up the clinic after treating the last patient. That's when John Gruber and an exhausted and wheezing Max, puffing on his pipe, came searching for them.

Gruber fidgeted with his hat while they both shifted on their feet. Neither one could look the women in the eye.

"What's up, guys. Can I help you with something?" Kitty asked.

Familiar with the face of impending bad news, Maggie cautiously approached. "What happened? Is Simon okay?"

They both attempted to talk, but stopped. John, his face a mask of misery, deferred to Max.

Maggie gripped Max's arms and shouted. "Say it. Right now. What happened?"

At that moment, Max would've given anything to be somewhere else. "There was a flood, Missus, a flash flood at the practice range. Several of the men got washed away. When the water settled, we searched the whole length of that creek bed, but only found one of the soldiers. We never found your husband."

Maggie's hands slid down his arms as her body collapsed towards the floor. Max caught her, holding her head on his shoulder as she sobbed.

Kitty stared in shock, her feet glued to the ground, her brain sparking as if it had short-circuited. John Gruber came to comfort her, but she felt like a rag doll in his arms. "I'm sorry, Miss Kitty, your brother was a good man."

Confused, she pushed back a few steps. "No, he can't be. Simon can't be dead. He can't do that." All the tension and frustration of the last few months culminated in this moment, igniting the sparks in her head into fireworks exploding colors behind her eyes. With her voice escalating, and her last wispy thread of sanity unraveling, she shook Gruber by his sweaty shirt and shouted the longest, most vile string of obscenities imaginable into his face. Then, in shameful defeat, she sank to the floor in tears. "He brought us here. He did this to us. We can't get home without him. He can't die and leave us like this."

Maggie knelt beside her as they rocked and sobbed in each other's arms. She'd lost the love of her life. Kitty had lost all hope of regaining the life she'd once had.

Max and Gruber let the women cry for a few minutes before escorting them back to their tent. With no appetite for supper, they guzzled the alcohol the men offered from their flasks, trying to numb the open wound in their souls. Their sleep came fitfully that night as they huddled close to each other for comfort.

***

Colonel Kane visited them in the morning offering his condolences. "Sergeant Reiger's efforts in training the new recruits to use their weapons will have an impact on this war, I can assure you. As for your positions here, our regiment sincerely appreciates the service you ladies have provided. But I will be glad to offer an escort to the nearest rail-line to board a train for home if you so desire. Please think about it and let me know your wishes."

After breakfast, the grieving family and their friends gathered at the river's edge where Chaplain Lawrence held a heartwarming memorial service. Even Kitty was moved by his prayers.

In no mood to talk or eat, Maggie kept to herself that whole day. She greeted those who came to offer condolences with vague stares and nods. At twilight, the heavens paid tribute to the missing soldiers with fiery slashes of reds and golds across the darkening clouds, as if the spectacular show could atone for Mother Nature's iniquity.

Kitty handed Maggie a cup of dandelion tea before taking her own seat, then broached the important subject. "What do you say, Mags? Should we take Colonel Kane up on his offer to send us back to civilization?"

Maggie watched the tiny leaves as she swirled them in her cup. "You mean return to Camp Curtin?"

"Oh, hell no. I'm not going back to that cesspool. But maybe we can retrace our steps at that tree outside Harrisburg. We'll find whatever door we fell through and go to our real home."

Maggie's head stayed down, but her eyes flared up at Kitty. "You know Simon tried that a zillion times, and he never found anything." Maggie paused, sitting up and gathering her composure. None of this was Kitty's fault. She didn't have to snap at her. "Besides, how will we live while we're looking? The whole idea of staying with the army in the first place was for food and shelter. Simon's savings won't even last long enough to get us through the winter. Then what will we do?"

"Get jobs? I don't know. There must be something we can do."

"This is the nineteenth century, Kitty. Women don't just go out and get jobs. We have to be sensible about this. I think we should keep living off the army and putting aside our hospital earnings until the spring and then go back to Harrisburg. If we have to live out on the street for a while I'd rather not do it in winter."

"Good point." Kitty sipped the last of her tea. She reached over, covering Maggie's hand with hers. "We're in this together, Mags. We'll wait till spring."

Still listless, Maggie went through her daily chores with the dead eyes of a battle-scarred vet. Kitty often caught her staring off in the direction of the river, as if hoping Simon would miraculously emerge, and it shamed her. Maggie's grief over the loss of her love certainly trumped her self-pity. Maggie needed her. The words of her parents, her teachers, her counsellors, her friends, everyone who had ever tried to help her past her feelings of inadequacy, all rang in her ears. She had to step up to the plate, now, for Maggie's sake and for her own sanity. She needed to be strong for both of them.

CHAPTER 13

General McCall issued orders for the regiment to advance across the Potomac to Langley, Virginia. Kitty knew Maggie harbored the irrational thought that Simon might return and wanted to stay put, but Kitty insisted they move ahead. They'd resigned themselves to staying with the army. They also needed to commit to the life ahead of them.

Letting Maggie rest inside the tent, Kitty took their belongings outside to be organized and packed. In the distance she noticed John Gruber striding across the grounds, his movements easy and fluid as if gravity had no effect on him whatsoever. Even from this far away she could see he'd spiffed himself up with a clean uniform, his shirt tucked in and jacket buttoned. *Hmm, I'd bet no one made fun of him in school.*

She tried to keep her interest from being too obvious until she realized his route took him straight to her tent with Chaplain Lawrence struggling to keep pace. The torrent of profanity she'd unleashed on him the other day came echoing back to her. They didn't have armed guards with them, so most likely they weren't coming to take her to the looney bin. Were they coming for a soul-cleansing or exorcism?

As they approached, Kitty stood wavering on her feet ready to bolt with the first splash of holy water. Though her greeting was cordial, her mind stayed on high alert.

Gruber's face flushed as he drew himself up to his full height and thrust a small bunch of wildflowers at her from behind his back.

"Miss Kitty, I am truly sorry for the loss of your brother and I'm here to offer myself to you for protection and support. Chaplain Lawrence has consented to perform the ceremony."

"What ceremony?" She felt her eyes bug open as they darted around for the easiest escape route.

Gruber's face flushed a deeper red, and he stammered. "Why, the um, uh, wedding of course. Forgive me, Miss Kitty. I'm not good at this sort of thing. I've come to m… marry you."

"Marry me?" She never saw that coming. Relieved, she tried not to laugh in the poor guy's earnest face. This was her first proposal, ever. But it didn't come from the soulmate she'd dreamed would sweep her off her feet and carry her off to a lifetime of wedded bliss. Sure, there was a physical attraction, but nothing else. And what did he mean by support and protection? Did he think she needed a man for that? "I don't want to sound ungrateful, John, but aren't you already married? I've heard you mention your wife. Her name is Linda, right?"

Gruber's gaze lowered to his shoes and remained there as he shuffled his feet. "The smallpox took her right before I enlisted, Miss Kitty. I know how it is to lose someone you love."

Kitty shared his grief and heard Chaplain Lawrence mumbling a prayer for him. "I'm sorry, John. I appreciate your offer, but I can't accept. It's way too soon to consider such a huge step."

"But you must, I insist."

"Insist all you want, the answer is no. Look, why don't you give me and Maggie a chance to recover from the shock of losing Simon? Perhaps you can ask me again, another time."

Without giving Gruber a chance to answer, Chaplain Lawrence cut in on the conversation. "That's an excellent idea, Miss Kitty. Mr. Gruber's intentions are admirable and I'm sure he understands it's best to wait until you're past your grief."

Dejected and confused, Gruber allowed Chaplain Lawrence to lead him away.

Kitty expected to get a chuckle from Maggie when she broke the news of Gruber's misguided offer. Instead, her shoulders sagged and her eyes got that distant gaze again. "We'd lay awake at night planning how we'd get married for real, me and Simon. He'd been putting away money from his paychecks and his winnings from gambling with the other men. He thought if we held out for a year with the army, the three of us could go back to Harrisburg with a stake for a new life." Her tears burst through and she sobbed out the rest. "He honestly had no idea how he got us here and tried every day to wish us back, but it didn't work."

"I'm sorry, Mags. I know you loved him and I'm sorry I gave him so much grief over bringing us here. We can still go on though. We'll find a way to make this work, you'll see."

***

As she mulled over John Gruber's naïve proposal, it occurred to her that, without Simon around as a deterrent, she and Maggie might be viewed as fair game. She began to pay closer attention to the faces of the men around them. The ones they'd been friends with since the beginning, expressed sorrow and sympathy for their loss. But she saw John Leahy lurking around again. He and a few others followed their every move like predators readying to pounce. She didn't worry so much for herself, but, without the training she'd had, Maggie was more vulnerable. She'd have to be more vigilant now, for both of their sakes.

To be safe, Kitty sneaked the revolver Simon had taught them to use in case of emergency, into her rucksack. She didn't want to frighten Maggie any more than necessary.

Only a few friends still joined them for dinner. Chaplain Lawrence, Lulu, and their faithful friend Max always visited. The others were too uncomfortable being around the women after Simon's death. One night, after everyone had returned to their quarters, she lingered with Maggie enjoying the coolness of the evening, her rucksack close at hand for security.

Aware of her sudden attachment to the carryall, Maggie raised the question. "Why on earth do you carry that ugly bag wherever you go, Kitty?"

Kitty tried to deflect her curiosity with a flippant answer. "Ugly? No, it's a fashion statement." She held it up between them for scrutiny. "Besides, if anyone gets too close, I can hit them with it like the old ladies in the park at home."

Maggie's suspicious eyes narrowed, and she snatched the bag away to rummage through it. Kitty's heart flipped over while her mind scanned its repertoire of excuses for a plausible fit.

"Aha!"

"Maggie, I…"

Her hand pulled out the silver flask Max had given her. "Seriously, Kitty? You're hiding alcohol in your bag?"

Bingo, excuse number 243. "Well, it's not that I need it all the time, it's just that… you know… sometimes… it helps. Especially with the heavy burden of stress we've had. Are you disappointed in me?"

Maggie put her arms around Kitty, holding her head against her shoulder. "Oh, honey, I'm sorry. This nightmare has been hard on both of us, I know. Just promise me you won't let it go too far." Her voice caught in her throat. "I need you now more than ever."

Phew, that was a close one. Kitty hated lying to her, but it was the lesser of two evils. The gun must've fallen to the bottom of the bag. She'd have to make sure it stayed accessible for when she needed it.

Kitty didn't sleep well anymore, her ears always attuned to the sounds of the night. Often she'd hear Maggie sobbing in her sleep and wished she could do more to reassure her they'd be okay. But to do that, she'd have to believe it herself. They were strangers in this place. While Kitty admitted to herself that she missed Simon's company, what she missed the most, and had come to rely on, was his extensive knowledge of the culture and customs of the era. Her jumbled nerves were a constant reminder of their precarious position.

Slow and sluggish one morning, Maggie didn't want to get out of bed at reveille. "I'll get breakfast for both of us, Mags," Kitty told her. "But make sure the tent stays closed, so no one knows you're here alone."

The quilt over her head muffled Maggie's voice. "You worry too much. No one's going to bother me."

"Just stay in bed, I'll be right back." She waited for a moment in front of the tent before leaving for the commissary to make sure no one noticed that she'd left alone.

***

One of the few wooden structures in the camp, the cafeteria-style commissary served the soldiers a close version of nutritious meals. The meager rations, though, always fell short of being satisfying. While waiting in line with the others, hoping for something other than salt pork, Kitty heard someone cry out for a doctor. Her curiosity piqued, she shoved her way through the crowd to see if she could help until a doctor arrived.

A man lay on the floor, his tray of food scattered around him, in an obvious seizure. While one person ran off for the doctor, the others stood by murmuring, afraid to get too close. As the tremors subsided, Kitty knelt beside the soldier. He wasn't breathing. Everyone who worked at a hospital in her time learned CPR so, by reflex, her brain flipped into rescue mode. She cleared the airway, gave two full breaths, and started chest compressions.

An angry outcry swelled around her. Horrified, everyone thought she was assaulting the poor man, and they tried to drag her away. She lashed out at the one nearest to her, knocking him off his feet. "Stop, you don't understand," she screamed. "I'm not hurting him, I'm helping him."

Kitty dropped back to her knees, managing a few more compressions before the doctor arrived. He paused for a moment, studying her technique, and then nudged her aside. A quick assessment showed the soldier's pulse had returned, and he enlisted two bystanders to carry the patient to the hospital.

The doctor's eyes narrowed as he studied her. "Who are you? What you did saved that man's life, but how did you know what to do?"

She couldn't answer him. What would she say? Without a word she backed away and turned to the food service counter filling her satchel with enough food for her and Maggie. She left amid a rumble of scornful remarks and sharp stares.

As she walked the hundred or so yards back to their quarters, she berated herself for letting her guard drop. Up to this point she'd been careful not to display any knowledge she'd brought from her century. But now she'd committed the cardinal sin of using a rescue technique that wouldn't be developed for another hundred years. *Well, screw it. I saved a life.* That had to count for something.

"Maggie look, they had apples…" Maggie lay sprawled on the floor exposed and moaning, her skirts hiked up to her waist, her face a swollen mass of bruises. The apples spilled to the floor as Kitty dropped to her knees. "Maggie, oh my God, Maggie, look what they did to you. I'm so sorry. I should never have left you."

Kitty's heart squeezed tight in her chest as a wave of dizziness washed over her. Still she forced herself to keep focused. After restoring her modesty and wrapping her in a quilt, Kitty bathed Maggie's battered face while she wept. She tried to keep calm, but fury raged inside her. Only a depraved animal could violate a woman with such brutality. As if grieving over her dead husband wasn't enough. "What bastard did this, Mags? Who hurt you?"

One faint word came from Maggie's swollen lips. "Leahy."

Kitty sat on the floor with Maggie's head in her lap, stroking her hair while she cried. Guilt overwhelmed her. She'd seen the danger, yet she'd left her alone. She'd failed her for the last time, though. They will not be at anyone's mercy, nor will they be the target of anyone's abuse.

Once, Simon had sought revenge on a soldier who'd attacked her with a knife. He'd dismissed their questions, but Kitty worried that, someday, they'd discover Barnes' body lying in a shallow grave on the camp grounds. She had the gun, but killing Leahy was too easy. She needed to feel his bones crunch and see the pain on his face. They would not be trifled with, and she needed to prove that to the other men.

As Kitty changed into her trousers and shirt, Maggie woke and struggled to get up off the floor. "Here, Mags, let me help you." She held the quilt tightly around herself as Kitty guided her to the cot. After she had Maggie settled in, she put the flask of whiskey to her lips. "Take a good swallow honey. It will help with the pain. I'll get a dose of morphine from the hospital for you." She reached into her rucksack again and put the revolver into her hand. "Here, take this. If anyone comes into this tent, do not hesitate to pull the trigger. Remember how Simon taught us?" The mention of his name clouded Maggie's face, but she nodded in agreement and held the gun with shaking hands. "I won't be long, I promise."

***

Kitty found Leahy in a clearing playing horseshoes with a few other soldiers. Good. She wanted witnesses. Spying from a safe distance, his casual, relaxed manner as his friends cheered a winning throw, strengthened her resolve. He raised his arms in triumph as they exchanged wagers amid a flurry of backslapping congratulations.

The group quieted as Kitty approached, her eyes intent on Leahy. His shoulders squared, his feet a few inches apart, only his twitching mouth hinted at his nervousness as he watched her.

Kitty took a firm stance two or three feet away to challenge him. "You enjoy beating up on women, Leahy? Want to try your luck with me?"

His snicker mocked her as he glanced around at his circle of friends. She stood her ground, staring into his eyes. His face grew serious as his open hand flew up to her face. It was the only invitation she needed. The unexpected kick to the mouth staggered him and drew blood. In her element now, her moves were quick and sure. Minutes later, he lay on the ground writhing in pain from the broken arm, cracked ribs, and missing teeth. She figured he'd be pissing blood for the next week at least.

As she circled in a warning stance to his friends, they backed away in awe, not wanting to test her further. She spit in Leahy's face, but she directed her threat to the whole group. "This was just a warning. If any of you try to hurt me or my sister again, you will die." Her head held high, a slight swagger in her step, she turned towards the hospital to get the morphine for Maggie.

CHAPTER 14

When they arrived in Langley, the distinct buzz of excitement and anticipation vibrated in the air. Doctor Freeman, the regiment's surgeon, issued urgent orders for the construction and organization of the field hospital. A scouting party had sent back word of an unguarded Confederate camp just over the river at Ball's Bluff and awaited reinforcements to attack. A battle was coming, and they needed to be prepared.

Being so close to an actual battle for the first time brought the reality of the war home for Kitty and Maggie. They busied themselves scrubbing surgery tables, lining up bottles of chloroform and the masks to administer it, and preparing dressings and bandages. Still, they were not prepared for the onslaught of patients that arrived. They came all afternoon and into the night, over two hundred men and boys, brought from the landing by the wagon ambulances. Most of them were already sedated with opium and moving like zombies. The worst cases, the ones diagnosed as not dead yet but definitely in the checkout line, rested in another section where orderlies kept them as comfortable as possible during their last moments. It didn't upset Kitty one bit to find John Leahy there.

Inside, the large hospital tent reminded her of a scene from a horror movie with blood all over, and now useless limbs flung into a corner to be disposed of later. Kitty dutifully sedated the patients using a dome-shaped basket covered with a cloth soaked in chloroform. Meanwhile, the four doctors in attendance feverishly sawed off the men's ravaged limbs in a desperate effort to save their lives. Noticing the doctors only gave their cutting instruments a casual wipe on their aprons between patients, Kitty tried her best to wrest them away for at least a quick cursory rinse between uses. It did not win her any favor with the doctors. But, in her mind, even this small effort may have increased the chances for a successful recovery for the patient.

Between the sharp metallic smell of the blood mixed with the sweat of fear and poor hygiene, and the accidental inhalation of the chloroform that kept getting on her hands, Kitty had to step outside on occasion to clear her head. During one of these quick breaks she saw Cal Jackson and David Isaacs sitting glassy eyed up against a tree.

"Hey guys, how's it going? Do you want a drink of water?" She brought the canteen up to Jackson's mouth, but being so out of it, his lips lacked the strength to press against the opening, and the water dribbled down his chin. She hadn't seen anyone so seriously stoned since college.

After inspecting the bandage for seepage, she saw that the bullet had hit below his shoulder missing the artery. Only a minimal amount of blood showed. As she went to take her hand away, Jackson's weak fingers clutched it. His dilated eyes searched hers as his slurred, muddled words made their plea. "Please Miss Kitty, the bullet, you have to take it out or I'll die for sure. Please, take it out."

"What. Me? You want me to do it? Noo… no I can't do that. I'm not a doctor, I haven't had any training. I'd probably wind up killing you if I tried it. No, no you have to wait for the doctor."

"By the time the surgeon sees me it will be too late. Please Miss Kitty, you have to do it."

A quick scan of the grounds showed what he meant. So many men waited their turns out there the chances of him being seen by any of the doctors today, or even the next day, were slim. In the meantime, the wound might become infected and with no antibiotics, he'd likely die of sepsis. On the other hand, if she went digging for the bullet and nicked the artery, she'd kill him. *Shit, either way he's screwed. If I hesitate too long, I'll talk myself out of this. I need to act, now.*

"Okay Cal, lie still and take it easy, I'll be right back." Inside the tent she filled her haversack with supplies—forceps, lint, bandage, needle and suture thread. Kitty deposited the forceps to soak in a soapy basin she'd laid near one of the instrument tables, and hurried back to Jackson before the opium had a chance to wear off.

After removing the bandage, she washed the tender and red wound site well, the caustic soap making him moan. Putting the flask of whisky Max had given her to his lips, she urged him to drink. After taking a good gulp herself, she poured most of the remaining alcohol onto the wound, reserving only a little to pour over the forceps. Even drugged, Jackson writhed with the sting of the alcohol on the open wound and she had to call over one of the male attendants to help her subdue him and hold him still before continuing.

"I'm going to use these forceps now to try to find the bullet Cal, are you still okay?" He was panting but determined to have it done. "Yes ma'am, do it, please."

Steeling herself, and praying for all the cosmic energies of the universe to guide her hand, she inserted the forceps into the wound. Sweat stood out on both of their faces—his from pain, hers from nerves—prompting the attendant to put a light dusting of morphine powder on Jackson's lips to relax him and allow her to probe for the bullet.

"Cal, hold out your hand." She deposited the ball into his hand and sutured the wound closed with a few stitches.

Kitty concentrated to see through the tears clouding her eyes. She washed the wound again, covered it with a dab of Hilda Maxwell's herbal tea mixture for good measure and re-bandaged it. Hilda's herbs had done wonders on other ailments. With any luck they'd do their magic here. Kitty's whole body shook as she sat back on her heels and let the wracking sobs escape. She buried her face in her hands. *I did it. God help me, I did it.*

Jackson strained against the sedatives, reaching out with his uninjured arm to pat her knee. "Thank you Miss Kitty, you saved my life for sure."

But did I do the right thing?

A wailing scream from Maggie interrupted Kitty's doubts. She rocked in anguish over a body not fifty feet away. What new hell did she find now? Drying her tears on her apron, she ran over and, as she knelt beside Maggie, her mouth dropped open in shock.

Simon lay unconscious on the ground, his uniform a bloody mess. Kitty's shaking hands made it difficult to undo the buttons on his jacket and shirt, but she had to find the wound to control the bleeding. She searched his entire chest and his arms finding no sign of a wound, but she did confirm he was breathing.

"It's okay, Mags. He's not wounded. The blood isn't his." Kitty called for an orderly to stay with them while she ran inside for a doctor.

Her anguished tears and pleading made Doctor Freeman take pity on her and he agreed to take a look. The scene hadn't changed since she'd left and the orderly had to pry Maggie away for the doctor to do his exam.

"This man is dehydrated," he said, "most likely from dysentery. I see he's been given opium. Good, that will help him for now, but get him out of the sun and try to get as much fluids into him as possible. If I have time tomorrow, I'll look in on him."

No shady spots remained, but they found room near a tree where Maggie arranged one of her petticoats as a canopy to block the sun. What a rotten time for the cloudy skies to disappear.

Like a feral cat with her litter, Maggie kept everyone else away from Simon. Kitty brought her a pan of water and rags to bathe him and cool his fever, then left her alone to care for her man.

A huge weight lifted off Kitty's heart seeing Simon alive. She hoped they could keep him that way. With the little influence she had, she managed to find him a bed inside the hospital and out of the elements.

When she couldn't stand upright anymore, Maggie agreed to let Kitty help her care for him. Still, days passed before Simon was lucid enough to talk. The fever and diarrhea had left him weak, his sallow complexion underscored by the dark circles around his eyes.

***

Colonel Kane allowed Max and the women to stay at Simon's bedside while he debriefed him on his miraculous survival.

"The water came out of nowhere," Simon started, his voice still husky from the dryness in his throat. "One minute I stood on dry ground helping this boy load his rifle and the next I found myself carried away by a raging river. It kept dragging me down over the rocks and brush and swirling over my head until I nearly lost consciousness. Then I saw hands reaching out to me." Simon's face took on a haunted pallor as he paused to sip his water and take a few breaths before he continued. "I knew I'd be dead if I went under one more time. The hands stretched out a branch, and I hung on for all I was worth. He used it to pull me out of the current and drag me back onto dry land."

"Who was it?" Max asked. "We searched for hours, but we never found any survivors."

"I only got a glimpse of his face before I passed out, and when I awoke I found myself in a Confederate camp."

Gasps and murmurs went around the room.

"The Rebs… maybe twenty of them… were in sorry shape themselves. They wore ragged uniforms and half of them didn't even have shoes. Their only food was what they could catch or trap. I did recognize their captain, though, as the man who'd rescued me."

Kitty moved closer to comfort Maggie's struggling tears as Simon's story unfolded

"Their plans to send me back to their command as a prisoner fell through when I got sick. The water may have been contaminated, or it's possible I caught something from one of the Rebs, I'm not sure. But the captain seemed relieved." Simon's gaze turned towards his hands as he picked at his ragged cuticles.

Colonel Kane nodded his head in deep thought. "Relieved, yes. If his men were in as dire straits as you say, he surely didn't want you infecting them with whatever ailed you."

A spark of suspicion hit Kitty as she watched Simon speak. She'd been around Simon long enough to recognize that when his fingernails became interesting, he was hiding something.

"It may only have been my fevered perception, sir. I'm not sure. After a while I drifted in and out of consciousness, so I don't know how much time passed before I heard the artillery in the distance. After that I only have a vague recollection of being on the ground with someone on top of me, then I woke up here." Maggie reached for Simon's hand and squeezed it in reassurance.

Colonel Kane stood to leave. "Well, Sergeant, it sounds as if you've had a harrowing ordeal. We're glad to have you back and we appreciate the intelligence you brought us on the condition of the enemy soldiers. Come, Corporal, let's leave Sergeant Reiger to his family."

After they'd left, Kitty stood at the bedside with her hands on her hips. "Okay, now tell us the rest."

Simon's mouth twitched and he avoided her obstinate glare. "Yeah, you're right, there's more. But it involves my memories, so I'm sure you won't want to hear it."

Kitty blew out a deep breath, a clear resolve in her mind. "No, go ahead and tell me. If we're to move forward and make a life here, then we need to be able to support each other. We can't have any secrets hanging between us."

Simon's eyes flashed at her changed attitude. "Okay, well for the most part, the memories I experienced as a child were things I knew to be true in my gut. At times I'd get flashes of scenes, battles, faces…" He glanced over at Maggie and kissed the hand he still held. "Later, this dream—or to be more exact, this nightmare—began scaring the daylights out of me. I'd wake up each time in a cold sweat and have to run and vomit. The damn thing repeated so many times, it haunted me." Even the memory of the dream made Simon's face pale and the sweat stand out on his lip. Repositioning himself in the bed, he reached for more water to soothe his parched throat. Then he continued to speak, his head swaying back and forth as if not believing his own words. "In the dream I saw myself being carried by the water, felt the coldness of it. Even the pain in my chest from not being able to breathe felt real. The nightmare never showed me the man's face, but I'm positive now it was that Confederate captain. He saved me from the flood and I'm sure he was the one who carried me onto the battlefield where he knew I'd be found. It sounds insane, but I think I experienced, in real time, a vision I'd had since I was a kid."

The tear that escaped the corner of his eye and rolled down his cheek made Kitty uncomfortable, but his words chilled her spine and made her queasy. Instead of rattling off her usual smart-ass remarks and finger pointing jabs, she plopped into the chair and held her head in her hands.

Maggie sat on the edge of Simon's bed, her head spinning. "Simon… I don't even know what to say. That's the most frightening thing I've ever heard. Are you sure this didn't come to you in your delirium from being sick? Maybe your mind was playing tricks on you."

"Maggie, that dream is crystal clear in my head. I had it over and over again for years. I've seen it before, all of this, everything around us. And if it was just a fevered dream, how do you explain me showing up here again when everyone thought I was dead? It's almost as if the things I saw weren't memories at all, but prophetic visions of my fate."

Kitty straightened up in her chair. "I have to agree with you, Mags. I've never dealt with such incredible, mind blowing stuff. It's like being trapped in a Stephen King novel. But, how can we dismiss it? I mean, look where we are for crap's sake!" *And listen to me defending Simon.*

"I know, you're both right, it's just that… I love you, Simon. And I'm so afraid we're not going to survive this."

Simon pulled her closer and kissed the side of her head. "I love you too, Mags. And I promise we'll make it through. One way or the other."

That statement echoed in Kitty's head. What's 'the other'?

***

During Simon's recovery time, Maggie and Kitty had discussed how to tell him what happened with John Leahy. They expected an awkward discussion, for sure, but Kitty was sincere about not having secrets. At least the fact that Leahy had been a casualty of the last battle meant Simon wouldn't be seeking him out for revenge.

Kitty gave Maggie the signal to go ahead. "Simon, something happened while you were… missing, that I need to tell you."

His eyes went from Maggie to Kitty and back again. He could tell by their downcast eyes they had upsetting news, and his body stiffened in anticipation of hearing it. "Tell me," he said flatly. "What happened?"

"Well… I…" Maggie couldn't get it out and cried instead.

If she wasn't going to say it, Kitty would. "It was my fault, Simon."

"No, Kitty, it wasn't, you can't blame yourself."

"It was, Mags…"

Anxious to get to the heart of the matter, Simon intervened. "Will you two stop arguing and just tell me for Christ's sake?"

Maggie continued in a small sniffling voice. "I… was raped."

The shock of this revelation caused his whole body to jerk upright but, still weakened by the dysentery, a wave of dizziness forced him back on the bed. Maggie rushed to his side, and he held her tight against his chest, his jaw rippling with suppressed anger and his eyes fighting to contain his tears. "Who?"

Kitty's guilt had her riveted to the spot, and she answered for her. "He's dead, Simon. It's my fault. I should never have left her alone."

"Tell me who did this. Even if he is dead, I need to know."

"It was John Leahy. The Confederates killed him for us."

"Leahy, that sadistic son of a bitch, even the men hated him." Simon squeezed Maggie tighter, "Oh, God, Mags, did he… hurt you?"

"He roughed me up pretty good, but didn't do any permanent damage."

"Damn, I wish the Rebs hadn't killed him. I want to tear him to pieces myself."

"I thought of killing him," Kitty admitted, "like you did Barnes, but I needed the other men to see me beat the crap out of him to make sure they didn't think we were easy marks."

"Barnes? I didn't kill Barnes. Yeah, I went looking for the kid to teach him a lesson, but his friends told me he'd gone AWOL. He'd been threatening to do it for a while and the embarrassing incident at the hospital pushed him over the edge. They saw him sneak out the gate. I'm sorry I gave you that impression."

Maggie sat up again wiping her face on her sleeve. "And stop blaming yourself, Kit. I know how hard you tried to take care of me, but you could only do so much without sealing me up in a bubble."

"Maggie's right. Come here." He motioned for Kitty to come closer and awkwardly embraced them both. "You women have been through so much, my heart aches for both of you. It's hard to stay strong with so much going against us. We will survive this, though, I promise."

CHAPTER 15

Kitty's body had been fighting off a bug she'd picked up and had been making her feel crappy for days. At least they had Simon back on his feet now, and their Bucktails friends, as well as Chaplain Lawrence and his wife Lulu, gathered at their campfire again for supper. Simon and Maggie had already told Kitty their good news, but they were eager to tell the others.

Kitty watched them rise in front of the group, arms around each other's waists, and the glow of love clear in their faces as Simon spoke. "First, I want to thank each of you for the kindness and courtesy you showed my wife and my sister while I was missing."

Max dismissed his thanks. "Ach, no thanks are necessary, Reiger, Bucktails take care of their own."

"In any case, since tomorrow is our anniversary, Maggie and I have decided to reaffirm our vows to each other with another wedding ceremony. Chaplain Lawrence, if you don't mind, we'd love for you to officiate."

"Why yes, Sergeant Reiger, I'd be honored."

"Good, then it's settled. My beautiful bride and I want everyone to come back here tomorrow…"

Simon's words sunk in just as John Gruber raised his cup for a toast. "Tomorrow? Why wait for tomorrow Reiger? You've got the Minister, the woman and the witnesses and as big a feast as we're likely to have already here right now. Get on with it man, do it now. Who's with me?"

Kitty recalled Gruber's impetuous marriage proposal. *That is one impatient man!*

Chants of 'Do it now, do it now, do it now' surged from the gathered messmates and Lulu looked as though she'd lose her mind with excitement.

Simon looked questioningly at Maggie whose blushing smile brought cheers from everyone. "It's settled then, Chaplain…"

"Wait, wait I at least need to brush my hair and change my dress. Just give me a few minutes to tidy myself up, okay?" Maggie ducked into the tent and, after a quick wash, scrambled for the calico dress Carole Brunswick had made for her. Once dressed, Kitty helped pin up her hair like a dutiful maid of honor. Maggie brought the rose locket out of hiding for the occasion and, slipping it onto a thin hair ribbon, tied it around her neck. Kitty loaned her the jade earrings to wear.

Kitty waved off any concern over her sudden coughing spasm. "It's okay. I'm just choked up over my sister getting married. Here, let's see what we've got. Something old, the locket. At least it was old in our time. Something new, the dress Carole just made for you. Something borrowed, the earrings. And I'll want those back please. And something blue… what do I have that's blue. Let me look… oh, there's the blue hair ribbon, but it doesn't match the dress."

"Seriously Kitty, do you think anyone cares if I match or not?"

"I know. I just want it to be perfect for you. Here, tie it around your ankle. It doesn't matter if it's hidden, as long as you're wearing it. There, now you're all set. And now I'm crying. I'm so happy for you." They hugged again for the umpteenth time.

As the women cleaned themselves up and got ready, the men had also been busy. They'd gathered sticks and branches to make an arbor for the happy couple and the chaplain to stand under for the ceremony. Chaplain Lawrence wore the coat he reserved for Sunday services and Lulu picked what flowers she could find growing nearby for Maggie's bouquet. A very handsome Simon waited at the makeshift altar with his hair slicked back and a clean shirt borrowed from Isaacs. As Maggie and Kitty emerged from the tent ready for the ceremony, murmurs of appreciation rose from the men at Maggie's glowing beauty. It seemed her feet didn't touch the ground as she floated up to Simon and reached for his hand. A puffed up Max stood beside Simon while Kitty took her place at Maggie's side.

Lulu sniffled loudly as Chaplain Lawrence began. "Dearly beloved, we have come together in the presence of God to witness and bless the joining together of this man and this woman in Holy Matrimony."

Kitty struggled to contain the emotions that welled up inside her. Afraid she'd start blubbering, she tried to distract herself from the chaplain's words. How mind-blowing. The woman who'd been like a sister to her was marrying the man who'd become her brother. *Wait, is that incest?* She cleared her throat to mask the nervous giggle. This was too solemn an event to be ruined by her distraction. Keep it together Trausch, for everyone's sake. She tried to focus on anything else she could. Multiplication tables, nursery rhymes, whatever took her thoughts away from the emotionally charged scene that threatened to send her into a meltdown.

Out of the corner of her eye she glimpsed John Gruber standing off to the side with his hands clasped in front of him. Even though she'd refused his offer of marriage, she still found his broad shoulders and dark features very attractive. *I wonder how it would've been to… okay back to the multiplication tables.*

The couple repeated their vows and Chaplain Lawrence asked for the rings. To prepare for the public announcement, Simon had purchased two silver bands from one of the peddlers that hung around the camp gates. He handed them now to Chaplain Lawrence for his blessing

Then, slipping it on her finger, Simon said, "Margaret McGrail, I give you this ring as a symbol of my love, and with all that I am, and all that I have. And with this ring I promise to love you and hold you from this day forward, for better, for worse, for richer, for poorer, in sickness and in health, to love and to cherish, until death…"

"Stop, don't say that part." Slipping the other ring on Simon's hand Maggie made her vow. "Simon Reiger, I give you this ring as a symbol of my love, and with all that I am, and all that I have. And with this ring I promise to love you and hold you from this day forward, for better, for worse, for richer, for poorer, in sickness and in health, to love and to cherish you… forever."

"Now that Maggie and Simon have given themselves to each other by solemn vows, with the joining of hands and the giving and receiving of rings, I pronounce that they are husband and wife, in the name of the Father, and the Son, and the Holy Spirit. Those, whom God has joined together, let no one put asunder."

Their gentle yet passionate kiss sent a shower of happiness raining down on the gathering as they cheered and hugged and kissed each other. Carried by the emotion of the moment, Kitty even let her emotional wall slip and kissed John Gruber with more passion than she had planned. There might even have been a little tongue action there which surprised both of them. As she guiltily turned away clearing her throat, she saw Maggie smile and nod in her direction. Kitty's face burned with embarrassment with the realization that someone had noticed her little indiscretion.

Max broke out his banjo, Carlyle the homebrew, and soon the party was in full swing. Gruber spun Kitty around in a polka that made her dizzy, so she sat the rest out, but the music and dancing went on for hours. Once the food and beer disappeared, the guests stumbled off to their own quarters. Simon put his arm around both of the ladies' shoulders to lead them into the tent.

Kitty planted her feet on the ground refusing to move. "No, I am not sleeping in there tonight. I've been a third wheel for a long time with Sonia and Carlos, and now with you two, but I am not sleeping in the same room with a couple on their wedding night. That is not going to happen. I'll stay at the hospital tonight; I'll be fine there."

Simon didn't need any arm twisting. "Okay, but it's dark, I'll walk with you to make sure you get there safe."

Gruber stopped him with a hand on his shoulder. "Wait Reiger, you don't need to do that. Stay here with your wife. I'll walk with her."

"Thanks Gruber, I appreciate it."

***

After a last congratulatory hug and kiss to her little family, she left with her bodyguard for the hospital. The half-moon shone enough light that they could make their way along the path holding hands, their shoulders brushing. The closeness of him made her earlier musings return. Though he hadn't captured her heart, he'd certainly stimulated her other parts.

Kitty found an empty isolation room for her bed and stood awkwardly at the door waiting for Gruber to make a move. As he stepped closer, tingles of anticipation rippled through her body. But instead of a repeat of the passionate embrace they'd shared earlier, he placed a chaste kiss on her forehead. "Goodnight, Miss Kitty." He turned and left.

Okay then, she sighed. After another extended coughing fit, Kitty sat on the bed with her back propped against the wall in reflection. With so many consequences to consider, it was just as well he left. Without penicillin, STD's were rampant and, even if she didn't catch anything, what if she got pregnant? That thought made her shudder.

She'd fallen asleep in that same position until a new round of coughing spasms woke her. Her damp clothes stuck like a second skin from her profuse sweating. Stripping down to her chemise she made herself more comfortable in the bed.

Kitty slept fitfully, her body alternating between extreme bouts of heat and shaking chills. Images of Richard Delaney came to her in her dreams. They'd met at Beth/Gen Hospital and were lovers until the day he'd tired of her and asked her to move out. In her dream, though, everything was still perfect between them. Wrapped around each other in the bed, his tongue left damp tracks over her whole body that made her squirm with anticipation. Her chest hurt from the pounding of her heart. His smiling face wavered in front of her as Kitty reached out to touch him. When reality threatened, she willed herself back, the dreams becoming more intense each time. Her shuddering climax was so strong it forced her eyes to flutter open and returned her to consciousness.

***

Maggie sat beside her on the bed, caressing her head with a cool, damp rag. She smiled as Kitty focused on her worried face.

"Are you okay there, Ethel?"

Her vision clearing, Kitty saw that the camp hospital had replaced Richard's apartment. This confused her because Richard's wandering kisses were still damp on her skin. "I'm… wet," she said, her deep, gravelly voice surprising her. "And naked."

Maggie cleared the sand from Kitty's eyes with the cool cloth. "You have pneumonia, Kit. Your fever spiked so high, for a while we thought we might lose you. You scared the crap out of us. You were burning up so Lulu and I took turns bathing you with cool cloths to keep it under control. Are you in any pain?"

"My head hurts, and it feels as if someone's sitting on my chest." Maggie's words finally registered in her mind. "I have pneumonia?" She'd cared for several patients with pneumonia. They'd all died for lack of antibiotics. The sadness in Maggie's eyes confirmed her fear. "I'm dying?"

"If you do, it certainly won't be my fault." Doctor Freeman leaned against the doorway of the small room with his arms crossed, watching them.

Maggie gave him a sideways glance, her lips thinned in agitation. "You can leave us now, Doctor."

Kitty's tears were hot on her face. "I don't want to die here, Mags, I want to go home." A sob caught in her throat and turned into a painful cough.

"Shh, I'm not going to let you die." She wiped away her tears with the cool cloth. "The doctor tried to use his archaic medicine on you that even I knew would do more harm than good, so he's angry at me. Pay no attention to what he said." Maggie returned the cloth to the basin, her eyes fixed on Kitty's. "You are a fighter, Kit, and you've got me in your corner. No, we don't have antibiotics, but with common sense and determination we'll beat this. I'm not giving up on you and you need to promise me you won't either, okay?"

Kitty only nodded, her lips trembling too hard to speak.

"Max sent over a pouch of Hilda's tea for you. Do you think you can sit up to drink it?"

Maggie propped up the pillow behind Kitty as she scooted her aching body back. At first the liquid warmed and soothed her throat, that is until a spasm of wracking coughs made her gag and throw up a wad of disgusting green stuff.

Maggie patted her back as Kitty hung over the basin. "That may not feel good right now, but getting the crap in your chest moving up and out will help. We'll work on that. Keep trying to drink this tea and I'll ask Lulu to get you a bowl of soup from the commissary. A fighter needs to keep up his strength." She kissed her cheek and went off in search of Lulu.

Kitty slept on and off for the next three days, surprised at how much stronger she was each time she woke. Maggie and Lulu brewed gallons of tea for her, some from Max's stash, some from dandelions gathered from the field, and as much willow bark as they could find.

At times Doctor Freeman stopped in to check on her, but only if Maggie wasn't in the room. He eyed her with caution and always kept his distance. Kitty wondered if he hoped she'd die just to spite Maggie and prove her wrong. The thought made her more determined than ever to survive.

As sitting up to talk and drink her tea became easier, she told Maggie about the strange dreams she'd had at the peak of her fever. Maggie blushed a deep crimson red as her hand flew to her mouth. She laughed until she cried.

"What? Is it that funny I'd have an erotic dream?"

She struggled to get the words out and couldn't meet Kitty's eyes. "No, no. But that explains it. Please don't be upset, Kitty, you were out of your mind with fever and had no idea what you were doing."

With slow, rigid motion, Kitty put the cup on the table next to her bed. From the way Maggie hesitated, she knew she had to prepare herself for something awful. *Is that why Doctor Freeman has been keeping his distance from me? Did I let loose a barrage of profanity on him like I did with Gruber? Good God, I hope I'm not going from this hospital bed to the one in the cuckoo's nest.* "Go ahead, tell me. What did I do?"

"Well, for a while you were so delusional that you… um… called Doctor Freeman Richard and… you groped him." Maggie giggled again. "Did you know that's really his first name?"

Kitty's body melted deep into the bed as she buried herself under the blanket. Why couldn't she have only cursed him out? *Okay, universe, you win. I don't want to go home anymore. Just let me die right here, right now.*

CHAPTER 16

In spite of, or as punishment for, her embarrassing gesture, Kitty lived. The diligent nursing care and the gallons of tea helped her body fight off the infection. Just in time, she returned to work at the hospital being careful to avoid Doctor Freeman at all cost. The cold, rain, and food shortages over the winter months kept the clinic hopping and Maggie and Kitty fell into their beds exhausted every night. Aside from the usual nasal miseries and miscellaneous infections, several men suffered from frostbite and trench foot. The sight of these maladies gave the women the skeevies more than any of the battle injuries. They'd even heard stories of men dying in their sleep from the cold.

Their tent, shored up with logs and mud, stayed cozy with the wood stove and the extra quilts and blankets Carole Brunswick sent them. None of them suffered any more weather afflictions worse than the common cold. And, though they were obviously thinner, at least they didn't suffer the ravages of malnutrition either.

***

With budding trees and warmer temperatures signaling the advent of spring, the time came for the company to break camp and get ready to move on to another battle campaign. Encouraged by a series of Union victories along the Mississippi, the Union strategists planned to end the war by taking the Confederate Capital. Only the three of them knew for sure that wouldn't be the case. The division's new commander, General McClellan, planned to go by ship from Alexandria to Fort Monroe in Maryland. From there they'd advance overland meeting up with reinforcements somewhere close to Richmond for what the brass thought would be the final definitive battle.

For the women, there was only one minor complication. They sat outside mending their sparse wardrobe getting ready for the next journey when Maggie told Kitty the news.

"I'm pregnant."

"What? Oh my God, Mags, are you sure?" Kitty's heart stopped for a moment, and she hesitated before gasping her first thought. "It isn't Leahy's, is it?"

"Not a chance. That happened way too long ago."

Thrilled to the bone, Kitty reached over and hugged her with all her might. "That's such wonderful news. You and Simon will be the best parents in the world. And I'm going to be the greatest aunt in the world. How far along are you?"

"Oh, it's still early yet, but I'm two weeks late which is weird because I'm never late. You can almost set your watch by my cycles."

"Well this is a good sign at least. I'm sure Simon must be excited, isn't he?"

Maggie looked around everywhere except at Kitty's face. "I haven't told him yet, he doesn't know."

"Oh, but you're going to, right? I mean you have to tell him. And soon. The regiment is gearing up for another battle."

Maggie bent to pick up the errant button that had slipped out of her hand. "And that's the reason I can't tell him." She gazed off to where the troops practiced their formations. "We can't leave the army yet, Kit. We're not ready and, if I really am pregnant, we need their support." Her eyes came back to the task at hand and her voice took on a stern, lecturing tone. "I can't be traipsing around the countryside with no money and no home in that condition. Simon has to stay with his regiment and do whatever is necessary until we're in a position to leave." Maggie broke the thread with her teeth, plopped down Simon's shirt, and plucked the next piece to be mended from the basket.

The words came from the practical Maggie that Kitty loved, but her actions spoke to an underlying anger and frustration.

Maggie's hands shook so hard Kitty had to help her thread the needle. "And I'm not even sure that this thing is a reality yet. I mean, there are so many reasons why I might be late. Malnutrition for one, we've been eating crap for months. Or maybe just this once I'm late." She took the threaded needle back, calming her voice. "I needed to tell you so we could discuss it, but I can't tell Simon. He worries about us so much already, especially after what happened when he wasn't around the last time." She still shuddered at the memory. "I can't give him anything else to stress over now. Please, Kitty, promise me you won't say anything either."

"All right, no problem, I won't. This is between the two of you anyway." Kitty tried to be upbeat to ease her mind. "I'll just keep my fingers crossed. Aunty Kitty, that sounds awesome. I hope it's a girl. You can teach her to sew and I can teach her to fight. We'll spoil the crap out of her."

Maggie glanced back at the troops. "Yeah, we will."

***

Three days later the regiment left Langley for Alexandria where they boarded the ship taking them downriver. The cruise was short and, since they all stood the rocking seas without getting sick, they disembarked in good spirits.

"This place is the largest stone fort ever built in the United States." Simon lectured with pride as their ship arrived. "It was built in the early eighteen hundreds to protect the Hampton Roads and inland water from attack by sea."

The sprawling complex housed numerous barracks, a balloon airfield, a naval port and a hospital. After being stabilized at the front line of nearby battles the sick and injured Union soldiers and Confederate prisoners wound up at this hospital for treatment. The patient capacity of the main building and the surrounding wings seemed overwhelming to Maggie and Kitty. Nurses here had their work cut out for them. But, after living in tents for so long, even the stark real living quarters they'd seen were like the Waldorf in comparison.

After his briefing, Simon joined Maggie and Kitty on the grass in front of the main building. "So what's the scoop, Simon, what are we doing?" Kitty asked.

Simon picked a blade of grass, hesitating before giving them the news. "The command told us this is only a staging area, so we're moving out again tomorrow." Simon talked faster now, blurting out the rest. "Look guys, don't get upset, I know you're used to going wherever our regiment goes, but this time I want you two to stay here where you'll be better protected. I'm sure the hospital can use your help and this way I won't be stressed over your safety."

Kitty's heart jumped for joy. It would be nice to live indoors for a change. But Maggie's face went dark and her hands shook. "And you think we won't be concerned for yours?"

Well aware of what she meant, he grasped at any argument to convince her. "At least you won't have anyone shooting at you while you're distracted with worry. Besides, look at the clouds. There's another storm brewing, and that means more heavy rain. It may be a long, wet slog through muddy roads before we get to Richmond."

Kitty had been trying to stay quiet and let the two of them talk it out, but she hoped that last statement caught Maggie's attention the way it caught hers. She'd done enough 'slogging through the mud,' and, if this pregnancy turned out to be real, Maggie needed to take better care of herself for the health of the baby.

Maggie paused for a moment before voicing her appeal. "Please Simon, tell me you'll be careful and not take any unnecessary risks. I lost you once. I couldn't bear for it to happen again."

Simon took her hand and brushed her knuckles with his lips. "I love you Maggie McGrail Reiger, and there's not enough hell fire on this earth to keep me from coming home to you. I just need to know you're safe."

Maggie glanced over at Kitty and, for a split second, it seemed as though Maggie might tell him about the possible pregnancy. But she didn't. Even if they couldn't go, he had to, and fighting a war was enough of a burden.

***

The women stood in the pouring rain before dawn the next morning, to say farewell to Simon and their friends. Lulu gave them a tearful hug before leaving with her husband. As Kitty turned to say goodbye to John Gruber, he embraced her longer and tighter than the others as he whispered in her ear. "I hope when we return from this battle you'll let me call on you, Miss Kitty."

She'd have to check with Maggie later, but it sounded as if he'd just asked her for a date. "Sure, that would be nice. You just be careful and come home safe."

The bugler called the troops to formation so, after a quick chaste kiss, he ran off to take his place leaving Kitty to stand under the tarp with Maggie for their mutual support.

"What was that all about with you and Gruber?" She asked as Kitty joined her. "He ran off with such a huge smile on his face, if I didn't know better, I'd swear you promised him more than a hot meal when he came back."

"I did no such thing. He said he wanted to 'call on me.' I think that's a date, right?"

"Sounds like it. And you said yes, right?"

"I said he could call on me, nothing more."

"Good for you."

The drums started their cadence, the pipes and flute their song, and more than a hundred thousand men, horses, and wagons began their march onto Richmond. The women pasted their stock fake smiles of bravery on their faces, and ignoring the heaviness in their hearts, stood under a leaky tarp like drowned rats and waved, what for some would be their last goodbye.

***

Maggie and Kitty had changed into their whites and reported for duty to their new boss. As head nurse and administrator, Mrs. Dickson oversaw the operations of the entire hospital, from budget and supplies to staffing and logistical issues—a formidable job. If appearances meant anything, she no doubt had the skills to handle it. A woman in her mid-to-late forties, she wore her grayish-brown hair parted in the middle and drawn up in a tight bun in the back. Her stern face showed dark, deep-set hooded eyes, thin lips and heavy jowls. A slender woman, tall for her time, she matched Maggie in height and wore a plain black dress with a narrow white collar. The overall effect spoke of no-nonsense efficiency. Maggie and Kitty hurried to keep up as she escorted them to one of the post-op wards. Mrs. Dickson gave them a brief, but firm, rundown of the policies she had instituted concerning discipline and expectations of conduct, then handed them over to the nurse in charge, leaving her to explain their specific duties.

The fast-talking young woman pumped their hands as she introduced herself. "I'm glad to meet you. My name is Rory, we're so grateful that you're here to help us. For the most part we've had male attendants looking after our patients, so it's wonderful to see more women around here. Wow, you're really tall, aren't you?"

A dizzying little bundle of energy, Rory had dark hair tucked under a white cap and plain, but not unpleasant, features. She dug through a drawer of linens as she spoke, at last coming up with the goods. "Ah, here they are." She gave them each the same starched, upside-down cupcake-holder caps she wore, telling them that, as part of their uniform, they had to wear them every day. "Unless your name is as distinctive as mine, we've gotten into the habit of calling each other by our last names as the men do, so what should we call you two?"

Rory had been talking nonstop since they met her, so they waited a beat to be sure she had finished before answering. They'd been Simon's wife and his sister at the other camps, so everyone assumed they had the same last name, but that would be too confusing here. "I'm Kitty Trausch and my sister is Maggie Reiger or if you'd rather..."

"Okay, well there are forty men in this ward, all of them amputees of some sort and needing care." Rory continued her instruction as she led them down the aisles between the two rows of beds, pointing out specific care duties as they walked. "Every morning we give the men their morphine to ease their pain and check the stump sites for signs of healing. If any of the men develop fevers, we need to tell doctor right away so the soldier can be moved to the isolation ward. So make sure you make an entry in the logbook on what you saw, and if you gave any medication, for the doctor to see. It's good that you're here now to get acquainted, 'cause I expect we'll be getting many more patients once General McClellan reaches Richmond." That was not a comforting thought. "By then they'll need to move this ward to a bigger room, but for now, here we are. There are supply closets at either end of the ward. The locked one is for linens and bandages and such, and the other for stocks of medicines. You'll find the quinine, morphine, laudanum and medicinal whiskey in there. Just make sure you knock before entering any of the closets. Any questions? Okay, well I have an appointment now, so Sloan there will help you with anything you need." And with a rustle of skirts she disappeared.

Maggie and Kitty just stood and stared at each other in stupid disbelief. "What did she say?"

"I'm not sure, but let's start cleaning up this place. It's a mess."

Sloan, a rather quiet black man, presumably from one of the 'Colored Units,' proved invaluable. After he returned with the cleaning supplies they'd requested, he unlocked the linen closet for them. Without hesitation, he started out with the mop and bucket while they opened windows, changed and tidied up each bed. As she went along, introducing herself to each soldier, Kitty found many with wound infections that weren't being treated. First she checked for a key, and Sloan directed her to the medical supply room at the other end of the ward. As a bizarre twist, she found it unlocked. Was it a sign of the time that blankets were more valuable and more prone to theft than morphine or laudanum?

Armed with several bottles labeled tincture of iodine, and a couple containing morphine, Maggie and Kitty made their rounds. First they administered the morphine, then painted the wounds with the dark red iodine and re-bandaged them with clean dressings. Kitty remembered reading a chapter on using iodine in her research to help her sister, Patty, with a nursing school project. Although an adequate antiseptic, it stings like crazy when applied. Even though they gave a dose of morphine before the treatment, the patients needed an extra little top-off afterwards.

Rory never came back. It took the whole morning to finish the cleaning and wound treatment for all forty patients, leaving the women exhausted and starving. Again, it was Sloan who directed them to the mess hall for dinner.

***

Maggie and Kitty found an empty table in the cafeteria where they could savor their meal in peace. The two male attendants who took the seats across from them at the table, though, soon squashed that plan.

"Good afternoon ladies, I hope you don't mind us joining you, the seating here is limited as you can see."

Maggie gave a polite, but short, answer. "No, of course not, enjoy your dinner."

The outspoken one put his hand out first to Maggie and then to Kitty, introducing himself and his cohort. "My name is Pete Yeager ma'am, and my cousin here is John Donnelly. We're both of us from Boston, here with the First Massachusetts."

Kitty sized them up at about average height for the time, in their low-to-mid-twenties, with fresh, eager faces and upturned noses that showed a family resemblance. The Boston part she caught right away from the accent. "Nice to meet you, gentlemen. My name is Kitty Trausch, and this is my sister-in-law Maggie Reiger. I hope you don't think us rude, but we've had a difficult morning and we're just looking for peace and quiet."

"Oh yeah sure, I get it, we just haven't seen you around here before and wanted to say hello is all. So are you ladies from Washington?"

"No, Pennsylvania."

The conversation went on that way the whole time. Either Kitty or Maggie gave one-word answers to the incessant questions while they scarfed down their food. It was nice that the soldiers were trying to be friendly and welcoming, but the women had asked for peace and quiet.

***

Later that afternoon, Kitty spied Rory coming out of the linen closet with one of the male attendants, both of them looking flushed. Rory, you ignorant slut, is that why the linen closets are locked instead of the medicine closets?

They emerged with perfect timing as the attending, Doctor Moorfield, came on to the ward. "Nurse Blandford, where is the logbook for this ward? I need to examine it."

Maggie and Kitty were on the same wavelength as their eyes grew wide with recognition and they turned to each other giggling and whispering. "Nurse Blandford? Rory short for Aurora? Holy crap, old man Blandford's daughter's a whore!" They got stunned, blank stares as they went into their high-five, fist-bumping routine, but this long awaited validation helped restore their spirits and renew their energy.

Since they had completed most of the necessary tasks that morning, aside from dispensing a little more morphine where needed, they spent the afternoon relaxing and socializing. The soldiers weren't sick, only injured, and bored with having to lie around all day. Experience taught them that boredom led to depression and restlessness, which undermined the patients' attitudes and delayed healthy recovery. As at Camp Curtin, they read to them, helped write letters and sang songs with, and for them. To lighten the mood, they encouraged the men to sing along with the popular songs everyone knew and the women had learned in camp. It turned out that Rory had talents for outside the linen closet as she strummed a guitar and sang songs in a clear and pleasant voice.

Weeks dragged by with the same routine. They'd seen Rory coming out of the linen closet several times, always with someone different, eliciting secret snickers from both of them. Each discharged patient felt like a personal triumph, but new admissions never lagged. For their after-dinner breaks, they found a quiet bench that overlooked the bay to enjoy the view and the clean smell of the salty spray. But they worried over Simon and their friends on the battlefield and prayed to whoever was listening for their safe return. Though there'd been rumors of battles, they still held their breath waiting for news of his unit.

***

Early one morning Kitty awoke to the sound of Maggie retching her guts out into the chamber pot. "Mags, are you okay? Do you need something?" The only response from that side of the room was more heaving. She rushed to help hold Maggie's long hair out of the way. "Maggie, have you gotten your period yet?"

She flung herself back on the bed panting from the effort of emptying her stomach. "No, not yet."

"Woo hoo!" Kitty jumped up, danced around the room, and did a poor imitation of a moon walk. "I'm going to be an aunt, me, Aunty Kitty. We're going to spoil the crap out of this kid."

Another round of puking left Maggie curled up on her bed, crying. "I wish I could be as happy about this as you. Do you realize that women die in childbirth all the time here? What if I need a Cesarean? Do they even do that now? And what if Simon gets killed or maimed, how will we live?"

That brought Kitty back to reality. *Shit, I hadn't thought about any of that.* Even if Simon fought in the army at home, they'd still have family and friends nearby for support. They were completely on their own here. Since she'd never had a child herself, the thought of complications had never occurred to her. Could fate really be that cruel?

Kitty knelt by her bed and rested her head on the pillow beside Maggie's, her arm draped around her shoulders. "I won't let you die, Mags. We're fighters, remember? And fighters never quit. I'll always be here for you, no matter what." She sat up and smoothed the hair from her face. "You stay here and rest and I'll bring you something to eat later. There's water here in the jug if you want it." Kitty poured out a cupful and put it on the night table next to the bed.

Late for work, Kitty rushed out the door with one nagging thought on her mind. I sure hope Simon is okay, and that he makes it back safe. And soon.

***

Without Maggie, the workload doubled and, as usual, Rory disappeared when Kitty needed her the most. Sloan, though, helped a lot. Kitty had shown him how to change the dressings, what to look for, and to alert her if he saw something that needed treatment.

Kitty stood in the linen closet trying to find clean sheets when she heard the door latch closed behind her. As she turned to make sure it didn't lock her in, she found John Donnelly standing against the door watching her.

Spooked by his sudden appearance, she reached for the closest stack of linens, and cradled them in her arms. "Oh, hi, Mr. Donnelly, could you please open that door? These have to go out to the ward."

In a flash he'd crossed the small gap between them and had her back pinned against the shelf. With his hand at her throat and the stack of towels in her arms squished between them, Kitty couldn't move.

"No."

Spinning her around and shoving her against the shelves, Donnelly pressed up against her to hold her in place while he fumbled trying to hike up her skirt, his onion laced breath hot on her neck.

Though the struggle had started off in his favor, the advantage shifted. Kitty shoved the towels onto the shelf and elbowed back hard with a good shot to his ribs. The blow forced him back a step, giving her space to turn and launch her knee into his groin in one swift move. As he jerked forward, grimacing and holding his injured crotch, she forced his head down and rammed her knee into his face. "I did not give you permission to touch me."

Sloan heard the scuffle and yanked open the closet door just in time for Donnelly to collapse unconscious at his feet. Kitty tiptoed over him with the armful of sheets she'd come for in the first place.

"Are you all right, Miss?"

"Yes, Sloan, I'm fine. He's not though. Could you please help Mr. Donnelly off this ward?" *And into an open ditch.*

Sloan's face shone with amusement. "Yes Miss, whatever you say."

Concerned for Maggie's safety, Kitty told her later that night about the incident in the closet. She had to make her aware that the two guys who kept showing up at dinnertime were not as friendly as they seemed and to make sure she stayed out of the linen closet. Apparently anyone in there was fair game.

"I don't understand what it is with men named John here," she whined. "Gruber tries to force you to marry him, Donnelly tries to rape you and…" Without thinking, her hand stroked her face where Leahy had beaten her. "You be careful, too, Kitty. Some men are just ruthless."

***

Mail call, that illusionary contact with home, always brought smiles to the patients' faces. The few illiterate soldiers listened with rapt attention while they read the letters to them with reassurances of a patiently waiting lover, news of spring plantings or Uncle Harold's piles. Sometimes they'd ask the nurses to read them over again, their faces wistful, as if imagining the author writing the words. Then, the replies transcribed, and envelopes addressed, the nurses made sure they got posted.

After dinner, Maggie showed Kitty a letter she'd received that day from Simon. She'd waited until they were together and alone before opening it, in part because she knew Kitty wanted to hear what he said, but, also because she feared it might contain bad news. They sat on their peaceful bench, overlooking the bay as Maggie read the letter aloud.

"My dear Maggie and Kitty,

Knowing how much you worry, I'll tell you first off that I'm fine and so are all of our friends. You may hate me for it right now, but I'm sure I made the right decision having you two stay behind at Fort Monroe. It was absolute torture slogging through the mud and muck for a week, and I'm glad you didn't have to go through it. You've both been through so much already and I can't tell you how grateful I am for all your support.

Even the best battle plans are fluid and this one is no exception. Instead of taking the direct route to Richmond as planned, McClellan has made a stand at Yorktown. I don't know how long this siege will continue, so I want to prepare you that it may be a few more weeks or even months before I get back. But I will be back.

Lulu misses you both and sends her love.

I haven't held you in my arms for weeks Mags, so I'm sure you can imagine how I'm feeling right now and I'd prefer you keep the rest of this letter to yourself...

Love,

Simon"

Maggie read the rest of the letter with silent trembling lips, while the word 'months' reverberated in Kitty's mind. Would he even be back in time to be with Maggie when she had the baby? She'd be there to help her, of course, but she's no substitute for her husband.

Maggie dabbed tears from her eyes, her face transforming into a mask of false bravery. "Well, so far so good. At least they're still in one piece."

After working in the post-op ward it was interesting to Kitty how, in war time, any war time, that simple statement could be taken literally.

***

Just as Rory had predicted, once the siege at Yorktown got under way, their ward was inundated with new casualties every day, most of them Union soldiers, but others were Confederate prisoners of war who needed medical treatment as well. Though given humanitarian care and medical treatment, the prisoners stayed confined under guard to their own isolated ward.

Other nurses and orderlies they'd met complained that many of their patients had developed severe infections and fevers. The doctors then gave instructions to move them to isolation wards to stem the spread of the illness. Ignorant of the concept that germs and bacteria were the culprits, the doctors reasoned that the 'malady' had to be airborne and thus required isolation. As with everywhere else they'd been, their preaching of hygienic and antiseptic care drew only polite nods. But the fact remained that few of the soldiers on their ward developed such severe fevers, or met the hospital standard for isolation. Kitty boasted that their ward had a recovery rate at least double that of any other. She tried to use that statistic to show the wisdom of such treatment, but to no avail.

Mrs. Dickson, the head nurse, made her rounds every afternoon to make sure the wards were in order, and to give the patient and supply logs a cursory check. A strict, no-nonsense woman, she kept her visits brief, and to the point allowing the staff to get on with their afternoon social activities. So when Kitty saw her lingering over the supply book, and double-checking the medicine closet, it worried her. *Crap, I thought I'd been keeping good records, I hope I didn't screw up somewhere.*

"Mrs. Dickson, can I help you with something?"

"Yes Madam, you can tell me what happened to the large stock of iodine you ordered for this ward?" Without warning, she thrust the log book up to Kitty's face to see the order entry. "There's only half this much in the closet, the rest seems to be missing. Have you been misappropriating government supplies, Miss Trausch?"

"It isn't missing Mrs. Dickson, we've used it. These patients came in here with infected wounds and I've been applying the iodine as an antiseptic to stop the spread and worsening of the infection. It's been working, too."

When she saw Mrs. Dickson's crass assault with the log book, Maggie came to where they were standing for support. "She's right Mrs. Dickson, look at our statistics. This ward has the fewest number of patients requiring isolation than any other. By using antiseptic on the wounds, it makes a huge difference in their recovery."

"Are you a doctor now Mrs. Reiger or a…" The way Mrs. Dickson stopped mid-sentence and stared at her, made Maggie uncomfortable. "You're with child aren't you?" It wasn't so much a question as a statement of fact.

"Uh, yes but how…"

"But nothing. I can't have a woman who is carrying a child working as a nurse here in my hospital."

"What, you're firing me? But… but… you can't, you can't do that. My husband's off fighting with General McClellan. Where will I go if I can't stay here? How will we live?"

Kitty wanted to seize the old biddy by the throat and shake her, but she knew that would only make matters worse. "Really Mrs. Dickson? You're going to throw a woman in her condition, whose husband is laying down his life for his country, out in the street? Are you that heartless?"

Indignant, she took a deep breath and straightened her back before answering the charge. "My job is to ensure the safe and efficient running of this hospital and I accept that responsibility with the utmost dedication. But I certainly am not heartless. I have no intention of throwing either of you out into the street although I am not wasting any more of the government's money by resupplying you, Miss Trausch, with any more iodine. Mrs. Reiger I will see to it that you are given work to do in the kitchen where you won't be around any of the patients. For now I want you both in your quarters until I've arranged your transfers. Go, now, you're relieved of your duties here. Mr. Sloan, where is Rory? I need to inform her of the staffing change."

Poor wide-eyed Sloan moved his mouth, but nothing came out. He knew where Rory could be found, but he didn't want to be the one to get her in trouble for not tending to her assigned duties.

"Check the linen closet" is what Kitty called over her shoulder as she and Maggie walked off the ward en route to the cafeteria for coffee and a snack.

***

With an obvious reason for transfer, Maggie's paperwork slid through with ease. The administrators assured Kitty she'd still be assigned somewhere in the hospital, but not in what capacity. Only that it would take a few more days to get past the red tape.

Reassignment to the kitchen turned out to be a blessing for Maggie. She'd have free access to nutritional food anytime she wanted it to keep her healthy. Also, the more mature women who worked that detail had more experience with pregnancy issues. That was a major relief for her. Maggie's only reference points on the subject came from what she'd learned in school, and even then they focused on how to avoid the issue entirely rather than how to manage it. The good women in the kitchen took her under their collective wings with motherly words of advice and encouragement that, without Simon nearby, meant so much to her sense of security.

Maggie wasn't free for a break until after everyone had eaten dinner and the kitchen spit-shined, so they met later at their favorite spot along the bay to talk. At long last Kitty had received her work assignment and wanted to share it with her.

"I don't mind working in the kitchen, it's fine. In fact, I feel more at home there since it's so much like Sammy's. But it's tough being around all that food. Sometimes the sights and smells overwhelm me and I have to run out and puke. Especially those oval-shaped white things that

chickens put out. Don't say the word or I'll hurl right here."
She'd brought along pieces of hard tack that she'd
crumbled with a mallet and tossed it out to the waiting gulls
along the walkway. "The women I work with say they
understand, but it sure turns off the people who come to
eat, to hear me barfing my guts out in the back room."

"What about you, Kitty? Have they told you yet where
you're going and what you'll be doing? They aren't going
to split up our living quarters are they?"

"I did get my assignment, just today in fact. And no,
they're not splitting up our living quarters. We lucked out
there. I'm going back to the hospital, but they transferred
me to the ward where they keep the prisoners of war, the
Confederate soldiers." Kitty held a piece of Maggie's hard
tack in her hand, turning it over and examining it as she
spoke. "I kind of have mixed feelings about that, Mags. I
mean, these are the guys that Simon and our friends have
been fighting. Maybe one of our friends even wounded
someone I'll be taking care of, or maybe someone I'm
taking care of might have wounded one of our friends.
There's no way to be certain, but it makes me uneasy. Do
you know what I mean?" Smashing the hard tack against
the bench, Kitty managed to break off a piece small enough
to feed to the birds.

"Huh, yeah I do, that's a sticky situation. I think you have to look at the assignment as just another soldier needing medical care. Regardless of how he got wounded or by whom. I'm sure that's what the doctors must do." Maggie took a break from the birds to give Kitty's shoulders a sisterly squeeze. "You'll see, once you get in there and start talking to them you'll find they're the same hurt and lonely men we've been taking care of all along. They've just worn different clothes and, for whatever reason of circumstance, stood on the other side of the line."

"Yeah, I guess you're right. Wars have been fought over much less important issues than this and, as we're well aware, will continue to be. Thanks, Mags, my little niece is so lucky to have such a smart Mom." Kitty moved to return the hug when a glop of bird poop fell on Maggie's hand. Maggie's lunch spewed to the ground followed by Kitty's.

CHAPTER 17

Bright and early the next morning Kitty reported for duty at the POW ward. Although smaller in size, the ward had the same basic layout as the one she came from, only with fewer patients. One of the male attendants showed her around, explaining that they held twenty prisoners here in the general ward, some recovering from miscellaneous minor wounds, others with amputations and only one, a captain, required isolation for a festering chest wound. The organization being the same, she started by taking stock of the medication cabinet. True to her word, Mrs. Dickson had all the iodine removed from the closet and left only a meager supply of morphine and laudanum on the shelves with the lint and bandages. Kitty gathered what was left into a bucket, and started at the far end of the ward introducing herself and frugally dispensing what little medication she had.

Maggie was right. Most of these men had a distinct Southern drawl that Kitty found interesting, but their complaints and needs were the same as the soldiers she had cared for in the amputee ward. The only difference being the fear these men harbored in their hearts. They weren't sure yet if they'd be sent to prison camps, exchanged, paroled, or left to die of their wounds.

Although Kitty tried to be as comforting and reassuring as possible, without antibiotics, the pitiful condition of their wounds thwarted any hope in her heart that the ones who were already glassy-eyed with fever might have a chance. The best Kitty could do for them was to wash the affected areas, change their dressings and dispense what little pain medication she had to keep them comfortable.

After washing her hands, and applying lotion to keep them from getting chapped, she steeled herself for whatever horror awaited her in the isolated captain's room. Even so, it was impossible to prepare herself for what she saw. The captain's feet hung over the edge of the six-foot long bed, the vague outline of his ribs showed through the blanket, and the skin visible around the beard and moustache looked pale and haggard. So weak, his eyes half open, he lay in his bed moaning with pain and fever. Kitty had presumed the attendant sitting at the desk outside the isolation room's door to be responsible for this man's maintenance care, but if that was the case, he'd done a damn poor job of it. She berated herself for not starting in this room first. If anyone had needed her, he did.

After moistening the dressing and peeling it away, the putrid smell of pus and necrotic tissue nauseated her. As she examined the surrounding tissue, she noticed red streaks radiating out from the wound. A foreboding sign. With the possibility of sepsis looming on the horizon, comfort care was the best treatment Kitty had for this poor man. She smoothed his dry lips with wax, helped him sip his dose of laudanum, washed the infected area and replaced his dressing with a clean one. All the while feeling so inadequate and frustrated with a medical system that refused to consider antiseptic care.

Kitty spent the rest of the morning in that room trying to reduce the fever with cold compresses and make the captain as comfortable as possible. She gave the attendant outside the door the benefit of the doubt as far as training and enlisted his aid to help her. Together they bathed the patient, trimmed and debugged his beard and change the linens on his bed. No doubt it was the most care given to the man since he'd been there. Most likely he'd still die, but that didn't mean he couldn't go with a little dignity.

***

The stressful morning had frazzled her nerves. Kitty needed to be alone for a while, so instead of meeting Maggie after dinner as usual, she went to her quarters to rest. What she needed more though was to pound on something or someone to get all her pent up anger out. Without access to a gym or a punching bag, her pillow would have to do.

Back in her room Kitty paced the floor, a stream of curse words flowing in a low voice in case anyone nearby should hear. *What good am I doing here?* It seemed she'd been beating her head against a wall trying to convince this primitive medical system that their methods didn't work. People were dying for no good reason and she was powerless to help them. One thing was certain, when Simon finished with the army, she never wanted to step foot in a hospital again.

She tried centering herself with yoga poses and, when that didn't work, she tried Tai Chi. Still unable to relieve her frustration, she collapsed in her bed to cry herself out. While lying there waiting for the tears to start, Kitty spotted the package sitting on top of the wardrobe at the foot of her bed and bolted upright. *Shit! Why didn't I think of this earlier?*

In a flash she moved the small box to the table to open it. Inside, Kitty found the letter from Hilda Maxwell describing the contents. After Cal Jackson's shoulder wound healed so well she had written Max's wife thanking her for the herbs. Kitty told her how she thought they'd been instrumental in Cal's recovery. In reply, Hilda had sent her this case full of little jars and tins of medicinal herbs with instructions on how to use them. The original plan was to save them in case any of their friends fell injured. But surely, no one cared if she tried using them on the wounded captain, right? Who knows, he'd most likely die anyway, but at least she'd be satisfied knowing she'd used every tool available to her.

Kitty took out and examined each jar and tin. After matching them up with the instructions, she found one tin marked 'healing salve' that the letter said to use on infected wounds. She sniffed the contents and thought she smelled rosemary, but didn't recognize any other scent. Well, she'd seen first-hand the results Hilda's tea had on other maladies. She'd trust that this balm would also do the trick. After adding the pouch of herbal tea mixture to the other items in her rucksack, she returned the box to the shelf. Kitty now strode back to the ward with a renewed sense of purpose and determination. *So they won't let me use anymore iodine. No problem. Thanks to Hilda, I have my own resources.*

***

Over the next two days, Kitty applied the salve and changed the dressing four times a day and helped the captain drink a cup of the herbal tea each time. That might've been overkill, she wasn't sure, but she needed it to work and, if some is good, more is better, right? Debriding the black necrotic skin from the edges of the wound so the good tissue could grow together gave her the heebie-jeebies. It made her hands shake so hard she thought she'd never finish. Kitty knew it had to be done though. She took a deep breath and reminded herself that she'd once found the strength to remove a bullet from Cal Jackson's shoulder. *If I could that, I can do anything.*

When Kitty arrived at his door early on the third morning, she found the captain propped up in bed with the attendant, whose name she'd learned was Foster, feeding him soup. The fever had broken during the night, leaving him still weak, but with the delirium gone, at least able to speak and take food. Gratified that he had improved enough to eat something, Kitty let Foster finish the feeding while she gathered her supplies.

Kitty sat in the chair next to the bed finally able to speak to the man she'd been hovering over for the past couple of days. "I'm glad to see you're awake, how are you feeling?"

As he turned his head towards her, the most startling blue eyes she'd ever seen, met hers. The color reminded her of the sky on a clear summers' day. Seeing him awake and focused for the first time, an instant and unsettling fascination with this man hit her. His longish, dark-with-a-sprinkle-of-gray hair now clean and combed, his trimmed beard darker at the chin and grayer on the sides, and those incredible eyes, stimulated urges she'd only had recently in dreams. This was a good life to save.

Even though the infection had subsided, he still struggled with pain making his slight, but noticeable, Southern drawl sound strained and husky. "They tell me you're the one to thank for saving my life."

"I was only doing my job." The shyness in her own voice surprised her as she peeled the dressing from his wound to check it.

He smiled, amused at her blushing face. "Will you tell me your name? I want to be sure to get it right when I tell everyone about the wonderful nurse who saved my… ouch… my life."

"Sorry, I didn't mean to hurt you, I'll try to be gentler. My name is Catherine Trausch, most people call me Kitty."

"Huh, I didn't realize Kitty was a nickname for Catherine."

"Well, you know, Catherine, Cat, Kitty… how about you? Everyone here calls you 'the captain'. You must have a name." The redness encircling the wound had disappeared and Kitty applied only a slight touch of Hilda's salve at the edges before redressing it.

"It's McCabe ma'am. Captain Sampson McCabe. What is that stuff you put on under the bandage? It smells like the pot roast my mother used to make."

"Mmm, yes, I'm seasoning you before we roast you outside on the spit." Her smirking smile settled the alarm that bloomed in those gorgeous blues. "And please, Captain McCabe, don't call me ma'am, it makes me sound old. Make it Catherine or Kitty, whichever suits you. I like that better."

"Okay… Catherine, if you'll dispense with the formalities and call me Sam."

Finished with the dressing, Kitty sat up straighter in the chair, her eyes narrowed with interest. Sam McCabe, S.M. Nah, it was too much of a coincidence. "Um, do you happen to have a middle name Sam?"

"Atticus. Sampson Atticus McCabe." He rolled his eyes as the distasteful name fell off his tongue.

"Nuh uh!"

"Yes I know." He shrugged with embarrassment. "Mother thought it was clever. Not too many people catch on to it though, you're very perceptive."

Perceptive? She was freakin' flabbergasted! "Well our mothers must've gone to the same school," she chuckled, "because my middle name is Abigail. Catherine Abigail Trausch. C.A.T. hence, Kitty."

Sam's laugh turned into a grimace as the movement caused sharp pains to spread from his wound.

"Here, let me get you a dose of morphine for the pain." *That was dumb instead of helping the man, I made him hurt more.*

Rushing back with the bottle of morphine Kitty poured the measured amount into his cup and, as she brought it to his mouth to drink, his hand closed around hers. It may have been her imagination, or static buildup, but she swore an electric charge sparked when they touched. And those damn gorgeous blue eyes boring into hers. This wasn't fair. How the hell was she supposed to stay professional when just brushing by his hand set her on fire? *I wonder if he knows what he's doing to me.* On purpose she gave him an extra dose of morphine to knock him out and let her take a breath.

Once he'd gone unconscious, Kitty sat back in the chair a moment, fanning herself and letting her heart rate slow. *Phew, cool your jets and take it easy there, Trausch.* This was neither the time nor the place for those kinds of feelings, and with a prisoner to boot. He may just be trying to win her over so she'd help him escape, and she was not falling for any of that crap.

The progress of his healing wound pleased and amazed her. Hilda sure knew her stuff. Kitty made a mental note to write another letter tonight telling her how well her concoction worked and send her money for another supply.

Kitty lingered at his bedside for one last moment, brushing the hair back from his face. His eyes fluttered open for a second before returning to his drug-induced stupor. "Who am I kidding? Anyone with your looks must have a wife and a half dozen kids at home waiting for him. Maybe someday I'll find someone like you."

***

When Kitty returned to the ward after dinner that day, three new patients had been admitted. One had a shoulder wound requiring an amputation of the arm from the shoulder joint. By sheer luck he hadn't bled to death. Although Kitty didn't see how he'd ever be fitted for a prosthetic with that much tissue loss. As she inspected his wound, more memories of removing the bullet from Jackson's shoulder flashed in her mind. She tried to mask the fresh shiver that went down her spine to save the injured man's feelings. That image may never leave her. Another soldier lost an ear to a bullet that had grazed his head, and the third had a bayonet slice a healthy gap into his thigh. It took Kitty and the attendants two hours to get them washed, re-bandaged, medicated and settled in their beds leaving less time than usual for socializing.

Close to quitting time, Foster came to get her as Kitty tidied up the last bed. "It's the captain, Miss Kitty. He's asking for that tea you've been bringing him, but I don't know how to make it."

"Oh that's okay, Foster, I'll get it. I wanted to check in on him one more time before I leave for the day anyway." That was a lie. She'd been avoiding his room as much as possible. He was healing well and didn't need her as much and, to be honest, the erotic fantasies he'd stirred up were embarrassing.

Kitty stood in the doorway for a second holding the steaming brew while trying to keep her heart from leaping out of her chest.

"Catherine, I'd hoped it would be you bringing the tea. I want to talk to you if you have time. Can you sit with me for a few moments?" He reached his hand out for the cup as she approached, and again their fingers met, creating that same spark that jumped right to her heart making him smile. "If we keep sparking like this every time our hands meet, we may set each other on fire."

So he felt the spark too. Was he aware though that she was already on fire? "After the work I did to get rid of your fever that would be a shame." Kitty eased herself onto the chair, trying hard not to meet his eyes. "Um, did you have something specific you wanted to discuss, about your wound perhaps, or do you just want company? I mean I'm okay with whatever, either way." *Good grief, Trausch, quit blathering.*

He paused for a moment, caressing her hand. "I wanted to tell you that I do not have a wife and kids waiting for me when I get home."

Her eyes flew open and her head snapped around to stare at him as if it were on a rubber band. She opened and closed her mouth but no sound came out. Instead, the all too familiar glow of mortification crept up from her toes. Kitty wanted to run out the door in humiliation, but she knew that if she stood she'd be tripping over her feet and only shame herself more. Her voice, though somewhat strained, came back, but facing him was out of the question. Kitty searched the room looking to focus on something else. "I'm sorry, I thought you were asleep, I didn't mean for you to hear that. I guess I should go."

"No wait, please. I didn't say that to embarrass you, I guess I just wanted you to understand that. Please stay, I promise I won't bring it up again."

He had no idea of her nervous balance affliction. Only she knew that the only way she'd get out of that room without hurting either her body or her pride was on her hands and knees. Besides the lost contact lens excuse would never work here. "All right, I can stay and talk awhile."

They started with small talk. Kitty avoided the question of her life before the war. She only told him that her brother, Simon, was off fighting, and she and his wife stayed behind to help at the hospital. Sam confessed that he had been married, but, when his son died in an unfortunate accident with a horse, his wife went berserk and left him. Although born and raised in Virginia, when his life fell apart he didn't want to stay there any longer. He'd been on his way to California when the war broke out. It wasn't the issues that made him join the army, he said, only the need to fight out his anger at life. Kitty understood those sentiments well.

***

Kitty didn't make it back to the room until after dark and found Maggie up and pacing. Her arms flailed about as she scolded her. "Where have you been? You had me so worried. I had visions of you being held hostage in a linen closet somewhere being gang-raped by twenty men named John. I thought of going to look for you until I realized I don't even know where the prisoner ward is and I'd only wind up getting lost myself. Don't do that to me again."

Kitty understood the memory of the abuse she'd received at Leahy's hand haunted her. She didn't mean to trivialize her concern, but the cloud she floated on kept her from mustering a serious apology. "I'm sorry. I didn't mean to make you worry, I stayed at the hospital talking to one of the patients and time just flew by." Deciding her uniform was still wearable another day, Kitty hung it in the little closet they shared. "I wish you could meet him Mags, he's so good-looking and has the most gorgeous blue eyes, and he's a great conversationalist too." She filled the wash basin from the pitcher of water and picked up the bar of lavender soap to wash her hands and face. "Oh, and get this, his father is this bigwig with a Southern railroad and, when I mentioned I'd met Jerome Brunswick from the Pennsylvania Railroad Line, he said they'd been family friends for years." Still miffed, Maggie slapped the clean towel into Kitty's hand. "Anyway, he's so smart he kept me on my toes the whole time, challenging everything I said, and when he told me he'd heard me telling myself that he's probably already married when I thought he'd fallen asleep, I got so nervous I had to stay because if I tried to leave I'd trip over my own feet and then the strangest thing happened…"

"Stop talking for crap's sake, you're going so fast I can't keep up with you. Wait a minute." Her fingers dug into Kitty's arm. "Oh my God Kit, are you telling me you're falling for a Confederate prisoner of war?"

"Ow! Stop. No, I didn't say that." Kitty pulled her arm away and sat on the bed to brush out her hair.

Maggie stood over her with her hands on her hips. "No you didn't use those words, but that flow of oral diarrhea you released said it for you. I know you Kitty Trausch, and you don't get worked up like this over just anybody. You should see your face! I've never seen you so ecstatic." She sat next to her on the bed, her hand resting on Kitty's knee. "Honey, sure these things sometimes hit out of the blue, but do you think this is such a good idea?"

Kitty put the brush down and turned to face her. "Mags, I am not in love with this man. It's just that he put me at ease so fast and had me smiling and laughing and when our hands met, I felt this tiny electric shock, you know, like when you turn a door knob after you've been shuffling your feet on a carpet, and when he said he'd felt it too before I'd even said anything, it surprised me because, obviously, I'd touched him before when he was too doped up to realize it and, I don't know, maybe I focused too much on caring for his wound then, but it seemed important to him to tell me that he isn't married and... shit. Shit, shit, shit."

"Uh huh, just as I thought."

"Trust me Mags, I would never do anything to jeopardize our safety. I don't know, it might be that he's playing me thinking he'd get me to help him. But I sure as hell don't want to be stood in front of a firing squad for being the idiot nurse duped into setting a prisoner of war free."

"Good, remember that. It's bad enough I have to worry about Simon getting shot, I don't want to be worried about losing you, too."

"You're right. I'll try to keep my distance as much as possible before I get in too deep. In any case, it doesn't matter. The chances of him being around much longer are slim. He's healing so well now, I'll bet the doctor will discharge him soon and he'll be sent off to some POW camp or something and I'll never see him again." Although that statement placated Maggie, Kitty's heart sank with the reality of what she'd said.

***

When Doctor Gallagher sought her out on the ward the next day, Kitty assumed her words had been prophetic.

"Nurse Trausch is it?"

"Yes sir."

"The captain's wound has made remarkable progress, but I'm concerned about his pain level and I'm not happy with the way he's breathing. He may have residual fluid in that lung that I'll have to reduce. I want you to check his breathing and heart rate at least every two hours and send for me if his condition changes, understand? And I want every one of your findings recorded in this log. You're lack of documentation is making my job harder and risking the patients' lives."

"Yes sir." His words were crystal clear. They meant she couldn't avoid being near him and that her efforts to save his life may have been for nothing. And that she was a terrible secretary.

After retrieving the wooden tube with the flared bottom that passed for a stethoscope, Kitty headed for

Sam's room asking Foster to go to the medicine room and bring her the morphine. If she had to be close to him, she'd at least have someone else in the room to help keep it on a professional level. She would not let him get under her skin and trick her into doing something stupid.

"Good morning Sam, Doctor Gallagher tells me you're worse today. I'm going to listen to your heart and breathing and give you a dose of morphine if you're still in pain, okay?"

"Yes, thank you, Catherine."

His voice sounded very raspy and his breathing more labored than it had been last evening. The sudden overnight change surprised her. Kitty hoped their little laugh fest hadn't caused this. Just baring his chest to use the stethoscope sent butterflies to her stomach, and she had to concentrate to keep her facial expression from giving that away. His heartbeat sounded strong and even a little fast. Or was that hers? And though she couldn't hear any rattling in his lungs, it might have been her lack of experience or training, or maybe his lungs actually were clear.

Kitty sat back in the chair with the stethoscope on her lap, confused. "I don't hear any unusual sounds in your chest Sam, how do you feel? Are you in more pain today?"

Sam signaled Foster to come closer. "Sir, do you mind leaving the room for a moment? I have something of a personal nature to discuss with my nurse."

Embarrassed, Foster looked to her for approval, then made a hasty exit.

After Foster left, Sam reached for Kitty's hand, smiled with a devilish sparkle in his eyes, and spoke in a soft normal tone. "I learned this morning I'm to be paroled, sent home. It'd only take a few days for the paperwork to be processed so, during that time, I'd be confined to quarters. But, if I still needed medical care, I'd stay here in the hospital until the doctor released me." He met Kitty's eyes with a sheepish look as he turned her hand over in his. "I made myself sound sicker than I am so the doctor would keep me here longer and I could still be near you." Seeing the surprise in her eyes, he talked faster. "Catherine, I realize we've only just met and the circumstances are not the least bit ideal, but I really enjoy your company and I want to continue spending time with you. That is, if it's okay with you."

"Well, that's a relief. For a moment I thought I was losing you. I mean, that you were getting sick again." *Be careful, Trausch.* "What you said is sweet, but I'm not sure how wise it is. Just now the doctor told me he might have to open you up to relieve the fluid pressure in your lung if your breathing doesn't improve and, trust me, you don't want him poking around in there if it isn't necessary."

"You could tell him my recovery has slowed. It might give us time to become better acquainted. Look, I understand I can't prolong it forever, but I hoped we'd have even a little more time together." He reached up and caressed her cheek with his thumb. "Catherine, last night I thought I felt something starting between us. Look me in the eyes and tell me I'm wrong. Tell me you want me to leave and I'll go."

She didn't want to, but she needed to tell him to go. He was a Confederate prisoner of war for Christ's sake. No way could she get into a relationship with him. At least being paroled was a good thing, he didn't need her to help him escape, but how could they be together? Staying here wasn't an option, and no way was she leaving Maggie. Especially with her being pregnant and alone. Why does everything have to be so damn difficult? Kitty pressed his hand closer on her cheek. "My heart wants you to stay Sam, but my brain says to let you go. Our lives are going in different directions. Yours is taking you home." Home, her voice caught on that word. "And I need to stay here. Maggie and Simon are my family now and I can't leave them. I'm afraid there's no hope for a future for us. And I need that hope, Sam."

"Perhaps if we give it a chance, we may decide to go home together to the same place, whether it be yours or mine, it doesn't matter. Or we can choose a different place altogether where we can start a new home. Regardless, it's too soon for either of us to make any promises, but there's always hope for a future, Catherine."

"Wow, I can see I'll have to step up my game if I'm going to argue with you. Listen, there's too much I can't tell you right now and I have to go see to the other patients. I'll be back later though and we can talk more, okay?"

"I'll look forward to it." He kissed her hand as he let her go, making the butterflies in her stomach behave like Chinese acrobats.

Kitty spent the rest of the morning doing her usual medication and wound care rounds. The patient with the shoulder amputation required an extensive dressing change that took a lot of time. She only popped her head in to Sam now and then to make sure everything was status quo there and to fudge a few lines in the log for Doctor Gallagher to see.

The whole time she worked Kitty mulled over what Sam had said. Lost in this Land of Oz, Maggie and Simon were her only family. They were the only remnants of the life that this anomaly stole from her. She could never leave them. But Sam did say he'd go wherever she wanted. He could come with them to Harrisburg. With Simon? Simon's been fighting the Confederates, what would he do if she brought one home? And what if he and Maggie figured out a way to go back to our time? What would she do with Sam?

***

Kitty waited on pins and needles for their after dinner break so she could get advice from Maggie on how to handle her dilemma.

As soon as they sat on the bench, a flurry of sea birds gathered around them waiting for their hard tack crumbs. At least the cement-like crackers were good for something. "Are you serious? You want to tell him where we're from?" Maggie's eyes flew open in shock when Kitty broached the subject.

"I don't know, Mags, that's what I wanted to discuss with you. Right now there's an infatuation between us, that's all I'll say. But I'm sure he'd see right through it if I lied and said I wasn't attracted to him. I mean, my God, just being around him takes my breath away. So I feel this obligation to be honest with him, now, before things go any further, and when he decides that I'm out of mind and it scares him away, I won't have wasted our time. I'm just afraid that if I don't do or say something, I may get in too deep and then, when he learns the truth, I'll be left with a broken heart."

Maggie dumped a large handful of crumbs on the ground to keep the birds busy for a few minutes. Worried, she turned and made Kitty look her in the eye. "Are you serious? Kitty, you hardly know this man. Is it worth exposing yourself to him? I mean, what if he tells somebody and they lock you up in a loony bin somewhere? Or worse yet, what if he decides he doesn't care how crazy you are and he still wants you or even that he believes you? What will you do? Will you leave with him?"

"No! You and Simon are the only family I have left; I can't leave you. If any more family dwindles away, whatever shred of sanity I have left will disappear as well. No, you guys are stuck with me, whether you like it or not." Kitty leaned forward with her elbows on her knees gazing at the ground. "You're right as always. I should let him go. But I don't want to Mags."

Maggie paused for a moment caressing Kitty's back. "Because you're in love with him, honey, aren't you?"

She nodded her head, sighing. "Remember what you said about Simon? How you knew right away in your heart that he was the right one for you? Even when you weren't sure he felt the same way? Couldn't it be possible that Sam's the right one for me? With all the insane things that have happened to us over the last year, couldn't this just be one more? What if coming here in the first place was our fate all along and I was supposed to meet him? Simon had a dream about being rescued from a flood and it happened to him here, maybe this is one more thing that's supposed to happen."

Maggie's arm drew her closer, and she kissed the side of her head. "Maybe, honey, but that's a lot of what if's. My mom used to tell me when I was a kid that if something's supposed to happen, it will. Don't worry, I'll support whatever decision you make."

They sat that way for a long time, Maggie's arm around Kitty, her head on Kitty's shoulder, watching the afternoon light dancing on the waves in the bay. As usual Maggie had it right without even having to say it. Kitty's heart just didn't want to accept the truth of it.

***

Kitty pretended to listen to the men's stories of home, going over in her mind what to say later to Sam and tried to anticipate his reaction and questions. She ached to tell him her life story, who she really was, about her parents, her friends. If any shred of hope existed that they could be together, it had to be with complete honesty. This wasn't something you spring on a person ten years down the road, 'Oh, by the way, honey, the reason I already know so much about what's going to happen in the future, is because I read it in the history books.'

She couldn't sugarcoat it to make her story more believable. How long did it take her or any of them to believe that they had, in fact, travelled back in time? Without any way to prove it… prove it… wait, she did have a couple of remnants of her life hidden away that might do the trick. Kitty excused herself from the ward, leaving the attendants in charge and hightailed it to her quarters.

***

By the time Kitty made it to Sam's room, her head was ready to explode. Even so, she was determined to make a stand right then and dive in with both feet, regardless of the consequences. The smile on his face as she entered the room warmed her, and she almost changed her mind. She didn't want to scare him away. She wanted to keep this moment, right then when he still thought of her as a sane and desirable woman, forever locked in time.

Kitty sat in the chair next to his bed, using the stethoscope to listen to his heart as a distraction. "How are you this afternoon?"

"Better now that you're here. I began to wonder if I'd scared you away with the things I said this morning. Have you given it any more consideration? I've been hoping that your heart won the argument with your brain and you're here to tell me you want me to stay." The hope she saw in his face gave her the courage to continue. She couldn't lie to him.

This time she took his hand, so rough and calloused from years of hard work. Kitty took the little container of lotion she kept in her apron pocket to keep her own hands from drying out, and massaged the softening liquid into his, giving her time to think how to respond.

"Remember when I said there were a lot of things I needed to tell you?"

His face fell by a mile and he withdrew his hand from hers. "You're the one who's married aren't you?"

"No, no I'm not married. I never have been. Remember, I told you, it's my, um, brother who's off fighting? I'm waiting here with Maggie, his wife." In her nervousness she'd fallen back on the familiar half-truth.

"Oh, I see." His expression didn't change. He sat staring at the wall waiting for her to continue and drop the other shoe.

Still edgy, she peeked outside the door to be sure they couldn't be overheard. When she returned this time, she sat on the bed to be closer to him. Continuing in a low voice, Kitty felt the blood rush to her face as she poured out her heart.

After several false starts and rambling explanations, and several sniffling nose blows, the whole story of how the three of them had come to be in this place, at this time, unfolded. As she purged her conscience of the lies and half-truths, regardless of whether he believed her or not, it took a weight off her shoulders that she didn't even realize she'd been carrying.

Though Sam's passive face never changed, he broke the silence after a long awkward moment. "That's a lot to take in. Is any of what you said even possible?"

Kitty pulled the first of her treasured items out of her pocket and put it into his hand. The battery in the cell phone had died long ago from Kitty's tearful agonizing over the photos of her parents and friends. But no one in the nineteenth century had ever touched plastic. As Sam moved his fingers over the strange object, Kitty explained the communication device and how people used it. When he looked up at her, his narrowed eyes showed what? Fear? Disbelief? She couldn't tell.

The key fob from her mom's BMW was her last piece of evidence. She pointed out the little engraving of the car with the trunk open and attempted to explain the most common mode of transportation from her former life. In doing so, she realized how little she knew about cars.

"You control the speed with your feet and steer with your hands." That summed it up.

Sam's gaze remained on the strange artifacts in his hand. "If you came here by accident, as you said, how will you get back?"

Kitty's strangled sobs threatened to break loose at this question. "I don't know, Sam, but if we do find a way, we're going. This isn't our time and we can't stay here."

"So, being from a future time, you've already seen the outcome of this war?"

"Yes. There are many bloody battles yet to come and many people on both sides will die. It's good that they granted you parole Sam, please don't fight anymore, the cost is way too high."

Sam took a deep breath, started to speak then paused, passing the phone and key back to Kitty. "Catherine, I think if you truly wanted me to leave, you could say so without tears and without making up such a crazy story. Though, I have to admit, you do make it sound very convincing. So rather than appeal to your logic, I'll appeal to your heart. I'm not sure how long they'll let me stay, but I can tell you I will treasure every moment you spend with me for all my days."

How do I say no to that? I realize it's not forever, but for once in my life I'm choosing the now option. Overcome with emotion Kitty lowered her head towards his, placing a feathery kiss on his mouth. "I will spend whatever time we have with you."

The noise in the hallway outside the door reminded Kitty where she was before she lost her head and went any further. The attendants were changing shift, and it was her responsibility to make sure everyone had their assignments before she went off duty. Although instead of leaving this evening, Kitty picked up a deck of cards and headed back to Sam's room. Too bad they couldn't pick up where they'd left off, but they could still spend a few hours of quality time together.

***

Just making curfew, Kitty slipped into the nurse's quarter's and found Maggie pacing again. "I told you where I'd be, why are you still worrying?"

"Because you missed curfew for crap's sake. How did you even get into the building? Don't they lock the doors at nine o'clock?"

"I made it to the door right at nine and the guard let me in with a warning. I talked to him for a few minutes and told him I'd been taking care of a sick patient and he was cool with it so it wasn't a problem."

"Well you'd better not be teaching your niece any of your little deceptions or Simon will have your head."

Kitty probed Maggie's small baby bump with her fingertips. "How is my little niece today anyway?"

Happy tears came to Maggie's eyes. "I think I felt her move today or else I had big gas bubbles breaking in my stomach, I'm not sure, but I mentioned it to one of the women I work with and she said it was most likely the baby starting to move. Isn't that exciting?"

They both screamed with excitement as they hugged, making their next-door neighbors bang on the walls for them to shut up so they could sleep. They lowered their voices and the lamp and sat huddled on Maggie's bed to talk without getting in trouble.

***

The battle at Yorktown still raged on and new patients arrived every day. Doctor Gallagher appeared to be under the gun to make room in the wards, because he began showing up every day, looking to discharge patients as soon as possible. Kitty had been fudging Sam's log for the last couple of weeks as much as she dared without having him undergo any unnecessary surgery. She spent so many evenings with him in his room that the attendants caught on and gave them as much privacy as possible in a prison ward.

Kitty's suspicious worrywart cousin had one of her kitchen buddies, who had connections in that department, verify Sam's parole story to make sure he wasn't just playing her to get out of a POW camp transfer. At first Maggie didn't tell Kitty she'd made the inquiry, only when she received word that Kitty's trust had been vindicated by the officer confirming the parole.

Kitty's ruse with the log could only go so far before Doctor Gallagher caught on and pushed through the parole paperwork. It had become her habit to visit his room first every morning, bringing him a cup of Hilda's brew that he liked so much. Today Kitty found him out of bed, dressed and sitting on the chair with his hat in his hand. "Today's the day isn't it? You're leaving." Her hands shook so hard, she had to put the cup on the bedside table so as not to spill the hot liquid all over herself.

"Yes. They brought me the paperwork this morning. They want me to leave today."

It had been easy to fool herself into ignoring the inevitable. But now, faced with the reality of his departure and the end of whatever relationship they had, Kitty was unprepared for the wrenching pain of her heart being crushed like so many dry leaves. As she reached out to him to keep her balance Sam moved closer, embracing her fully for the first time. Their mouths sought each other's with weeks' worth of pent up passion. Kitty stepped back deciding right then, that if these were to be their last moments together, she'd make the best of them. She led him by the hand, checking to make sure no one saw them as they escaped into the linen closet and locked the door behind them. If Rory Blandford could do it, so could she. Birth control be damned.

Up to now there had only been the opportunity for brief stolen kisses and soft caresses, but their hunger for each other now bubbled over like a shaken bottle of carbonated soda. Without knowing how much time they had before someone either came looking for them or needed something from this closet, they skipped the pleasantries of the romantic picnic and went straight to the Fourth of July fireworks. And the fireworks were spectacular. Sam put Richard to shame.

***

With Sam gone, Kitty was not in the mood to deal with someone else's injuries when she felt so raw herself. So, feigning illness, she left the attendants in charge and went to the cafeteria looking for anything that might substitute for rocky road. Even a big bottle of whiskey to take back to her quarters to mope around and cry into would do. When Maggie saw her come in looking so miserable, she arranged for a quick break so they could talk.

Maggie joined Kitty at their favorite table near the window. "So he's gone? I'm so sorry, Kitty, you must be devastated. But you know letting him go was the best thing to do, right?"

"Yes, it was the best for both of us. So why do I feel like I just got run over by a bus?" Kitty watched the leaves swirl in the cup of tea Maggie had brought her. The taste of Sam's warm kisses lingered in her mouth and she didn't want to wash it away.

"Don't worry honey, it'll get better, just give it time."

"Time, I hate that freakin' word."

"I don't have any alcohol or ice cream to offer you, but here, we made cookies today, why don't you soothe your nerves with them back in our room. I'll come check on you during the break, okay?"

"It'll take more than cookies to soothe my nerves."

"Well, you could always go look for anyone named John and beat the crap out of him just because."

"Huh, you say that in jest, but seriously, that's not a bad idea."

"You're not going to do that. But if it's exercise you need, why not put on your trousers and go for a run around the base? When I'm sad or I need time with my own thoughts, running always helps me. Why not try it?"

"Yeah okay, that sounds like the best idea. And I'll meet you at the bench where we always sit later. Thanks Mags."

CHAPTER 18

Kitty had been in her room only a few moments when a nurse from the post-op ward came searching for her. "I'm looking for Miss Reiger. Kitty Reiger, is that you?" She hadn't been called that since Simon's unit left.

"Yes, yes, I'm Kitty Reiger. What's happened? Who's looking for me?"

"It's your brother, Miss Reiger."

The heart she thought had been smashed into bits now jackhammered in her chest as she shook the nurse by her shoulders. "Simon? What's the problem? Is he okay? Where is he? Tell me damn it!"

"Please, Miss Reiger stop shaking me. He's wounded. The surgeon is with him now, but he won't let anyone near him unless you're there. He said only you, no one else."

Thank God Hilda sent me a new supply of her healing salve. Kitty paused only to snatch the tin from the box, then ran with the nurse to the surgery. He'd said only her. Did that mean his wound was so severe that he didn't want Maggie to see it? *Oh dear Lord, Carl Sagan, or whoever's up there, please don't let him die.*

When she rushed in she found Simon strapped to the surgeon's table with an attendant getting ready to put the chloroform mask over his face. The doctor stood poised over his leg with the amputation knife. "Stop! What are you doing? You can't amputate that leg."

Startled, the surgeon turned to see who had made the fuss. Using the momentum from rushing in, Kitty charged forward into a leaping right cross to the surgeon's jaw, grabbing the knife from his hand. The blow to his skull as he hit the floor knocked him unconscious. With the long knife brandished over her head, she threatened to amputate the arms of the other two attendants as they tried to restrain Simon from struggling against the binding straps. "Get away from him right now or, so help me, I'll cut you all into little pieces." Kitty felt wild with fear and anger and she must've looked even worse because everyone stepped back from the table. The nurse who'd brought her there ran off out the door, wide eyed and horrified.

"Both of you, get the doctor tied up into that chair. Now! Be quick about it. Don't make me use this knife."

Doped up with laudanum, Simon struggled hard to keep hold of his senses. "Thanks Kit, I knew I could count on you."

"You look like shit Simon, what happened?"

"Don't swear. The bullet, get it out of my leg."

Kitty picked the field dressing off the wound just a few inches above the knee. It was filthy and flaming with infection, the red lines creeping up the thigh. So that's why the doctor wanted to cut it off, to save him from dying of sepsis. "How long have you been this way?"

"Shot three days ago. Took that long to get here."

As they stood at the surgery door, the attendants argued over what to do with her. To keep control, Kitty commanded one of them to fetch soap and water, clean dressings and morphine. Another made a move to wrestle the knife away from her, but it only took a single glaring look to make him reconsider. It would be a huge mistake to test her resolve right now.

Visions of Cal Jackson's shoulder crept back into her brain again, turning her into a sweat machine as Kitty scrubbed her hands, then Simon's leg, with the soapy water. The sting of the soap on the open wound made him cringe, and Kitty instructed the attendant to take the edge off with a touch more morphine. She didn't know how much laudanum or whatever else he'd had so she needed to be cautious of over medicating him. She washed the forceps and applied a smear of Hilda's salve on the instrument. As she steeled herself, Kitty prayed in silence to all the forces of the universe, along with any and every deity, for the strength to do what had to be done. Her forceful behavior must've fooled the attendants into thinking she knew what she was doing, because they became more cooperative and followed her instructions. If they only knew.

"This is going to hurt Simon, but I'll try to be as quick as I can, okay?"

"I trust you, just do it."

Unable to see, Kitty poked the forceps into the hole the bullet had made, while one attendant just about sat on him to hold his shoulders and the other two held his leg steady. With Jackson she had hit on the ball and removed it right away. This time was harder, and she had to probe around inside the wound to find the metal piece, making Simon squirm. The more he squirmed the more nervous she got, so she allowed him another dose of morphine. She wished she had something to take for her own nerves. The doctor, now recovered from the assault, hurled furious insults and threats to have her arrested for interfering with his work. When that had no effect he resorted to egging on the attendants to stop her from 'butchering' his patient. Still unsure of her sanity, they played it safe and followed her orders.

Kitty stopped only to wipe the sweat off her face and eyes then began again after the attendant gave Simon the medication. Another minute and she felt the hard metal piece hit the forceps, and seconds later she had it out along with a small piece of fabric from his pants. With quick fingers, she sutured the wound closed and slathered on a generous application of Hilda's wonder drug, finishing just in time for the nurse to return with the guards. Kitty feared the doctor might still take the leg off if they took her away so, positioning one of the attendants in front of her, she held the knife to his throat, threatening to kill him if anyone came close. Whispering in his ear, she assured him she had no intention of hurting him as long as he helped her. Too scared to do anything else, the attendant played along and begged the guards to stay away.

The ruckus attracted quite a crowd in the hall and Kitty called for anyone who could hear her to go get Maggie from the kitchen. She knew she couldn't keep up this standoff much longer. Maggie would have to keep watch and make sure no one laid a hand on him. At least the bullet was out, now Maggie only had to keep changing the dressing and using the salve to get rid of the infection. It worked with Sam, it had to work on Simon.

Maggie arrived at the surgery frantic with fear. They'd only told her that her husband had been wounded, and that Kitty was being arrested. She flew into the room, shielding Simon's semi-conscious body with hers.

"Here Mags, change the dressing every couple of hours and put this salve on the wound. I know it looks gross, but trust me, this is the stuff I used on Sam and it worked wonders. Just keep doing it and he'll be fine. And whatever you do, do not let them take off his leg. No matter what Mags, promise me okay?"

"Yes of course, I promise. Will you be all right?"

Kitty wanted to reassure her she would, though looking around at the room full of furious people, she wasn't so sure of that.

Still holding the knife to the attendant's throat, Kitty whispered to him. "You stay here and help her, understand? And God help you if anything happens to my brother because there is nowhere on this earth you can hide from me. I will find you, cut your balls off and stuff them down your throat. Is that clear?"

"Y'yes ma'am. I'll stay right here. Don't worry, no one will touch your brother, I promise."

Reluctantly she let him go with a warning glare and gave herself up to the guards.

***

The massive stone barricade that protected Fort Monroe from a sea attack housed the prison. Kitty's cell reeked of mold and mildew and the narrow, barred window high on the wall let in the only light. A cot with a thin blanket and a small side table provided the only comforts. With the thick wooden door shut tight, the only sounds that could be heard were the sea gulls over the bay.

At first she thought the quiet might be good for her. As the days passed, though, with her only other human contact lasting five minutes twice a day, her thoughts wandered into dangerous territory. Self-pity took hold and, in her mind, she wrote long, tortured letters to her parents apologizing for the grief they must be suffering from her disappearance. Kitty missed them terribly. She worried about Maggie, her yet-to-be-born niece, Simon's leg, Sam. Her last moments with Sam stayed fresh in her mind and made her ache for him. *Am I doomed to live the rest of my life alone, an outsider in a world where I don't belong?*

One of Maggie's friends from the kitchen, Maria, brought Kitty her meals and the few snippets of information she had on Simon and Maggie's conditions. Maggie, she said, had been spending every day and night at Simon's side, nursing him back to health. With the infection in his leg improving, his fever subsided and he could sit up and eat his meals.

When the guard's keys rattled in the door, Kitty expected to see Maria with her meal tray. This time, though, two more guards entered the room, their rifles pointed at her. The third guard shoved her up against the wall, securing her hands behind her with iron cuffs.

Kitty was beside herself with dread, but the rifles pointing at her kept her from fighting back. "What are you doing? What's happening? Please, talk to me."

With a guard at each arm, and the rifleman at her back, they silently led her outdoors. When Kitty saw the enclosed prison wagon waiting for her, she dug her heels into the ground forcing them to drag her towards it.

Panic took over, and she screamed. "Maggie. Maggie, help!" Kitty tried to squirm out of their grip, but the shackles and the guards' firm hold made it impossible. "Let go of me. Please, don't take me away, please."

Her screams were muffled by the slamming of the door behind her as they hauled her up by the arms and pitched her into the wagon. Dazed from hitting her head as she flew into the dark interior, it took a moment to catch her breath before she could resume her pleading cries. It was too late. The wagon jerked forward knocking her off her feet. Kitty sat in the dark, her hands shackled, her hysterical sobs unheard.

They moved along at a slow pace over bumpy roads. Unable to use her hands or arms for balance, the movement knocked her from side to side until she gave in and stretched out on the floor of the wagon.

Sealed up like a coffin, her prison let in no light and her only reprieve came from the two overnight stops. During those breaks, they gave her food and water, and removed her cuffs allowing her a few moments outside to relieve herself. That was the only time the guard spoke to her.

He held his revolver on her the whole time. "My orders are to shoot you if you try to run away. And trust me, lady, I'll have no problem doing that. So hurry up, do your business, and get back in the wagon."

"Please, I didn't do anything. Can't you let me go? I promise I'll never tell anyone you helped me. Please?"

She might as well have been talking to herself.

They weren't taking any chances and, as soon as Kitty finished, and had her hands secured again behind her back, they rudely stuffed her back inside the wagon. The tears had dried up and only a deep heaviness in her heart remained.

From the very beginning, once the reality of their misfortune took hold, the one thing Kitty had feared most was being locked up and branded as crazy. She'd tried to conform, minimized her habit of swearing in public, kept her mouth shut as much as possible when she witnessed their primitive and often dangerous medical practices even though she raged inside, never divulged her knowledge of events to come. Yet, here she was on her way to an asylum. *Who knows what God-awful medieval terror they'll subject me to now?*

The closest mental hospital had to be in Washington. Alexandria was just a few miles south of Washington. When they'd left there, Kitty remembered Simon explaining that sailing downriver would save them from another two-hundred mile march. Assuming that statement was accurate, she taxed her brain with the mathematical calculations and came up with an estimate of only three more days before her permanent descent into hell. She had to do something fast.

During the past couple of overnight stops, the guards took care of the horses, ate dinner, then threw Kitty their scraps and let her pee. She expected the same routine tonight, but her plan would work better if she had more control of her hands. She wriggled and twisted, crushing her already bruised wrists against the outer edges of the cuffs to give herself more room, at last sliding her hands past her feet and in front of her. The wagon had been stopped for a while and, judging the right time, she readied herself at the door.

When she heard the chain rattle and the bolt slide out, Kitty kicked the door with all her might, smashing it into the unsuspecting guard's face and knocking him flat. She tripped over the felled guard as she jumped out, but quickly regained her feet and charged into the brush. Angry shouts swelled from behind her as she ran for her life. The brambles tore at her clothes and she stumbled over vines and branches. But she didn't look back and didn't hesitate, until the searing pain in her back paralyzed her feet, pitching her body to the ground. She couldn't see. Her breath slowed to a whisper. Vague voices came and went.

Then another man's voice spoke gently. "I'm so sorry. This is going to hurt… a lot."

The excruciating pain only lasted a moment before the blackness welcomed her.

CHAPTER 19

Kitty dreamed she felt someone brushing her hair. The sensation of the soft bristles being drawn across her scalp, felt so warm and comforting it made her sigh with pleasure. But a deep breath made thunderbolts of pain explode through her body and her eyes flew open in shock. Kitty lay under a thin quilt, in a somewhat comfortable bed. The room had a sloped roof and a sunny window with chintz curtains. A good deal more pleasant than the dark, dank prison cell at Fort Monroe. She scoured her recent memory, but had no recollection of the smiling woman sitting beside her holding the brush. Only the desperate escape attempt came to her. *Did they catch me and deliver me as promised? Is this woman my cellmate or was I lucky enough to get a kind nurse?*

"Your gentleman will be happy you're awake," she said. "He's been so worried about you."

Gentleman? Trying to breathe hurt, words were almost impossible. "Who?"

"I'm Mrs. Bailey. Or Sarah, you can call me Sarah, and you're resting in my home. Just a moment, I'll go get him." Sarah patted Kitty's hand and disappeared.

Oh, dear God, what version of hell did I fall into now? And why does my back hurt so much?

Sarah's light footsteps went down stairs, then heavier, quicker ones returned. Afraid to confront this newest horror, she kept her face towards the wall as 'her gentleman' approached and knelt at her bedside.

His breath sounded ragged and Kitty felt what might've been a tear as he held her hand to his cheek. "Catherine, thank God, I thought I'd lost you forever."

That voice lured her attention to a pair of startling blue eyes shining with tears. "S… Sam?"

"Don't talk now, I know it hurts." His thumb moved to wipe away the tear that escaped from the corner of her eye. "Those bastards shot you and left you for dead. You were lucky. The bullet hit a rib, so the wound isn't fatal, but that's why breathing is painful. Don't worry. The Doc said you'll heal up just fine."

Sarah had come back up with a bowl of soup which Sam gratefully accepted on Kitty's behalf. He moved his chair closer, explaining the events that brought her to this place while he fed it to her.

After only getting halfway home, Sam had returned to beg Kitty one more time to leave with him. He got thrown out of the fort when he tried to bribe the officials into letting her out of prison.

He shook his head and chuckled. "Did you really tell the attendant you'd cut his balls off and stuff them down his throat?"

The memory made her smile. "… was angry."

Sam wiped the soup that dribbled down her chin with a napkin. "Remind me not to make you angry."

Sam continued. "When I found out the doctor had arranged your commitment to the asylum in Washington, I searched after the prison wagon to free you. You were a day ahead of me so I had some catching up to do. I'd just gotten close when I saw you bolt out the back door of the wagon." He stopped for a moment, spoon in mid-air, and his eyes distant with the memory. "I heard the shot, watched you fall, and my heart exploded. This farmhouse was close by and the good people inside agreed to help."

Kitty waved the soup away and motioned for him to bring his head closer. His soft lips on hers were all she needed.

***

Sarah and Mr. Bailey were kind hosts and cared for both of them until Kitty recovered enough to be on her feet. When everything started, Kitty hadn't even changed out of her nurse's whites yet. It now hung in filthy tatters. Kind Sarah exchanged it for one of her dresses. Sarah frowned seeing the dress didn't even reach her ankles, but Kitty didn't care that her mended stockings and army boots stuck out from under it. She'd start a new fashion trend. The Baileys' showed them overwhelming compassion and generosity. At first they balked, then accepted, the few dollars Sam offered as payment for their hospitality. Kitty wished she could offer more.

***

Sam sold his horse in Richmond to buy their train tickets and, less than a day later they were on the streets of Washington. After buying the tickets and keeping a sum of cash aside for food, they had enough money left for a deposit on a comfortable hotel room.

They had two errands to complete. Sam had to arrange for a bank note transfer so they could pay for the hotel room, and then they planned to send a telegraph message to Maggie and Simon to assure them Kitty was safe.

Sam stopped and turned, searching the crowd for the familiar voice coming from behind him. "Listen. I think someone's calling 'Kitty.' You said people call you that, right?"

Surprised and wary, Kitty searched as well, clinging to Sam's arm for reassurance. A short woman with blond curls hurried along the crowded street and waved her arm to get their attention.

They recognized her at almost the same time. "Carole Brunswick, oh my heavens, it's such a surprise to see you here. You look wonderful, as usual, how are you?"

Out of breath from running to catch up, she hugged them both, panting. "Sam, Kitty, I didn't realize you knew each other, but I'm so glad to see you both, and just in time."

"In time for what Carole?" *Crap, are they looking for me? Are they coming to take me away again?* Kitty's eyes scanned the street for possible threats.

"It's Maggie, she's sick and they've quarantined her at the hospital. She needs you."

Sam's face was just as surprised as they both did a double take. "What? I mean, what? She's here in Washington? Where's Simon?"

"You haven't seen him? He's been going every day to the insane asylum to get you released. When I saw you I thought he'd succeeded. He told Jerome and me what happened to you. It must've been awful."

Sam slipped his arm around Kitty's shoulder. "It was sheer luck I found her in time."

With Maggie sick and nearby Kitty couldn't stand around any longer. "Sam you go on to the bank and take care of your business. I'll go with Carole to the hospital and we'll meet up at her hotel later." Directions given and arrangements made, she hurried off with Carole to the hospital to check on Maggie.

***

A male attendant sat at a desk outside the door with the quarantine sign on it refusing to let them enter. "Why is she quarantined?" Kitty demanded. "What's wrong with her?"

"I can't let you in there, Miss, it's smallpox. She's highly contagious."

"Smallpox?" Kitty didn't know whether to laugh or cry with relief. "She can't have smallpox, she's been vaccinated. We both were when we worked at Camp Curtin."

Leaving Carole outside the door to be safe, Kitty pushed past the attendant and found Maggie behind a screen at the end of the ward. She had several red blisters on her face and her hands had been tied to the bed so she couldn't scratch.

With her eyes shut tight, Maggie flinched as Kitty knelt and touched her hand. "Are you okay there, Lucy?"

Someone had used their code. First only one eye opened, then both, followed by a waterfall of tears. "Kitty, oh my God, you're safe. I'm not hallucinating, am I? Tell me you're really here."

Kitty laid her head across Maggie's chest and hugged her. "It's me, I'm here. We're all safe now."

Maggie's voice squeaked out through the sobs as Kitty dried her face with the sheet. "They say I have smallpox and they keep trying to force their medieval treatments on me that'll wind up killing my baby, but it can't be, can it? We were immunized for Christ's sake, remember?"

"You do have blisters, but they don't look as severe as the other cases I saw at the hospital. Mags, did you ever have chickenpox when you were a kid?"

"No, but I'm too old for that. Only kids get chickenpox."

"Hmm, it doesn't seem as if that's the case." Kitty examined the blisters on Maggie's face and upper chest. "At least it isn't as serious as smallpox. I'm not sure how long the rash is supposed to last, but many of these blisters already have scabs. I think that's a good sign you'll recover soon. What are they giving you for the itch?"

"They tried to give me opium, but I wouldn't take it. My baby's in enough jeopardy without doping it up, too. I thought for sure she'd die if I had smallpox. What will chickenpox do to her?"

"I don't know, Mags. We'll have to check with the doctor on that one."

Kitty pulled the sheet back up to Maggie's neck. "When I got into a patch of poison ivy once, my mom made a paste of baking soda and water. That might help your itching. You rest and I'll try to find some."

Kitty met Carole at the door and gave her the good news. Yes, Maggie was sick, but she'd live.

After buying the baking soda at the apothecary next door, Kitty sent Carole back to the hotel. Everyone would be relieved to hear Maggie's condition had been misdiagnosed. Kitty promised to meet her at the hotel before dark.

Kitty could tell her mom's remedy had helped right away when Maggie's whole body relaxed. She stayed at her bedside for hours, applying cold compresses to her head for the fever and headache while they caught each other up on their recent harrowing experiences.

Helping her eat the soup the attendant brought made Kitty's stomach growl so loud Maggie made her leave.

"Thank you, Kitty, for taking care of me, you've been so helpful. And I feel so much better now that I'm sure you're safe and well. Um, you know you still have work ahead of you to bring Sam and Simon together. Maybe with everything you've told me about Sam saving your life, Simon will be more forgiving of Sam's war service."

"Yeah, maybe." Kitty patted her hand as she stood to leave. "Anyway, I'll be back tomorrow to tell you how it went."

***

Joseph, the butler, met her at the door to the Brunswick's room and showed her into the large suite. Sam and Simon had been on opposite sides of the parlor when she entered and now they both rose to greet her.

They hadn't killed each other yet. She took that as a good sign.

Sam held back, allowing Simon to embrace Kitty with one arm while the other balanced him on his cane. "Oh God, Kitty, I'm so glad you're safe, I was so worried about you. To say I'm sorry for everything I've put you through just isn't good enough."

Kitty's eye caught Sam's smiling face as she assured Simon everything was good between them. "How's your leg, Simon? Is it healing okay?"

"It hurts like a bugger, but the cane helps." He motioned for Sam to come closer, struggling with a range of emotions as he embraced them both. Even with the cane, Simon needed help to a chair before his leg buckled.

The butler appeared with a tray of drinks for each of them and Kitty downed hers in one gulp. The alcohol hit the bottom of her empty stomach and killed off the butterflies swarming there. "Simon, are you okay? You seem... emotional."

"Emotional?" Simon's voice cracked. "You mean just because the man who saved my life is involved with the woman who saved my leg? Why should that make me emotional?"

Kitty signaled for another drink. Her injured rib had been killing her the entire day, but now her body felt numb as she turned to face Sam. "That was *you*?"

"It's an amazing coincidence, isn't it?" Sam said.

Kitty lowered herself into a chair, took the glass from the butler and downed the second drink. *Sam, my soulmate, is the man from Simon's dream? The one who saved him from the flood?* "Yeah, coincidence."

The Brunswicks interrupted their discussion as they emerged from their bedroom all dressed for dinner. They were relieved to hear Maggie's condition had improved and commented that Kitty's surprising reappearance must have been the catalyst.

In the midst of their polite chat Kitty's stomach issued another embarrassing roar for nourishment making the Brunswicks insist they join them for dinner. Carole and Kitty each linked arms with her husband as they entered the dining room. It was gratifying yet spooky as hell to watch Sam help Simon with his cane. At least the worry about them getting along had passed.

"How fortuitous it is that we're all here in Washington at the same time," Carole gushed. "Jerome had business here, and I tagged along to show my dresses at Lady Jane's Dress Emporium. Jane's a dear friend. She said the dresses should sell with ease."

Simon and Kitty nodded to each other. Yes, this day was chock full of coincidences.

Their entrée dishes removed, the waiter placed a thick slice of warm apple pie in front of Kitty. She couldn't remember the last time she'd had apple pie. The crust, thick with caramelized sugar, topped the warm juices that ran into the scoop of melting whipped cream next to it. Kitty stared at it with tender delight.

As Kitty sat panting and staring at the dessert, her imagination running wild, Sam took her hand and whispered in her ear. "Catherine? Shall we tell them?"

She tore her eyes away from the pie, gazing up into his beautiful blues. "Hmm? Oh. Yes, this is a perfect time."

Sam waited until he had everyone's attention. "Dear friends, we want you to be the first, well the second, to know that Catherine and I are engaged. Simon has already given us his blessing."

Kitty whipped her head around, her eyes bulging out of her head as Simon smiled and raised his glass to them. "May you both find the happiness that Maggie and I have."

The Brunswicks each offered their own well-wishing toasts as Kitty finished her wine. Carole was bursting with excitement. "I just had the most wonderful idea. Why not get married here, in this hotel? Do you think Maggie will be recovered soon enough? We'll only be in town another week, but I'd love to dress you."

It might have been the alcohol that made her head spin, or the recent uncanny revelations, or the anticipation of becoming Sam's wife, but only one word made it out of her mouth as she shrugged. "Okay."

***

The three of them couldn't wait to tell Maggie the events of the night before as Simon, Sam and Kitty rushed up to the hospital in the morning. When they arrived at her door, though, the attendant stopped them. "Your wife's not in there anymore, sir, she's been moved."

"Moved? What do you mean moved? She's too sick to be moved."

"The doctor saw her blisters had scabbed over," he explained as if they were children, "so she's not contagious anymore. He put her out on the open ward to finish her recovery."

Kitty couldn't believe it. The open ward with all those sick people? For crying out loud, what kind of medical system is this?

Men were not allowed on the women's ward so Simon, steaming mad, waited outside with Sam, as Kitty went in alone. At least it didn't have as many patients as the men's wards she'd worked in, but the familiar stench of dysentery hit her the minute she entered. Kitty passed five or six beds of hacking, moaning women before she came to Maggie.

The patient huddled with her head under a blanket at the far end of the aisle had to be her. Kitty recognized the calico dress sticking out at the bottom. She stopped and put her hand on Maggie's shoulder.

The hand was shrugged off and a muffled voice came through the blanket. "Go away. I don't care what you want, I'm not coming out. Leave me alone."

A stab of pain shot down her back as she knelt at the bedside. Kitty tried again. "Lucy, it's me, Ethel. Are you okay?"

Only a pair of eyes peeked out at her. "Kitty?" Tears spilled from those eyes and her shoulders shook from sobs. "They put me with the cootie people. I'm going to catch something else, I know it. I have to get out of here. You need to help me. Please, help me get out of here."

Kitty's anger threatened to boil over at how the hospital had treated Maggie, but she remembered where that anger got her the last time. "Leave it to me," she reassured her. "I'll be right back."

Simon had a carriage waiting as Kitty strode out of the hospital, Sam a step behind her with Maggie bundled in his arms. Two attendants came running out just as their carriage left to take them back to the hotel. Kitty could care for Maggie much better than anyone in that death trap.

Surrounded by her loving family and given a few days of nutritious food, Maggie's health returned. A few of the blisters had left marks on her chest, but her face still glowed with the same porcelain complexion she'd always had. Just in time, too. The arrangements for the wedding were complete, Carole had their dresses ready, and Sam's father had come to Washington for tonight's ceremony.

* * *

Mr. McCabe Sr. was just an older version of his son with the same brilliant blue eyes, only slightly hooded, and grayer hair. It was like seeing a portrait of Sam twenty years from now. And it wasn't a bad picture, at that.

While the men got ready in Mr. McCabe's room, Maggie and Kitty dressed in Carole's. It didn't matter that they hadn't seen the dresses yet, they were well acquainted with Carole's talented handiwork and trusted that whatever she'd created for them had to be spectacular. Carole brought Kitty's out first, a scooped neck ivory gown trimmed in lace and beads, with lace off-the-shoulder sleeves. She'd also brought along a corset for her to support that low neckline. Kitty cried when Carole gave her the low heeled beaded slippers that went with the dress. These were the first pair of shoes she'd worn in a year that weren't issued by the army.

Maggie's dress came out of hiding next and it knocked both of them flat on their butts. The deep purple satin dress with the sweetheart neckline and off-the-shoulder sleeves had patches of cream-colored lace scattered across the wide skirt.

"Purple and cream are my signature colors." Carole beamed with pride as she displayed the dress, smoothing out the wide skirt. "Your peaches-and-cream skin will set them off perfectly, Maggie."

Carole held the dress from the photo in Grandma Margaret's trunk. Dumfounded and unable to speak, Maggie reached out her shaking hands to touch it.

Still reeling from the inconceivable relationship between her, Simon and Sam, nothing surprised Kitty anymore. "The dress is beautiful, Carole, and I'm certain Maggie will look stunning in it."

The photographer waited with quiet impatience in the room while Maggie and Kitty argued over the rose locket. The original plan was for Kitty to wear it for the ceremony as Maggie had. They wanted to start a tradition that could be passed along to future generations. But now, with the dress from the old photo, it meant Maggie had to wear it. They struck a compromise and agreed that Maggie should wear it for the photo and then give it to Kitty to complete her ensemble for the ceremony.

Sam waited downstairs at the appointed time while his father and Simon came to escort the bride and bridesmaid.

Simon tilted his head and narrowed his eyes when he saw Maggie's dress. "Where have I seen you wearing that dress?"

"In the photo on my mantle at the house in Harrisburg. You saw it at my grandma's memorial."

Simon was lucky he had the cane to lean on to keep him from falling. Even so, his face blanched, and he had to tug on the collar of his shirt to make room to swallow.

Mr. McCabe led Maggie down the stairs followed by Kitty and Simon. They each took their places in front of the minister. During the short, sweet ceremony, Sam put his mother's thin gold band with a small diamond on Kitty's finger and they pledged their undying love. After that, tearful hugs from the emotional women followed while Sam had his hand shaken by more people than he recognized.

A blur of happy faces, music and dancing filled the evening, keeping everyone busy enough for the newlyweds to sneak away to their room. At long last they indulged in the romantic picnic they had forgone in the linen closet that fateful day. Although the fireworks had to wait until Kitty's rib healed enough for her to take a deep breath without cringing in pain.

Sam was more patient than Kitty. "Don't fret. We have a lifetime together. Just lying here with you in my arms is good enough. For now."

CHAPTER 20

Lying in his arms in the dark, listening to the soft, reassuring shushing of his breath behind her, Kitty wondered again how this all came to be. How did it happen that the man who rescued Simon from the flood in his dream, and then in reality, turn out to be her soulmate? And how did Simon's dreams and memories bring them to this time in the first place? There seemed to be a force at work here just beyond her grasp and calling it fate gave her the shivers.

In her haste to undress, Kitty hadn't removed the rose locket, and she brushed her thumb over it as she dreamed of her former life. It made her smile to remember how they'd found it after breaking into Grandma Margaret's old house that night. She'd been scared out of her wits, but Maggie knew it would turn out okay. That was only a few days before she'd left her family and her home for the last time. Tears started in her eyes.

At least things were settling down now. Simon's injury released him from the army, and Maggie was vibrant and healthy as ever. She'd have her baby surrounded by people who love her. Kitty and Sam looked forward to a long, happy life together.

Business plans in Harrisburg were on the drawing board. With Sam's contacts and experience and Simon's mechanical engineering skills, the burgeoning railroad industry would be their best bet. The four of them looked forward to living out their lives there in peace.

Many times over the last year, the dream of being home, seeing her parents, her sister, her friends, had kept her going. Kitty dozed off with the dream encircling her, the old room in her parents' house so close she almost felt it.

***

"Catherine, wake up." Sam's insistent voice in her ear brought a smile to her lips as she pressed her body back against his. *That's my husband calling me.*

His hand squeezed her shoulder. "Catherine, open your eyes."

"Ow, Sam, that hurts. What's the matter?" Her eyes blinked open. As they scanned the room, Kitty sat bolt upright gasping at the sharp pain that shot up from her rib. Sam sat up beside her.

Panting from the pain, Kitty clamped her hand on his. "Sam, what happened?"

"I was just going to ask you the same thing. What is this place?"

Sam climbed off the bed after her as she went around touching everything to make sure it was real. With no reference points to understand what he saw, he only stared wide-eyed at the foreign objects around him. Some things were obvious and familiar—the dresser, the mirror, the desk and chair. But the bed seemed higher and firmer than usual and there was an odd odor to the air. Opening a door, he jumped back from the avalanche of shoes that tumbled to his feet.

"Sam, be careful," Kitty warned. "There's a crapload of shoes in there."

Drawn to her trophy wall, he peered at the photo of a teenage Kitty holding a medal she'd won in a fight. Her beaming face showed metal bands on her teeth. The rich colors of her hair and eyes, even the blue of the ribbon and the gold of the medal stunned him. He touched it gently. "Is this you?"

"Yes." Kitty turned in circles, tears streaming down her face. "It's me, I'm home." She stopped mid-circle, hugging him with all her might, then stepped back. "I'm not dreaming, right? We're both here?"

"Now you're scaring me," he said. "Are you okay? I'll go get Simon and Maggie…"

"No, no wait." She held his arm to make him stay in the room. "Let me think." She still had the ring on her finger. "We got married, we had dinner with Maggie and Simon, then we went to our hotel room and… you know."

"Well, I'm glad you remember that part, but that still doesn't tell me what we're doing here."

In deep thought, Kitty twirled the locked around in her fingers as she recounted their steps. *We were in bed, Sam fell asleep, I missed being home….* Kitty's hand flew off the locket as if it were on fire, her eyes bugged out and her jaw fell open to her chest. "Holy…" She struggled to contain the swear words that bubbled up inside her and fought to get out. "It was never Simon at all. Well, maybe partly Simon, but it was the locket." Her fingers dug into Sam's arm as the stark realization that they were never stuck in time at all hit her. "All this time it was the freakin' locket."

Sam peeled her fingers off his arm and seized her shoulders. "Catherine, you have ten seconds to make sense and then I'm walking out the door to get Simon and Maggie and you're not going to stop me."

"Okay, but let me go, I need to pace to get this clear." Kitty took as deep a breath as she dared. "Remember I told you the three of us had somehow travelled through time? That we were actually from a future time and didn't know how to get back? Well, this is what did it." She stopped and held the locket out to him. "Maggie had this in her hand when we wound up in 1861. I had my fingers around it last night as I fell asleep thinking about home. It used to belong to Maggie's grandma and I remember now, she said something like 'just hold it very tightly and it will take you wherever you want to go.' It must be some kind of talisman and Maggie's had it in her pocket the whole freakin' time."

"So, what are you saying? We're in your future time? Now?"

Kitty took his face in her hands and gave him a huge smacker of a kiss. "Yes, that's exactly what I mean."

Kitty found everything she had brought over from Sonia's in the room. She opened the laptop on the desk to check the date. June 8th, 2015, the day she left for Harrisburg. And it was early yet. Most likely her parents were downstairs right now.

With the locket's miraculous secret exposed, Kitty no longer carried the weight of being trapped. Though she was free to move about the universe at will, if she stayed in her room for the rest of her life, she'd be just as happy. Kitty overflowed with joy until she saw Sam's uncertainty and hesitation. She had come home, but Sam had left his.

She stood before him, both of his hands in hers. "You are my husband; I am your wife. We'll always be together, no matter what. It won't be easy, that's for sure, but I ask that you at least give this a try."

Sam took a deep breath and nodded. "Just tell me what to do."

The first order of business was clothes. Sam couldn't meet her parents in his underwear. She tossed him a pair of sweats from her drawer, and a shirt she'd appropriated from Carlos that she used to wear while doing housework. It may be too warm for sweats, but they'd have to do for now. With both of them properly dressed for the time, Kitty led Sam down the stairs.

***

They waited in the doorway to the kitchen watching her mom and dad slow dancing, Mom's head on Dad's chest humming along to the song on the radio. After thirty-five years of marriage they were still so in love. Kitty hoped that would be her and Sam one day.

Dad noticed her first. "Morning Kitten, I'm surprised to see you up so early. And… you have company?" Dad's eyebrows shot up to his hairline.

Kitty wanted to run over and give each of them a bear hug but, without the corset to support her rib, she settled for a half hug and kiss to each of them while she kept a death grip on Sam's hand.

Kitty introduced Sam as a man she'd met at the hospital. Though they'd been dating for a while, Kitty had kept it under wraps until she knew they both felt the same way. And now that their connection was certain, he'd be coming with her to Maggie's. Mom winked at her while Dad gave his usual 'look before you leap, Kitten' expression. Before leaving her room, Kitty decided telling the truth about everything except the year and their marriage would work. Sam could say he'd fought in 'the war' just not which one, he could talk about his family and what they did and what his plans were. Everything was still relevant and Kitty could always inject an explanation here and there as necessary.

Mom gave her a scrutinizing stare. "Kitty, are you losing weight? Those jeans used to be skin tight on you. You'd better sit and eat something right now. And, Sam, don't you let her skip any more meals. She's going to waste away."

"Yes, ma'am, I'll make sure she eats."

Kitty's heart swelled as they talked like a normal family over the French toast, bacon and eggs Mom made. Sam impressed her mom with his Southern charm, as Kitty knew he would, while Dad's interest piqued when Sam mentioned his engineering degree from Harvard.

Although reassured she'd see them again, Kitty still got choked up when her parents had to leave for work right after breakfast. After they'd gone, Kitty took Sam around the house and showed him how everything worked. "You know," she chided him. "You didn't have to make up that story about going to Harvard. Although it sure grabbed my dad's attention."

"But I did go to Harvard. I have a degree in engineering from the Lawrence Scientific School. Whether you like it or not, Madam, you are married to an educated man."

Educated or not, the electric lights, running water, flushing toilet, washing machine and Kitty's beloved microwave oven, all brought exclamations of wonder and surprise. After doing the best she could to explain how the music came out of the radio, she introduced him to the TV which flabbergasted him. And they hadn't even gotten outside yet.

They spent the day exploring the wonders of the twenty-first century. As excited as a child at Disneyland, Sam marveled at the technological progress society had made, even though the environmental cost dismayed him. What bothered him the most, though, was the style of dress.

"Sam, you have to stop staring at the girls. They're going to think you're some kind of pervert or something."

"But look how they're dressed, for crying out loud. Do all women dress that way now? Do you go around half naked too?"

"It'll just take time getting used to it, that's all. Just try not to stare."

Once back in her room, they cuddled in the bed. "What do you think, Sam? Could you give it a shot here? The four of us could still do as we planned, put together a business in Harrisburg and live together as a family. Would it work for you?"

"I think I remember telling you once, that we could go to my home, to your home, to any home you wanted, as long as we're together. I still feel that way."

"I love you, Sam McCabe."

"I love you too, Catherine McCabe."

Kitty grasped the locket, wishing them back to the hotel they'd left on their wedding night in Washington.

***

Maggie and Simon were surprised when they joined them for breakfast in the hotel dining room. It wasn't the French toast, bacon and eggs that her mom had made, but the biscuits and pork gravy were tasty.

"We thought you two would sleep late this morning." Maggie's eyebrows waggled up and down.

Kitty glanced slyly at Sam. "Well, we were anxious to give you the gifts we'd brought for each of you. Close your eyes and don't open them until I tell you."

Simon closed his eyes, but Maggie giggled like a little girl. "Oh, for goodness sake, you two didn't have to waste your money on us."

Sam and Kitty had rehearsed this. "Okay," they said together, "open them."

Neither one spoke. Maggie's hands shook as she lifted the Reese's Peanut Butter Cups from her plate and Simon just stared at his Snickers bar.

Kitty moved her chair closer and covered Simon's hand with hers. "I owe you an enormous apology. I hated you for months, blaming you for getting us trapped here, when it was never entirely your fault."

Maggie's face paled, and Kitty thought she'd have a stroke. "Mags, are you…"

"How? How did you do it? How? Tell me, now!" Her voice started out weak, but grew in intensity until the whole dining room stared at her.

Simon woke from his stupor and hugged her to calm her down. "Shh, Maggie, don't create a scene. We certainly don't need an audience right now. Why don't we go upstairs to the room so Kitty can tell us what she found out without anyone overhearing us, okay?"

Kitty helped Simon with his cane and Sam escorted Maggie to the room where they could talk in private.

Maggie and Simon sat on the bed while Sam and Kitty took the only two chairs in the room. "Maggie, what's your last memory of that night at the karaoke club?"

"It was that fight in the parking lot with Doyle," she said. "He broke the chain on my locket and Simon hit him. Then we ran away and woke up here."

"Yes, that's what I remember, too. And Simon you said something about wishing you were 1861 so you wouldn't have to deal with Doyle, right?"

"Yeah," he said. "Something like that. Get to the point, Kitty."

Sam untied the ribbon around her neck and Kitty handed the locket to Maggie. "You had this in your hand when we woke up didn't you? When Sam and I went to sleep last night, I held it and thought of being home. Then… we were."

The light went on in Maggie's head as her mouth fell open. "Hold it tightly and it will take you wherever your heart desires. That's what Grandma said." She was on her feet in an instant. "I've had this freakin' thing in my pocket all freakin' year and this was the key? Are you freakin' kidding me?" Angry tears streamed down her face as she paced the floor stomping her feet and waving her arms. "All that time, sleeping in tents, in the rain, eating that slop, worrying that I'd die in childbirth, and I could've gone home all along?"

Kitty jumped up to calm her and let her cry on her shoulder.

"Sam," Simon whispered. "Am I losing my mind? Were you there? Really? Is it true?"

"Yes, Simon, it's true." Sam whispered back. "The things I saw were amazing. A tiny lever on the wall lights up the whole room. Turn a knob and steaming hot water pours out. And the women, they go around the streets half naked. Catherine says I'll get used to it, but I'm not so sure."

Simon laughed and cried at the same time.

Maggie gathered her composure. "Okay, but wait. Let's do this right. We can't just disappear and not, at least, say goodbye to the Brunswicks. Look at how much they've done for us—the clothes, the care packages, your wedding, the *dress*. They're part of this somehow. We can't ignore that."

"Of course not," Sam said. "That's why they're waiting for us now at their hotel."

"Oh, God, you guys thought of everything." Maggie kissed the newlyweds and helped Simon with his cane.

***

The Brunswicks and Sam McCabe, Sr. had finished breakfast and were lingering over coffee as the foursome arrived. During the hack ride over, they had agreed to tell everyone their plan to rejoin Simon's business in Wellsboro, only omitting the part about returning to the twenty-first century. Easy laughter and warm conversation filled their corner of the room until the inevitable time of departure came.

This wasn't just a casual goodbye. Centuries would divide them. Knowing it would be for the last time, Sam embraced his father longer and tighter than he ever had. For Maggie, Simon, Kitty, it was impossible to say everything that filled their hearts. Tearful thanks and warm, lingering hugs passed among them.

Emotionally drained from the heart wrenching farewell, there were still important matters to discuss as they returned to Maggie and Simon's room. Though they were eager to go home, the transition had to be carefully planned to minimize any chance of error or surprise.

The safest time to return, they decided, had to be the day after they disappeared. They had no idea what the consequences would be if there were two versions of them in the same place at the same time.

"I was holding you both by your arms when we ran from the club that night. I bet we have to be touching to travel together. Otherwise, only the person holding the locket would go." Simon reasoned.

"That's a good point." Kitty agreed. "Sam and I were… um, touching when we woke up in my room."

Maggie clutched the locket as they huddled close with their arms around each other, and wished to be in Maggie's house on June 28th, 2015.

EPILOGUE

On the first day of class her palms were so sweaty she could barely hold her briefcase. The registrar had told her the roster was not only full, but several students were on the wait list.

Kitty's preparations had been meticulous: the syllabus studied, lectures prepared and rehearsed, slides chosen. She'd even lined up a guest speaker for each side. Although she couldn't very well tell them how she'd come by it, she'd be offering a unique perspective on the subject. This class on the American Civil War would be the best Penn State had ever seen.

By the time they'd come back she'd had enough of hospital work in any century to last a lifetime. She did feel a need, though, to tell people not only what a soldier's life was like during that time, but also the lives of the women who supported them. Kitty had pitched that idea to the University, and they'd loved it.

Sam had been so patient and supportive while Kitty finished her Master's and beamed with pride at the graduation ceremony. For a man of his time, he was quite progressive.

So much had happened in the three years since they'd returned to the twenty-first century. The niece that Kitty had expected turned out to be a big, healthy, bawling, baby boy. Maggie had been so worried that coming down with the chickenpox would cause a birth defect, but little Max was perfect. Kitty forgave Maggie for ruining the girls club when she and Sam brought Cameron Abigail McCabe into the world.

Simon had been telling the truth when he told Doyle about his thriving business and Sam's degree in engineering won him an executive spot in the company. Of course, the fact that he'd saved Simon's life didn't hurt either. Simon's brother, Matt, knew a guy who knew a guy, and got Sam set up with an ID and credentials.

Sam found the adjustment to the technology of this century challenging, but met it head on with enthusiastic determination. Everyday things like cars, refrigerators and telephones, that everyone took for granted, were new to him. Watching him discover and master each new advancement helped bolster Kitty's own courage to follow her new path. Even his disdain for the current clothing styles had become a thing of the past and girls in their summer clothes were freed from his gaping stares.

The four of them had given up trying to unravel the complexities of how they were connected to Simon's memories, and if the "butterfly effect" of the lives they'd touched hadn't surfaced yet or had always been there. It would take greater minds than theirs to sort it out. Still, the bond between them remained strong, and the warm, dry house they all shared overflowed with love.

The infamous rose locket had been safely stowed away.

Authors Note

Dear Reader,

Thank you so much for purchasing *Fated Memories*. I know there are a lot of ways you can spend your entertainment dollars, so I'm grateful you decided to give my debut novel a chance. I sincerely hope you enjoyed reading it as much as I enjoyed writing it.

If you did find the book entertaining, I would like to ask you to do one thing: please go online and post an honest review. The reviews of satisfied customers are essential to the success of every author, and your extra effort will be greatly appreciated.

Thanks again, and I hope to hear from you soon.

Joan Carney

About the author:

A transplant from the concrete sidewalks of New York City to the sunny beaches of Southern California, Ms. Carney enjoys writing stories about women who are strong—whether by nature or circumstance—and the men who love and respect them for who they are. Bold coffee and dark chocolate fuel the artistic fire inspired by her family, friends, and psycho cat.

www.ingramcontent.com/pod-product-compliance
Lightning Source LLC
Chambersburg PA
CBHW071228200626
46817CB00017B/2201

* 9 7 8 0 6 9 2 6 6 3 8 6 8 *